SUBMISSION REVEALED

DIANA HUNTER

ELLORA'S CAVE
ROMANTICA PUBLISHING

What the critics are saying...

ℰↃ

4 **Lips** "This love story is intense, emotional, and touching. The characters are so very true to life that they could be your next door neighbors. The intense emotional connection between Phillip and Sarah will bring tears to your eyes and help you to understand their relationship. Diana Hunter once again delves into the world of Master/slave and brings it alive in a way that will have you sympathetic and understanding why this independent woman is being collared. I highly recommend *Submission Revealed* to anyone who enjoys the BDSM genre and likes a great love story." ~ *Two Lips Reviews*

An Ellora's Cave Romantica Publication

www.ellorascave.com

Submission Revealed

ISBN 9781419959059
ALL RIGHTS RESERVED.
Submission Revealed Copyright © 2007 Diana Hunter
Edited by Pamela Campbell.
Cover art by Syneca.

This book printed in the U.S.A. by Jasmine-Jade Enterprises, LLC.

Electronic book Publication May 2007
Trade paperback Publication May 2009

SUBMISSION REVEALED

ॐ

Trademarks Acknowledgement

ร๑

The author acknowledges the trademarked status and trademark owners of the following wordmarks mentioned in this work of fiction:

Corvette: General Motors Corporation

Hickey-Freeman: Hickey-Freeman Co., Inc.

Saturn: Saturn Corporation

Prologue

∽

Sarah always thought of this room as Phillip's dungeon, even though the surrounding cream-colored walls reflected the morning sunlight when it poured in through the room's only window. Every once in a while the sun's rays would fall just right and glint off the bars of an uncovered cage, making her squint against the glare. When the room was filled with light, only the furnishings gave away the more sinister aspects of the refurbished cottage bedroom.

No sunlight blinded her now, though. This Friday night, soft candlelight glimmered off the rich wood of the new contraption before her. Sarah shivered, goose bumps rising on her naked skin as she contemplated the black leather straps and padded surfaces that attached to the wood with solid metal brads. This was a piece of furniture designed to immobilize the unfortunate soul strapped onto it.

She smiled. Or the fortunate one. Her heart beat harder as the love of her life stepped behind her and slid his arms around her waist. Knowing enough to keep her arms at her sides, Sarah couldn't resist leaning back into the wonderful strength of Phillip Townsend.

"Cold? Or excited?"

His rich voice, soft and sexy, murmured in her ear. Sarah turned her head so she could look up into his wonderful brown eyes. "Both," she replied, gasping a bit when his warm hand slid along the valley where her belly met her thigh. With arrow-sureness, his finger dipped between her parted legs to find the evidence of her arousal.

"I'd say more excited than cold, my dear slave girl."

Sarah loved it when he called her that. She snuggled her back against him, brushing the side of her cheek against the soft material of his T-shirt. Although she wore nothing except leather cuffs around each wrist and ankle, Phillip remained fully clothed. The subtle statement of power was not lost on her. Especially not when he dragged his wet finger up along her belly, tracing her white cream in a line from her shaven mound all the way to her belly button.

"So have you figured out what it is?" Phillip's voice murmured in her ear, the caress of his breath weakening her knees. Trying to focus on the new piece of furniture, Sarah blinked hard and stared at the oddly placed pieces of wood and leather. The narrow top couldn't be more than six inches wide, she decided—only about two feet long and covered with black leather that gleamed in the candlelight.

Four legs supported the well-padded top, each leg splayed out for stability. Smaller pieces of wood, also padded in black leather, were bolted to each support. Black straps hung from several places on the contraption.

"It looks like a mutant sawhorse," she finally proclaimed.

Phillip's deep baritone laugh filled the room. "You're not that far off." Gently he guided her closer. "Come stand here at the end. Now, lean forward and kneel on the two back pads."

In order to do so, Sarah had to spread her legs wide enough to straddle the top of the horse, leaning on her hands to keep her balance. She could see two divots cut out of the top pad, making it look like one of those "Road Narrows" signs one always sees before an old bridge. A sneaking suspicion began forming in her imagination as to what was coming but she kept her counsel, preferring to let Phillip take her along at his own pace.

"Lie down."

His hand steadied her as Sarah shifted, putting her hands down on the lower front two pads to lie along the length of the padded top. The leather, cold on her skin, made her shiver as her breasts neatly fell into place on either side of the divot, confirming her earlier suspicion about that irregularity in the design.

She set her cheek on the cool leather and smiled as Phillip adjusted her position, thoroughly enjoying how he played with her body as if he were a sculptor molding clay. When he pulled her back along the top just a smidge and walked around, inspecting her from every side, Sarah watched him until he disappeared behind her. Suddenly she realized how vulnerable she was, kneeling on this bench with her rear end and pussy presented to him almost as if on a plate.

She felt Phillip bring the cold strap across her lower back. He slid the end through a metal buckle that hung on the far side of the contraption and she gasped as he cinched it tight.

"I do not want my slave to think she can escape."

Sarah resisted the urge to wiggle as he brought a second belt across her middle that strapped her chest tightly to the top of the bench.

Phillip adjusted the position of her left leg before fastening her calf to the pad with two more wide web belts, one across her ankle and one up by her knee. When he did the same to the other leg, Sarah found she was caught fast from just above her waist, down to her ankles.

He knelt beside her where she could just make him out in the dim light. The candle burned behind him and his shadow fell across her face.

"I like seeing you so open and vulnerable, my slave. So ready to do my bidding." His long fingers brushed her hair back so the stray strands did not get into her eyes. "You have no idea what I'm going to do to you. And yet you place yourself in my hands, ready to accept pleasure or pain."

"Yes, Sir," she murmured, knowing he had earned her trust.

Taking her hand, he laid her arm along the front pad before belting both forearm and wrist snugly against the leather. Satisfied, he walked around to fasten the other arm and she resisted the urge to turn her head and watch his panther-like tread. As usual, he wore no shoes or socks, allowing him to move silently when he didn't want her to know his exact whereabouts in the room.

"You like this bench, slave?"

His name for her never failed to produce an arousal. Had it been only two months since they'd kissed on the beach and he'd told her he liked his women compliant? Of course, at that time, she hadn't understood what he meant. After years of being a good girl, then a dutiful wife, Sarah had decided the time was ripe for her to be naughty. That he might mean sex with bondage had never entered her mind. Nor had submission.

Yet that first night, Phillip had demanded both. He'd bound her in several ways, each one taking her farther and farther along a path she had never before even imagined. Now strapped to the bench, she tested her bindings, unable to imagine life without Phillip's magnificent dominance.

The straps didn't give her an inch. She tried scooting forward but the webbing across her back held her too tightly. She had just enough play to allow her to wiggle her ass an inch or so back and forth. White cream gathered in the folds of her pussy when Phillip's hands slid off her shoulders and down along her sides to cup each breast.

"I like your nipples, slave. Feel how hard they have become?"

He pinched and twisted them, rolling the hard nubs between his fingers until she gasped and tried to squirm away. Not until she whimpered did he let go and move to her exposed ass.

The anticipation made her whimper again. How could he torment her like this? Would he spank her? Flog her? Insert a butt plug? Not being able to see his actions made her fidgety. The warmth of his hand on her back startled her and she jumped, then giggled, hating how nervous that made her sound.

Phillip's palm pressed gently against her back and Sarah took deep, cleansing breaths, calming herself, letting go of the world outside these walls. His hands massaged her shoulders, releasing her tension. Under his touch, Sarah felt her muscles relax as her mind shifted.

There existed a state of mind Sarah never quite had the words to describe. Soft, peaceful...a gentle lulling that warmed her spirit, like a warm blanket fresh out of the dryer wrapped around her soul.

In that mental state, she was free from society's judgment, free from her childhood lessons about what constituted "good girl" behavior. She was free to simply exist, to simply react with honesty and with pleasure. Here, nothing mattered to her except Phillip and the touch of his hands taking possession of her.

Her breathing slowed as his hands kneaded the muscles of her back, pressing out stresses with each exhalation and pulling in peace and contentment with each new breath. Sinking deeper into an almost trancelike relaxation, content to simply skim along the smooth path he laid out for her, her eyes closed. As her breathing became deep and regular, she almost fell asleep.

Which was why the crack of his palm across her ass made her squeal and jump so hard that her body slammed against the rigidity of the straps holding her down. Every muscle suddenly tightened in surprised shock. A second hard slap in the same spot made her wince. And when a third blow landed, just as hard and putting a third handprint right on top of the last two, she couldn't help crying out.

"Hurts a bit, my slave?"

She could hear the humor in his voice at her reaction. All right, so she probably shouldn't have been falling asleep on his new toy. Her new toy, she corrected as he now rubbed his palm over the stinging skin, easing the pain away.

"Since this is a spanking bench, it's only right you receive a spanking from me. Don't you think so?"

"Is that what this is called, Sir?" With her cheek pressed against the leather padding, her words came out muffled, although Phillip didn't seem to notice.

"It is, my slave."

The fingers of Phillip's hand dipped between her cheeks as he caressed her ass, sending fresh waves of pleasure straight to her pussy. To be so vulnerable to him still embarrassed her a little. The fact that the two of them were now engaged, with the wedding date a scant three weeks away, made little difference, the man still had the power to unnerve her in the most delicious fashion.

Sarah heard him moving toward the table he always kept covered with a dark blue velvet cloth. He had told her he kept the table covered for two reasons—one practical, one selfish.

"On the practical side, I hate dusting. On the selfish side," he had stepped in close to her, pulling her possessively into his arms, "I don't want you to run away in fear."

She remembered that conversation now as she heard him slide something out from under the blue cloth. Before she could puzzle it out, however, she heard the slap of the paddle against Phillip's palm and understood what was coming.

"I'm willing to bet a paddling is not punishment for you, slave. You have enough difficulty restraining your climaxes when I flog you and I suspect this will be the same. Shall we find out?"

"Yes, Sir." Sarah nodded even as fear clutched her stomach. Would it hurt? She had thought being flogged would hurt but then he had taught her how the leather thongs could caress or bite as he saw fit. And he was right. When he had warmed her skin to pink in the past, she'd often ended up begging like a rutting animal for his permission to come.

Phillip lightly rubbed the hard surface of the wooden paddle over the exposed skin of her ass. She couldn't see it—was it round like a ping-pong paddle? Long and narrow like a yardstick? The only sense that gave her information was touch and at the moment, his touch was featherlight.

She would not be lulled again. She remained tense, waiting for the first blow.

When it came, solidly on the fleshy part of her ass, the loud smack startled her more than the physical touch. Phillip circled the paddle around her ass again, lifting it and tapping it lightly on the other cheek. Sarah grinned.

Keeping his touch light, Phillip paddled her ass irregularly for several minutes. Sarah didn't know when the next one would land and the uncertainty begin to unnerve her. "Oh, my glory, Sir...just paddle me!"

Phillip's baritone laugh filled the room. "My, my...listen to the slut! Begging to be spanked."

Sarah tossed her head with the little movement she could manage but all she accomplished was to get her hair in her face. She blew it and it rose in graceful wisps only to fall back into her eyes. "It's the not knowing when the next one is coming that's driving me nuts." She blew again, harder and the hair rose farther but still settled over her nose, obscuring her vision completely. "Sir," she added when she realized she hadn't given him his title.

"Perhaps that uncertainty is exactly what I'm aiming for, slave. Consider that."

He punctuated his sentence with a hard smack on her right cheek and Sarah jumped, then giggled again at her predictable reaction, even as her skin stung.

She tried counting seconds between the paddles but Phillip was not keeping any rhythm she could fathom. The irregular tempo made her jumpy and several times she flinched even when no blow landed. A frustrated growl formed in her throat and came forth as a cry when two slaps in quick succession were followed by nothing for almost a minute.

"Did you say something, slave?"

Although Sarah could hear the amusement in his voice, she did not smile back this time. How could she explain that her ass wanted more? Or less? She wiggled in her bindings, knowing she couldn't move. That immobility made her pussy clench, however, and she whimpered in her need to come.

"Remember, you are not to come unless you ask, slave."

Sarah didn't trust her voice. She nodded instead, her hair in her face.

"Here..." Phillip gathered the brown strands of Sarah's hair and wound them into a ponytail. He didn't have a band to keep them in place, however, so he waited until she laid her cheek on the leather pad again and then let her hair flow down along the far side of the bench. Only then did he move behind her again and out of her sight once more.

Sarah took a deep breath, letting it out slowly and tried to settle herself again. She felt Phillip rest his warm hand on her ass for a moment before letting the paddle fall with a loud and hard slap on her ass.

Gasping, Sarah's body jumped, again held tight by the straps over her back and arms and legs. Seeming to take pity on her, Phillip now set up a steady tattoo—two short slaps on the right, two on the left, followed by a hard one right and left. Two right, two left, slap right, slap left.

Over and over he repeated the pattern and Sarah tried to squirm away, moaning in agony as her skin turned supersensitive. Her ass burned where the paddle repeatedly landed. Right, right, left, left, slap, slap.

"Oh, Sir! Please let me come!"

Phillip did not let up. "What was that, slave? You need to speak up."

"Please! Oh, please let me come, Sir!"

The tempo increased and Sarah's moans became cries. "Please, Sir! Oh, my glory, let me come!"

"Come for me now, slave. Sing to me!"

Sarah bucked against the straps, her hair falling unheeded as her head snapped back and her body convulsed. Stabs of pain accompanied each slap of the paddle now, stabs that gathered in her pussy to explode with a gush and a scream. She gasped for breath as warmth surged from her pussy outward, filling even her fingertips with pulsing heat.

When her breathing quieted and she could no longer hear her heartbeat in her ears, Sarah wondered when he had stopped spanking her. She'd never felt him stop. Her ass burned but Phillip's touch was absent.

* * * * *

Sweat poured down his brow and he wiped it away with impatience. His cock, hard as stone, pressed against his jeans, demanding attention. Tossing the paddle onto the soft cover of the "tool table", as he thought of it, he watched Sarah's body writhe and convulse in her bindings. He didn't move until her cries turned to whimpers, then he unzipped his pants and kicked them off and into the corner, pulling off the T-shirt and throwing that into the pile as well. Usually fastidious, tonight's activities had awakened the latent tiger that slept inside him. Already it pawed at the door of its cage, wanting out.

Stalking around her helpless body, the tiger inside Phillip watched as Sarah's body slowed, her breathing still coming in great gasps as she started to relax in the straps with which he had bound her, on the bench he had crafted with his own hands as a present for her. So open, so vulnerable, so trusting.

Phillip grabbed a handful of her tender ass and squeezed, gratified by the squeal it produced. He'd watched her cream over and over again as he played with her body and knew the time for tenderness was long past. With his free hand, he slid his fingers along his cock, feeling the rough bumps of the blood vessels turning his cock into a rigid shaft that ached to plunge into her ready pussy.

He mauled her ass and watched her come again, her mind slowly leaving her as he unlocked the cages that held both their wild sides. She pressed against the straps, trying to push herself back on him, his cock teasing her vulnerable entrance. Slippery with her hunger, he relished the heat that poured from her pussy.

With one hand he positioned himself, with the other, he reached forward and grabbed a handful of her hair, pulling her head up and forcing her back as he growled and plunged deep inside her inviting warmth. Her muscles protested at first but he persisted, forcing her to open more with each thrust.

"Come for me again, my little slave girl."

His voice, colored with his desire, pitched deep and gravelly as he took what belonged to him. Relentless, he hammered into her pussy, his balls slapping against her clit each time he buried himself. And when her body let go, the muscles contracting around his cock, the tiger burst from its cage and he rutted with her like the animal he was. Pressure exploded. Relief flooded through him. Warmth spread over and through every inch of his body, until at last he rested his body on top of hers as he gasped for air.

Her body warmed his and they breathed as one as passion ebbed. He luxuriated in the wonderful glow that surrounded them until his spent cock slipped from her warmth, the colder air bringing him back to earth.

Her hair had fallen in her face again. He'd have to remember to tie it back the next time. Gently he brushed it back, gratified when she gave him a weary smile. With tired fingers, he undid the straps that held her to the spanking bench and helped her to stand. She faced him, leaning against his chest in the romantic candlelight and Phillip gathered her into his arms, still a little amazed she had come into his life. And when she looked up at him and whispered, "Thank you," he scooped her up and took her to bed, sending his own prayer of gratitude to the power responsible for her presence.

Chapter One
Reservations

❧

"I know, Beth. I know it seems fast but you met him. He's wonderful."

Sarah Parker cradled the phone on her shoulder while she packed her old dishes into a sturdy cardboard box. In just under three weeks, she would become Mrs. Phillip Townsend. They had timed the ceremony to coincide with the end of her lease when she would leave this apartment, move into Phillip's cottage in the woods and became Phillip's wife and full-time sexual slave. The thought gave her a shiver all down her back and an excited tightness in her stomach. She could barely keep the giddiness out of her voice as she discussed the wedding arrangements with her best friend.

"Yes, we're going to have a civil ceremony. Please don't tell me you're backing out. I really want you to stand up for me." Sarah layered her old ceramic plates between cheap paper plates and listened with only half an ear to her friend's concerns. "Well, you're the one who told me to stop moping about Tom's death and to start dating."

Tom had been Sarah's first husband, the handsome daredevil who blew up bombs for a living and who had been killed when a drunk swerved into his lane, hitting him head-on. With her husband's five years of experience in the military bomb squad, the irony of his death had threatened to turn her bitter that first year without him.

Time was the best healer, however, and Sarah had moved on, taking this small apartment as the first of many steps toward finding a new future for herself. Who could have imagined that future would involve whips and chains? She giggled into the phone and covered her lapse with a cough.

"What was that?"

"Sorry, Beth...I'm packing while I'm talking...got some dust in my throat."

For good measure, Sarah faked a few more coughs. Although they'd known each other for decades, Beth would never understand Sarah's discovery that bondage was not only fun...but intoxicating.

"Tell me the date again, Sarah? I have my master calendar here."

"Three weeks from Friday at city hall, second floor. I'll talk to you before then, Beth, so I'll remind you. And please don't change your mind!"

"Fat chance. Although I still think you're rushing things. We need to talk, girl."

"All right. Meet me for dinner at Attie's? You can talk my ear off there."

"Can't be there 'til seven, though. That too late for you?"

"Seven o'clock sounds good. See you then."

Sarah hung up the phone and stared at the mess she'd made of her kitchen, a silly grin plastered on her face. That grin had become a permanent fixture since Phillip Townsend had asked her to marry him a week and a half ago. Hefting a large serving bowl, she remembered how she and Tom had shopped for this particular pattern. Now she packed her past with every wrap of newspaper.

After Tom's death, Sarah had dated idly, mostly men Beth fixed her up with, just drifting along, not really having a direction or sure what she wanted out of a relationship or, for that matter, out of life. Certainly, sexual passion had never been important to her and it wasn't anything she had ever expected to experience.

But then her hand had reached for an orange in the supermarket at the same moment Phillip touched it. While she had never been one to believe much in that spark of electricity the pulp romances always wrote about, she couldn't deny the instant attraction she had felt for the tall, dark and Hollywood-handsome man with the devilish grin.

She had agreed to meet him for coffee, which turned into a date, which led to…more. When one romantic, moonlit night Phillip had asked her back to his place in the woods, she had gone, figuring it was high time she was a naughty girl.

Sarah pulled a drinking glass from the shelf, absently wrapping it in newspaper as her mind turned over her new life.

That moonlit night, Phillip had opened an entirely new world to her, a world of bondage and sex where she had no control. He commanded her and only asked that she be willing to let him take her where he led. She had followed with a great deal of nervousness…and an arousal stronger than she had ever felt before.

Thus began a journey of discovery that had led her down paths she never knew existed in life. What began as just a sexual exploration of Dominance and submission with a strong dose of bondage had evolved into a stronger relationship over a month's time as Sarah accepted Phillip as her Master and called herself his slave.

In the privacy of her kitchen, Sarah's hand slipped to her crotch, rubbing her clit through her jeans as the words "Master" and "slave" echoed in her mind. She couldn't deny the incredible sense of wholeness that washed over her the moment Phillip clicked the lock onto her cuffs and collar. Especially the collar. When she wore the wide leather band with the four D rings, one at each compass point of her body, she felt like she had finally found home.

As Sarah stood in her kitchen, thinking about Phillip and the magnificent way he stood over her naked body at times, her panties dampened. She rubbed a bit harder, envisioning the wonderful ideas Phillip had given her to mull over as he slowly trained her mind to accept his dominance. She would never be able to explain to Beth that this wasn't brainwashing, that Sarah was fully cognizant of her actions. Rather, Phillip was helping her to "unlearn" all the behaviors she had used to build walls around the passionate wanton who lurked deep inside her. The woman Sarah still kept caged because of shame. From her mother's knee, in every magazine ad, in every Hollywood movie, Sarah had been taught that girls who expressed sexual passion were nothing more than Jezebels headed for trouble and Sarah had swallowed that story hook, line and sinker. She had squashed her feelings of discontent, her yearning for more excitement in the bedroom, constantly repeating the mantra drilled into her…*good girls don't.*

But Phillip's teaching was slowly pulling down walls and unlocking the wanton's cage.

Sarah closed her eyes and unzipped her jeans, sliding her hand inside and rubbing her clit harder and harder as her thoughts of Phillip's acceptance brought her closer to an orgasm right there in her kitchen. Two years ago, the thought of coming at her own hand anywhere but the bedroom would never even have occurred to her. Now, she rubbed eagerly, her clit engorging with desire as her mind turned over her relationship with Phillip.

Every once in a while, the titles of Master and slave still pulled on her sensibilities, yet she found the concepts too intriguing to ignore. At the moment, she held the position only on the weekends. After the wedding, she would move to his cottage in the woods and become a full-time, twenty-four/seven, total sexual slave.

Her pussy spasmed at the realization and Sarah gasped, grabbing on to the counter for support as her muscles contracted. A tiny whimper forced itself out of her throat as small waves of pleasure coursed through her. For a half minute of bliss, she kept only one picture in her head—her kneeling before Phillip's commanding presence, totally naked and with head bowed, submitting her body and mind to his will. Riding the waves, she enjoyed her orgasm as tingles spread all along her arms and down into her toes. Savoring the moment, she milked every last spasm.

And when she was done, Sarah opened her eyes, washed her hands, dried them, picked up another drinking glass and methodically wrapped it in newspaper, while her thoughts turned over the new life she would soon be leading.

* * * * *

"I like Phillip, I really do," Beth was saying around her barbequed ribs. "It's just not like you to be impulsive."

Sarah shook her head. "I'm not being impulsive, Beth. I've thought this through. Really."

"Where are you going to live?"

"He has a small cottage just outside the city. About an hour away."

"So you're gonna commute an hour each way to work? Sarah! Think of the gas that's gonna eat up!"

She had raised the same point with Phillip. Driving out and back once a week was a far cry from doing it every weekday. The two had discussed her options and Sarah had decided a monthly plan from the local transit authority would work out well. She tried to explain that to Beth.

"There's a bus that comes in from the mall out that way. I drive fifteen minutes to the mall, park my car and take the bus in. From the bus stop in the city, it's another ten-minute walk to work."

Shaking her half-eaten rib at Sarah, Beth objected. "Yeah, that'll be fine in the summer. But winter's coming. You're gonna freeze!"

With a laugh, Sarah feigned fear. "Watch where you're pointing that thing!"

Beth grinned and tore a hunk of meat off with her teeth, snarling like a barbarian. "I'll rip Phillip to shreds just like this if he doesn't behave himself!"

"Look, the total commute time won't be much longer than driving." Sarah started to take a bite, then stopped as another thought occurred to her. "Besides, if I take the bus, I'll finally have time to read through all those books you keep giving me!"

Even Beth couldn't find an argument for that. Beth avidly collected books the way others might collect stamps or coins. She had eclectic tastes and was always giving Sarah something new to "broaden her horizons". Unfortunately, Sarah didn't always have time to read them and return them in a timely manner.

"What about kids? You planning to have any? Your clock is ticking, you know."

Sarah rolled her eyes. "Now you sound like my mother." She pointed with her fork. "No kids. Tom and I had that agreement and Phillip and I have the same one."

Beth shook her head. "Never did figure out why not."

Sarah shrugged. "I want my career. I like getting out of the apartment on a daily basis and I like my job. I have responsibilities and some day might be CEO if I keep playing my cards right. Kids need their mothers. Don't get me wrong. I love kids. But I also love being able to hand them back to their parents at the end of the day."

Beth shrugged and Sarah knew her friend was arguing just for argument's sake now. Neither of them had chosen the family route—probably why they'd remained friends long after their other girlfriends had left them for a world of play dates and diapers. "Nope," she told Beth, "I'm staying on the Pill and am just going to have to get my hugs and kisses from Phillip, instead of children."

"So what does your Mr. Romance do for a living?"

"He owns a small dot com company."

Beth paused, frowning at her over a rib dripping with barbecue sauce. "Thought those all went bust after the whole Y2K problem."

"No, only those that didn't know what they were doing. Phillip and some friends created some sort of software that the libraries bought to help them inventory their collections. They've since expanded it and now it's used all over. He's mostly retired on the money they made, although he keeps his hand in. Said the company needs to stay current if they're going to continue to make money."

"So he's rich?" Beth's eyebrows went up along with her appreciation and Sarah laughed.

"Yes, he's rich." She toyed with the remnants of her salad. "Or well-off, anyway."

"You'd better get a pre-nup before you go jumping into holy matrimony."

"Why?"

"As I recall, Tom left you with enough to live on very comfortably. You work because you'd go nuts sitting at home all day long. I just don't want to see this guy get control of all your money, then dump you and you end up destitute."

Sarah sighed. "I love you, Beth. You always find the darkest, most unpleasant possibility and make sure I'm aware of it."

Beth wiped her hands on her cloth napkin before picking up her glass to take a sip of her diet soda. "I'm sorry. I don't mean to rain on your parade. I just worry about you is all."

Smiling to show she wasn't really angry, Sarah nodded. "I know. And I appreciate it, I really do. But Beth...I love him." She thought of how she felt when he held her in his arms after an especially passionate sexual play and knew the color came up in her cheeks.

Beth sighed. "I know. That's why I'm gonna be there at the wedding. Because I haven't seen you this happy in a very, very long time." She threw her napkin on the table. "But he tries one thing, hurts you in any way and I'm gonna rip his balls off and stuff 'em down his throat!"

Sarah laughed and the tension between them fell away. She was about to marry the most wonderful man in the world and her best friend would be by her side. All was right with the world.

* * * * *

All the same, Beth's questions nagged at her for the rest of the week. When you got right down to it, there were several conversations she and Phillip hadn't had yet. Yes, the sex was wonderful. More than wonderful, it was incredible. But twenty-four hours a day, seven days a week of sex? Not likely to happen. Even if she had the stamina.

She'd been making assumptions that she'd keep her position at work. Yes, it stressed her out sometimes, yet she actually enjoyed what she did and didn't really want to give it up. Except she and Phillip hadn't discussed that. Did being a total slave mean she no longer had control over her own money? And what about her job? If she gave control to Phillip, would that mean she'd have to stay home and service him whenever he wanted instead of going to work and using her mind?

By the time Friday rolled around, Sarah had most of her "extra" belongings packed in an assortment of cardboard boxes she had collected from the neighborhood grocery and the liquor store around the corner. She had also worked herself into a state of confusion. As she surveyed the mess before she left for work, she made a mental note to set up a time with Phillip to take all her things to the mini-storage mall. It was only a mile from his cottage outside of town so anything she later decided she needed wouldn't be too far away. But, then again, would she ever need any of these things if she were a slave? She growled as she shut the door harder than she intended. Damn Beth. She'd gotten too many questions swirling around in Sarah's mind, like so many autumn leaves in the wind.

At least she didn't need to look at the remaining mess in her apartment until Monday night. Only eight hours of work and then she'd be in Phillip's arms. She could ask her questions, he would have sane, sensible answers and life would be glorious once more.

* * * * *

Why did Fridays always drag? For the past twelve weeks, every Friday evening she would head directly from work to Phillip's rural cottage where he would immediately put her to use. She hid her grin behind her hand as the vice president in charge of her section droned on. Under her strict business attire, Sarah wore a tiny thong...and knew it had dampened as she thought about what the evening would bring. Questions about the future aside, she couldn't wait to tell Phillip that the mere thought of being with him that night put her on the edge of an orgasm while stuck in a roomful of stuffed shirts and laced-up women.

Escaping at long last, she sped down the highway and out of the city to Phillip's one hundred acres out in the middle of nowhere. The scenery turned from urban to industrial, from suburban to farmland and finally to a long, meandering country road bordered with trees and brush. Often she saw deer standing in the infrequent meadows, so she kept a lookout for them now. With winter coming, they would be on the move.

The scent of autumn filled the air and she hit the button to roll down her window as she slowed for the turn into Phillip's driveway. Beside the entrance, a climbing vine flashed up the telephone pole like a flame of scarlet fluttering in the late afternoon breeze and as she slowly drove along the dirt path, she noticed several trees beginning to change their colors from the tired greens of summer to fresh hues of orange and red. The colors ought to be at peak right around the wedding, she realized, making a mental note to figure autumn shades into the bouquet of flowers she would carry.

Practically bounding out of the car as soon as she parked beside the house, Sarah drew in a huge breath, filling her lungs to their utmost with fresh air untainted by harsh city life. Closing her eyes and letting her head fall back, she spent a moment enjoying the sun's warmth on her face.

Phillip watched her from the porch, stepping out of the cottage as soon as he heard Sarah's car turn into the drive. Watching her now, when she was still unaware of his presence, brought a smile to his lips. When they had first met, she'd been so guarded and careful, so concerned lest she frighten him away with her incredible passion for life. And now she stood in his driveway, soaking in nature's peace, her soul bared for all the world to see. How could he do anything but love her?

She slowly turned in the sunlight and he gloried in the sight of her long brown hair unbound now and cascading over her shoulders to fall free. He loved it when she draped that silky curtain over his cock, teasing him to distraction. And he loved it when she was bound, unable to move or have her way at all. Both giving her free rein and reining her in had unique advantages.

She turned to face the cottage, opening her eyes and his heart quickened at the sudden joy that leapt into her face. With a bounce and a skip, Sarah crossed the space between them and he gathered her into his arms, burying his face in the soft tresses of her hair to drink in her perfume as moments earlier he had devoured the sight of her. Crushing her to him, he held her tightly in his arms, never wanting to lose the precious gem she had become.

And when he mastered himself and stepped back, he was again undone by the soft sensuousness of her heart-shaped lips—lips made for being kissed. She looked up at him with eyes half closed with lust and his body responded. Bending down, he captured her mouth in his kiss, first gently tasting, then ravenously devouring her as the wild animal banged at the cage inside.

The birds twittered in the trees and a chipmunk paused in its mad dash across the clearing but Phillip and Sarah didn't even notice. After a week apart, with only emails to sustain them, they reveled in the sense of touch.

Phillip pulled back with a stern look. "See what you do to me, woman?"

She grinned. "I almost thought you might take me on the front steps again, my dear Sir."

Phillip cocked an eyebrow at her. "You liked that, as I recall."

Sarah nodded. "Yes, Sir, I did." She paused and a naughty twinkle sparkled in her eye. "A lot."

He laughed and the chipmunk skittered away. "A far cry from the time you walked the deck naked!"

Sarah colored and Phillip bent to kiss her again. Pulling the inner wanton out of her took patience, but patience he had in plenty. He loved testing her limits and finding her boundaries, knowing the journey was always more fun than the destination.

A gentler kiss this time. This one filled with promises of what was to come. He wondered if she would like the new toy he'd bought? Okay, maybe toy was the wrong word, even if he was going to have some fun playing with it. Them, he corrected in his mind.

Taking her hand, he led her toward the house. Sarah paused at the door, as she often did. One of these days, he'd have to ask her why she did that. This time, she looked up at him, a question in her voice. "Phillip, once we get married and I'm living here all the time, will you still greet me like that? Won't you become used to me? If I come home to you every day instead of every weekend, it won't be as special anymore."

Phillip took both her hands in his. "It will be special, but in a different way." He could see she was truly troubled. He set his plans for the evening aside for a few moments so he could ease her fears. Long ago he'd learned that small concerns could blossom into huge problems if ignored. That previous relationship had ended in disaster because he hadn't learned the lesson fast enough. Phillip was determined not to repeat the same mistake. "Come on over and sit down for a minute." He led her to the porch swing he'd put in two weeks ago so they could enjoy the sunset together. They sat and he started them swinging as he answered her questions.

"You were married before and you know passion flames brightly and burns quickly. What's left once the passion is gone?"

"That one's simple. Love." She reached over and took his hand. "The passion Tom and I shared was nowhere as intense as what I feel with you, though."

"It doesn't matter. Passion has many faces. There's an elderly couple I know who still hold hands when they sit down. Both need walkers to get along or I'm sure they'd hold hands even when they're walking down the hall. Their kisses are small but no less intense for all the infirmities of age. Their passion isn't as violent as ours can be, yet flames just as brightly after all their years together, wouldn't you say?"

Sarah nodded. "That couple has love to back them up, that's why." She shifted on the seat. "I loved Tom but our relationship was...quieter. The fireworks died early and life became...well...comfortable. More like an old sweatshirt or a favorite-pair-of-sneakers-comfortable."She laughed. "Something tells me that's not the kind of relationship we're ever going to have."

Phillip grinned. "Oh, I think you'll be surprised. There's something wonderful about putting on your favorite sneakers in the morning."

"Yes," she agreed. "And there's also something to be said for putting on nothing but a pair of cuffs!" She waggled her eyebrows toward the door. Phillip took the hint. Sarah only wanted her concerns noted and verified, not solved immediately. Apparently his intended was far hornier than worried.

"All right, you minx. If that's the way you feel." He paused to pull her to her feet. "Off with your clothes!"

"Right here?" She looked around in shock.

"Right here." The long, curved drive cut off all view from the road. No one would see her strip but him and that was just the way he liked it. He would share her beauty with others, but others of his choosing. Strangers had no business looking at her wonderful body. His cock stirred at the thought of Sarah on display for his friends to admire.

She wore a scarlet blouse today, with a full black skirt that fell below her knees. The severe cut of the blouse, coupled with the freedom of the skirt finished off with heeled sandals, gave her a look that crossed between carefree hippie and confident businesswoman. A look that showed she was not afraid to make her own statement in the world.

Phillip approved. He loved her independent spirit and the fact that she expressed it through her clothing. As she more and more became his sexual slave, he needed to be sure to allow her this freedom of expression.

In the soft light of the setting sun, Sarah unbuttoned her blouse. With a quick look around, she let it fall off her shoulders, revealing a sexy red pushup bra beneath. The blouse had been buttoned too high to show her cleavage, which, now revealed, showed like a dark line between two beautiful hills of white. The scarlet of the bra only accentuated their paleness, though it beautifully matched the color of her blushing cheeks.

He crossed his arms and leaned against the pillar of the porch as she unzipped her skirt and stepped out of it. Instead of pantyhose, she wore garters and hose with a thong covering her shaved mound. His cock rose, straining the fabric of his pants and he shifted his weight to ease the pressure.

Her seductive smile teased. "You like these?" Turning on the porch, she modeled her sexy underwear. He amended his description of her—carefree hippie mixed with confident businesswoman mixed with a healthy dose of wanton underneath.

"I like them very much, slave. Now take them off."

Phillip absolutely loved the way the color came up in her cheeks when he commanded her. Just as he expected, she took off the least-revealing item first, unsnapping her stocking from the garter and rolling it down her long, shapely leg. She'd draped her blouse and skirt over the porch railing, now she balanced the rolled-up stocking on top before bending and taking off the other. Once that joined its mate, she slid the garter belt down and off, then hesitated. Phillip grinned as she tried to decide which would embarrass her least...the bra or the thong.

A truck roared past the end of the driveway just as she unclasped her bra. With a start, she jumped and looked toward the road as if she expected the driver to magically appear in the small clearing. Phillip watched with amusement as she realized it was already long gone. Her shoulders slumped in relief.

"You will be naked in front of others soon, you know."

Sarah looked up, her eyes wide. Yet her voice was steady when she spoke. "I know. I'm almost ready." She grinned, her composure coming back. "The truck just surprised me, that's all."

Phillip nodded to the north. "Just my neighbor, who drives a big, souped-up truck to prove his manhood to the world."

With an enigmatic smile, Sarah just nodded. She pulled off the bra, then pushed down her thong almost as if she wanted to get the ordeal over with. Phillip recognized the signs. Whether it was something he'd said or just that she thought she'd almost gotten caught, he wasn't sure. But Sarah's sudden rush to get undressed and stand before him naked told him she wanted to be indoors. Fast.

Stepping to the door, he held the screen open for her as she gathered her clothes and brought them in with her. Pushing her to the edge of the cliff without pushing her off tended to be a delicate balance sometimes. Wondering what had suddenly turned her off and hoping he hadn't pushed too far, he followed her inside.

Chapter Two
Limits
ଚ

Sarah set her folded clothes on a chair just inside the living room door, then took the stance Phillip had taught her. Legs slightly parted, her hands clasped behind her back, her chin up and her gaze straight ahead and waiting. A slave's position.

Her nipples stood out in the cooler air inside the cottage and little goose bumps crawled along her arms, making her shiver. She shook herself and took a deep breath, mentally putting away the stresses of the week, relaxing into the role she loved. The questions in the back of her mind could wait until later. After they'd had wonderful sex. Her pussy twitched. Definitely after.

"Your cuffs are on the dining room table. Go put them on."

"Yes, Sir." Stepping lightly, she crossed through the small arch that separated the two rooms and saw the four leather straps lying in a neat row on the table. Four tiny golden locks glinted beside them.

Taking one of the cuffs off the table, she paused to inhale the scent of the leather deep into her lungs. The scent of her submission. She let the aroma settle her deeper into her mindset. Bending to circle her ankle with the cuff, she knew she exposed her pussy to him where he stood in the doorway. She didn't try to hide the naughty grin this time as she closed the lock. As she stood to pick up the cuff for her other ankle, she shifted her position slightly so Phillip could get an even better view. The small snick of the metal going home and locking the leather never failed to send a little shiver along her skin.

Standing again, she kept her legs apart as she picked up the shorter strap of leather designed for her wrist. The left cuff went on easily, fitting snugly. Each click of the little locks pushed her further and further along her weekly journey as she shed her public persona, allowing Phillip more and more control over her body and mind. She didn't even know where he kept the keys to these—and she didn't want to know.

The right cuff gave her trouble, however, as it often did. Being right-handed, using her left hand felt awkward and clumsy. Each time she pulled the cuff tight enough but then felt it loosen as she tried to thread the arm of the lock through the D ring that would secure the leather around her wrist.

"Here. Let me help."

Phillip was there, his fingers assured and comforting. Sarah smiled up at him, loving the way he knew just when she needed help. The soft light of the autumn sunset came in through the screen on the front door and lit the highlights in his dark hair making him look like an angel with a halo of golden light. The last vestige of the everyday mask she wore slipped off, baring her true nature to the only man she had ever trusted to handle it.

"I am yours to command, Sir." Her voice trembled with suppressed anticipation.

Phillip took her chin, tilting her face so he could look into her eyes. He weighed her, as if debating his course of action. Sarah put her now-cuffed arms behind her back, trying to wait patiently. When he spoke, his voice was deceptively soft.

"Each week you come and give so much of yourself to me, my slave. Soon you will live here all the time. Will you be so willing every night when you come home from work?"

"Every night?" Sarah thought of her unchanged, normal days juxtaposed with nights in sexual servitude and her heart beat a little faster. She thought about pushing aside the multitude of questions that had arisen throughout the week. But Phillip only ever wanted the truth from her, no matter how hard it might be to deal with. With regrets, she realized the sex would just have to wait. He knew her too well and wasn't going to let her off easily.

Taking a deep breath, she admitted, "I do want to serve you, however you need me. Every day and every night."

"But?"

All her concerns came out in a headlong rush. "I'm just not sure how. You see me at my best every weekend. All week all I can think of is what the weekend will bring. And I do the laundry and the dusting and I shave my legs and..." She hesitated only a brief second before plunging ahead and saying the word on the tip of her tongue. "My pussy. And I make myself as pretty as I can for you so that when you see me on Friday, you see me at my best." Her cheeks turned red but she didn't dare stop. This was too important and she needed him to know.

"But after we're married, I won't be able to hide all that from you. You'll see me when I'm grumpy and stressed during the week and you'll see me when I'm bloated and feeling fat. I won't be able to keep anything from you and I'm worried you won't like me when I'm...not at my best."

"All right, Sarah. Come here." Phillip took her hand and led her to the couch. Using her name instead of the endearment "my slave" had become his signal to her he wanted to talk to her as an equal. When he indicated that she should sit next to him rather than kneel on the floor, she knew she was right.

She tucked a leg up underneath her and sat facing him, her hands in his. He reached up, tucking a lock of her hair back behind her ear, running his hand down along her cheek to cup her face and she couldn't resist turning to place a kiss in the palm of his hand. He didn't begin until they held hands again.

"Sarah, when you were married to Tom, did he see you in all sorts of moods? Good ones and bad ones?"

"Yes. But that was different."

"How?"

Sarah tried to explain. "Tom and I had a more...well, equal relationship. We made all our decisions together, discussed plans for our future together, even decorated our apartment and then our house together." She shrugged and ducked her head as she always did when talking about sex out loud. "As far as the bedroom, well, we were young and both of us virgins. Neither one of us really knew what we were doing, so mostly we just acted from instinct and without a lot of imagination."

"And you think that's going to be different between us?"

"It has to be!" Sarah frowned. "I mean, I'm going to be your slave!"

"My *sexual* slave." Phillip's hands tightened around hers. "Sarah, you are an independent woman who has moods and thoughts and wonderful ideas all of her own. I am not out to squash that." He paused to look at her with a warning in his eyes. "And I don't want you squashing that either."

"You're my Master, though. When I come here on the weekends, I submit to you. Completely. Even to making you breakfast and sitting at your feet while you eat first." She remembered how angry that had made her the first time he'd asked. But then she'd understood the reasoning behind it and hoped to be able to serve him like that again every once in a while.

Phillip's eyes narrowed. "Okay, Sarah. What is it that's really on your mind? Something tells me you're skirting around an issue."

She opened her mouth to deny it and gave a wry chuckle instead. Her shoulders relaxed, making her wonder when she had gotten so tense. "Yes, Sir. You got me. I am dancing around something." She tried to explain. "I mean, what we've been talking about is really important too, but..." She sighed. "But, well...I want to keep my job." There. Blurting it out wasn't graceful but the issue was now out in the open.

Phillip looked puzzled. "Why wouldn't you keep it?"

"Do you want me to?"

"What difference does it make if I want you to?" Phillip shook his head. "Sarah, haven't you been listening? I love you. I want you. All of you. Your mind, your body, your spirit...everything. That means accepting you with all your good qualities and all the not-so-good ones as well. That also means accepting you with your strong independent streak. I'm not some monster who wants to beat that out of you. Your submission is a gift you give me every weekend. Once we're married, it will be a gift you give me every moment of every day. That doesn't mean you stop being a feeling, *thinking* human being!"

Sarah shook her head. "I just am not sure where the lines are. This is all so new to me."

For answer, Phillip pulled her into his arms, his voice soft against her hair. "I know, Sarah-my-slave, I know. I've made mistakes in the past, mistakes I won't repeat this time. Remember, this is a power sharing we're trying to find our way through. We'll find all our answers together."

Sarah leaned back, looking into his eyes, searching for signs of the power-hungry male she once thought all dominant men to be. Of course, Phillip had shattered that stereotype the very first night he tied her up. She had since learned he would not demand control over her. She had to willingly give it to him.

"So you're saying that, even though I'm your slave, it's possible I could still disagree with you? Or refuse you?"

He hesitated. "Yes...and no. In some things, you might definitely disagree with me or even refuse. In others, you might still refuse but there would be consequences."

"And a part of the journey is deciding which things are which?"

"Yes."

Sarah considered. "And I can keep my job if I want to?"

"You can keep your job if you want to."

"And my friends?"

"And your friends."

"And you'll still tie me up when we have sex?"

Phillip laughed. "And I'll still restrain you in the manner I choose when we have sex."

The rephrasing reasserted his dominance in the relationship and Sarah smiled. They'd work it out together. That was the important part. "Thank you, Sir. I really didn't intend to start our weekend this way. It all sort of…just came out."

Phillip stood and held out his hand and Sarah took it, letting him pull her up beside him. "Remember, slave. I always want honesty from you. Better to get this out of the way now than make me spend the entire evening trying to figure out what I'm doing wrong."

She cocked her head at him. "What do you mean?"

"You get a faraway look in your eyes when your mind isn't totally with me. Usually that means I've pushed a limit too far. Tonight I was afraid it was something I said. Promise me you'll always tell me when you have concerns?"

Smiling, she put her hands behind her head, shifted her weight so she stood with her legs slightly spread and smiled up at him. "I promise, Sir."

He grinned. "In that case, Sarah-my-slave, I do believe you're ready for this." He crossed to the buffet and picked up a thicker leather strap. Coming back to her, he held the collar in both his hands as he waited for her to lean forward and accept her servitude.

Smiling, Sarah gathered her hair and moved it out of the way so he could fasten the leather collar around her neck. The familiar snick of the closing lock flooded her pussy as it always did. She blushed.

Hooking a finger through the ring on the front of the collar, Phillip didn't say another word, only gently pulled her toward the dungeon room. Her heart pounding, Sarah followed eagerly, anxious yet excited at the same time. How would he use her tonight?

He motioned for her to stay in the doorway while he went in and arranged some items. She loved the way all the big pieces were covered in blue velvet, hiding their nefarious purposes, much as she hid her true nature under the everyday clothes she wore. Smiling, she realized she was very much like this room...rather plain-looking on the outside, yet such delightful secrets hidden inside. Just like her. What secrets would Phillip uncover tonight?

The autumn twilight faded quickly, filling the room with long shadows. The room's only window faced east and Sarah knew how cheerful it looked in the mornings. Now, however, as Phillip lit a small candelabrum filled with little white candles, cheerful was not an adjective she'd use. Romantic worked. So did erotic and sexy.

Jarred candles were placed around the room and Phillip lit each of those in turn as well. Only when the place was ablaze with light did he put down the lighter and turn toward where she still stood in the doorway. He held out his hand in a gesture that could not be denied.

Sarah stepped forward, trying not to look too eager, and placed her hand in his. He led her to the center of the room, then stepped back to examine her. Sarah saw hunger in his eyes, mixed with something else too. Something calculating. He definitely had a something up his sleeve tonight. The thought gave her a splendid chill.

"You need something to keep you warm, slave."

Sarah nodded, her hands at her side, loving how his voice deepened as he, too, settled into his role. Would he warm her skin with the deerskin flogger tonight? Or maybe the paddle? She glanced over at the table against the far wall but the blue covering prevented her from seeing the wonderful implements she knew he kept there.

"First, however, you need binding."

He turned back a corner of the blue velvet and picked up a small coil of white cotton clothesline. "Keep your hands at your sides, my slave."

Sarah did as she was told as Phillip threaded the rope through the rings of her wrist cuffs and pulled her arms close to her body. Winding the rope tightly around her belly, he tied it off in the back. "Wiggle," he commanded her.

Obediently, she tried to pull her hands out of the ropes. She could bend over and thence bend her arms but she could not get them free. After a few minutes, she straightened and stilled, her shoulder-length hair falling into her face.

"Hmm...we'll have to do something about that."

Phillip left Sarah standing in the middle of the room and she remembered the first time he'd left her alone while bound. Then she'd been locked in a cage and her thoughts had gotten the better of her. Tonight, however, she could hear him rummaging around for something in the bedroom. He was back in a matter of minutes with an elastic hair band.

"I want your hair out of the way tonight. Kneel."

With her hands bound to her sides, her kneeling wasn't nearly as graceful as she'd practiced. Phillip's hand steadied her and when she was down, he gathered her hair and pulled it into a ponytail near the top of her head. Once it was up, he pulled on the tail a few times, turning her head this way and that.

"I like this, slave." She could hear the grin in his voice, even though his hand on her hair prevented her from looking up at him. "You have lost control even of your head."

Her lips parted as he pulled her hair backward, forcing her to look up at him and she knew her pussy dampened.

"Completely at my mercy." He came around to the front of her, bending and steadying her as he pulled her to her feet. Once she was standing, his hand went again to her ponytail, taking control of her head. Using his other hand, he caressed the length of her exposed neck, putting his fingers around her throat and gently squeezing. Sarah swallowed hard against the sudden pressure. Her pussy flooded as she realized Phillip completely controlled her in everything—even her ability to draw a breath.

She felt his breath on the side of her neck, his tongue caressing the lobe of her ear. Of their own volition, her arms tried to circle him but the ropes prevented them. She couldn't get away and she couldn't actively participate. A low moan escaped from her stretched neck.

Phillip let her ponytail slide from his fingers and Sarah lowered her head, her lips searching, kissing his neck, his chin, finding his lips and opening to him, giving herself into his hands. His tongue, first softly exploring, turned to ravishment as the heat between them ignited, sending Sarah's mind reeling. And when he pulled away, she was grateful that his hands steadied her, knowing she would have fallen if he hadn't held her while the room came back into focus.

"You will be even more at my mercy very soon, my slave."

He was playing mind games with her, she knew that. It didn't matter. Her pussy gushed, filling the air with her musky scent.

Phillip turned away from her now, reaching under the cloth for something different. Not until he pulled a short length from the round tube did she realize it was ordinary cling wrap.

He placed it over her breasts, pressing them flat. "This will bind you tighter than any cords." He pulled it up and she watched her skin rise with it, only to fall back quickly into place. Phillip put it over her face, covering her nose and mouth and Sarah's heart jumped in panic. Without thinking, she opened her lips in order to gulp in air and instead got a mouthful of plastic wrap. Phillip quickly pulled it away but no remorse shone in his eyes. He liked what he was doing to her!

Sarah swallowed hard. This was much more extreme than anything he had done to her before. She watched as he picked up the small butterfly from the tabletop, not knowing whether to groan or cheer. He could keep her on the edge with this little toy for as long as he wanted. The torment, sweet and agonizing, often led to the most incredible orgasms she ever had.

"Spread your legs."

Oh, that command! Even as she shifted her weight and parted her legs for him, those words made her feel like such a slut. And the fact that she would open for him without hesitation showed just how far she'd come in the past few months. Still, her cheeks colored when his fingers slid along her slit and came away soaked with her juices.

Phillip held his fingers before her lips and Sarah didn't need any instruction. He wanted them cleaned. She opened her mouth and leaned forward, eagerly licking her own wetness from his dripping fingers. Once she had the last bit, he took the rubber butterfly and centered it between her lower lips. One end of the toy had a little nub that teased her pussy, the other end would torment her clit. Quickly strapping it in place, he picked up the cling wrap again.

"Close."

Again she shifted, bringing her feet together. The toy between her legs did not yet hum, although she knew from experience he had a wireless remote hidden somewhere that he would use to great effect later. Phillip now knelt on one knee and began wrapping the clear film around her ankles.

Each pass of the tube around her body bound her tighter and tighter. He rose as the wrap reached her knees, then her thighs. Once she tried to look down and watch but that made her overbalance. Phillip caught her but she learned not to do it again.

The plastic film now covered her entire body from the waist down. Her hands, already trapped by the rope, were further trapped by the plastic. She tried wiggling her fingers and found even that movement was difficult. And still Phillip kept wrapping.

He had reached her breasts, except instead of squeezing them flat, he pulled the wrap over and under them around her chest, pushing them together somewhat, while leaving them open for further play. Her shoulders now disappeared under layers of film before he ran out. He tossed the empty cardboard tube onto the blue velvet and turned back to her.

"Up on the table with you now."

For a moment, Sarah thought he meant he wanted her to hop over to the table, bound as she was. She looked at him like he was nuts to expect her to do that. But she should have known better. Phillip scooped her up and Sarah was surprised to discover she could actually bend in all that cling wrap. Not well but she could bend.

This table differed from the one with all the toys hidden on it. This one was closer in height and width to a massage table but with more padding and with eyebolts screwed into the sides that he could use to fasten parts of her body in various wonderful positions. Phillip now used these eyebolts to bind her to the table with a thick white rope crisscrossing her cling-wrapped body like a spider's web. When he was done, he stood back to survey his handiwork.

"Yes, my dearest. You are caught fast and going nowhere." He leaned in, his mouth only inches from her ear. "And in a perfect position for me to play with you all night long and hear all the sounds you make."

She heard him move away but he was back again in seconds, another tube of cling wrap in his hands. "You didn't think we were done, did you?" He grinned and waved the tube where she could see it. Her heart fluttered. Would he really wrap her face?

It seemed he would. The first few passes went around her shoulders again, sticking to the film already in place. She couldn't hold her head up very high and she had to strain her muscles to hold it up while he wrapped the film around and over her neck and mouth. She swallowed hard when Phillip put a gauze pad over each eye and continued wrapping up and over, around and around, taking sight away from her. She could feel him vary the pattern, coming down under her chin and continuing to wrap until her entire head was encased in the cling film. All that remained open was her nose.

A total mummy. Sarah tried to move just to see what movement was left her. Between the cling wrap and the ropes, precious little. If she tried, she could pick her head up but then the wrap around her neck cut deep and threatened to strangle her. Leaving her head to rest on the tabletop definitely was a better option. A strap or rope tightened across her forehead and Sarah sighed inwardly, accepting that even that decision had now been taken away.

The few senses Sarah had left became more acute. She tried to listen for any noise he might make but the wrap over her ears muffled all sounds. The perfumed scents of the candles filled her nose. Alone in her cocoon, she could discern little. Instead, she concentrated on breathing and on remaining calm.

If she could have, she would have smiled. Actually, she was in no danger of panicking. Phillip had left her a way to breathe and she trusted him implicitly. A warm, gentle breeze blew over her exposed breasts and her nipples rose in response. Where did it come from? It puzzled her only a moment before she decided she didn't care. Her body became nothing but sensation as she lay bound and expectant.

For what seemed like several long minutes, nothing happened. In her dark world, her mind eased as she slid into a state where she was comfortable with her bindings. Cocooned, she felt hugged by the plastic wrap, safe and secure from the world outside.

A sharp stab on her breast jolted her from her complacency. A second, then a third little prick made her wiggle. To no avail, however. Between the wrap and the ropes holding her down, she could not escape the torrent of hot stabbings that now tore across the top of her right breast.

A pause in the assault. Sarah breathed heavily through her nose, unable to ask Phillip what he was doing. She could only experience. Now that the small stings had stopped, she realized they didn't really hurt. The tiny pinpricks had stung for a second, then vanished as if they hadn't ever been there. She inhaled deeply as she settled herself and realized something pulled at the skin on her breast.

Before she could puzzle it out, another assault began, this time centered on her left breast. As before, tiny pricks that stung jumped all over her exposed skin. She tensed up as the stings circled the areola, thankful they did not approach any closer to her nipple.

Another pause. Phillip's voice beside her ear, sounding far away through the wrap. "Hot wax, my dear. The sting barely felt. I will cover your breasts in wax and listen to the moans that come from deep within your need."

Sarah's pussy clenched, a small spasm making her skin tingle. Damn, if she couldn't come from just this, he controlled her so well. But he hadn't given her permission and, wrapped as she was, she couldn't ask for it. One of the moans he wanted to hear escaped the confines of the wrap.

Drops of wax hit her skin. Knowing what it was didn't help. She wanted more even as she wanted them to stop. Each drop moved closer and closer to her nipple only to circle around and drip between her breasts or to make a lazy figure eight around the twin mounds.

And then one drop of wax directly on her nipple. Even with her bindings, the sudden tensing of her body was evident. Phillip waited a moment, then dropped another drip from directly above her other nipple.

The moans that came from behind the plastic wrap over her mouth didn't increase in volume but her need still came through loud and clear. Not letting up, he dribbled wax in a continuous flow from the candle, encasing her entire nipple in a sheath of white. He didn't stop until every inch of her areola was covered and then he paused only long enough to move from one breast to the other.

The moans had turned to whimpers now as he finished laying down an equally thick coat of wax on her right nipple. Her breasts heaved with her breathing and Phillip stepped back to examine his most beautiful slave.

Her body, stretched along the table and bound with white rope, glimmered in the light of the myriad candles. Her breasts, covered in white wax, moved slower now as he let her regain her composure and he thanked the power that had brought Sarah into his life.

For years Phillip had looked for the woman who could handle his passions and his desire to dominate in the bedroom. Although inexperience had doomed one relationship when he was still in his twenties and inflexibility had doomed another, with Sarah he felt as if he'd found the other half of himself. She not only took what he gave her but turned it around and gave it back to him fivefold. She deserved the best experiences he could design for her.

Picking up a stiff crop, he paused a moment more before bringing it into play. This would take her totally by surprise. The neck of the crop was much stiffer than anything he'd used on her in the past and the sting would be much stronger as a result. The end was also made of stiff leather, not floppy and soft like the one he'd used a few weekends ago. If he allowed her her voice, he was sure she'd scream first and scold later.

Without another thought, he slapped it down across her breasts.

He wasn't disappointed in her reaction. The guttural scream, cut off and muffled by the plastic wrap, still came out loud and clear in the silence of the room. He thwacked her breasts again, watching the wax pop off one nipple entirely to roll down off her breast, across the small space of the table and onto the floor. Picking up the candelabrum, he checked her breasts.

Two small pink spots showed where the crop had landed, but other than that, the now-cracked white wax had protected her skin. He set down the candles and snapped the crop across her breasts several times in quick succession. Wax flew off in several directions as he flipped it with the stiff crop. Even after the majority was gone, he continued slapping her breasts from side to side with the crop, listening to her cries.

Time to bring in his secret weapon.

Sarah had forgotten all about the butterfly between her legs. The stiff crop had prevented her from thinking anything at all, but the sudden vibration on her clit quickly refocused her thoughts. She wanted to come. No, she needed to come. Desperately.

The stinging on her breasts subsided as the vibration between her legs increased. Her hands tried to move, to press the toy against her clit and hasten her coming. Frustrated, her whimper became a sob.

The vibrations grew even stronger. Her attention, desiring to solely focus on her pussy, was torn by her inability to move and by the small, light slaps he now rained on her breasts. Her mind couldn't deal with all the sensations. Quick, small breaths balanced her on the edge of a precipice as her mind shut down everything but the tension that coiled ever tighter. A tension centered just beneath that little pink butterfly.

A hard slap across her breasts sent her hurtling over the edge, plummeting downward only to rise again as the spasms racked her body. As her muscles contracted over and over, her spirit dove and rose, released in total freedom from her bound body. She soared through the clouds, diving and dipping in their incredible whiteness, relief and joy intermingling in total freedom made possible only by the binding of her body. Even after the vibrations stopped and the ropes were removed, Sarah lay listless, her body contracting sporadically as her mind gloried in the ride.

Fresh air cooled her legs and dimly Sarah realized Phillip was cutting away the plastic wrap, allowing her skin to breathe again. Her soul was too contented to be disturbed by moving, however. Satisfied, she remained relaxed, letting him play with her as if she were a rag doll or a puppet he could control.

Does control, she amended, in a slow, buzzed sort of way inside her mind. She felt him push her right leg up until her heel just touched the back of her thigh. He must've tied it there somehow, she decided, when she realized she couldn't straighten it again. The thought didn't alarm her. She simply accepted whatever he would do, content to let him take his pleasure any way he wanted.

He did the same to the other leg, leaving the plastic on the upper half of her body, her fingers free to wiggle but her wrists still tight to her hips. She felt herself being pulled along the table and realized he must've brought her to the edge so he could take her. The thought of accepting his cock stirred her idle tolerance and tendrils of tension began to weave together again.

But it wasn't his cock she felt after he removed the wet butterfly. Warmth enveloped her and the aware part of her brain, which admittedly was still mostly asleep, realized he was washing her with a wonderfully soft, warm cloth. He dried her as well and if she'd had the energy, she would have smiled.

Phillip set the towel aside and picked up her favorite instrument, letting the smooth deerskin barely touch the skin of her thighs. Dragging the long thongs along her pussy lips, Phillip pulled the small flogger through her slit, watching her reactions. With her head bound as it was, he could not read the look in her eyes or listen to her words. While part of him missed those, another part enjoyed the total power she gave him. He pulled the flogger through her slit again and when she creamed, he knew she wanted more.

A heaving flogging was not what he had in mind this time, however. He pulled a stool over to the end of the table and sat down, arranging a few of the candles so her slit was fully lighted. With the flogger, he continued to lull her, not really slapping it against her skin but rather lightly landing it and pulling it through her legs.

Two minutes, three minutes…five minutes. He didn't change the slow pace or the lightness of the slaps. Her breathing settled into a regular pattern and he knew her mind was floating free once more. Time to up the ante.

Almost imperceptibly, he let the flogger land a little harder against her pussy lips. Not much, just enough to move her even deeper into the subspace she longed for. Every ten or so slaps he would increase the strength of the slap, still keeping the same slow pace.

A pace that became maddeningly slow to her. Phillip could tell by the whimpers that were really small moans in the back of her throat. He obliged her and picked up the pace. Her pussy lips turned pink now and fresh white cream appeared. He increased the intensity again and listened to the whimpers turn to muffled pleas.

He hit her tender flesh harder now, each blow making her soul swell with desire. She arched her back and he quickened the pace, watching her body's reactions. And when she came, he knew by the way her voice wailed in the back of her throat and by the way her pussy lips opened, inviting him in.

Phillip needed no second invitation. Dropping the flogger on the blue velvet, he stood and slid his pants off, his cock already hard. Long and thick, he knew she would take him easily, yet he tormented himself first, rubbing his cock head in her juices until it glistened.

Only then did he plunge into her tight hole, her swollen pussy lips enveloping him in a snug embrace. Her body accepted more than half his length in his first thrust. Pulling out, he pushed in again and again, feeling her take more of him each time until his cock was fully buried inside her.

He stayed there, pushing against her body, forcing her to stretch and accept his cock, his balls firmly against her body. His soul expanded as she bucked and cried out beneath him, her submission filling his spirit, his dominance fueling his power. Mercy was his to give or not give. Pleasure and pain were his to command. She gave him everything she had and he took it, savoring her willingness.

He gloried in the sight of her beneath him, her body still partially wrapped in plastic film and unable to stop him, her breasts heaving, stray pieces of wax still spotting the perfect globes of her breasts, her face covered, unable to see him as he took her, her mind floating and totally at his mercy.

With a loud groan, he came. Closing his eyes to the vision before him, he gloried in the power that coursed through him, releasing in swells of almost unbearable force. He gave himself to that power, letting it empty his soul as her muscles milked his cock, her cries muted echoes of his groans. They moved as one, their spirits entwined, their needs fulfilled in each other's passion. Their entire world existed in these eternal seconds.

His eyes still closed, Phillip lay forward, resting his head on Sarah's bound body. His cheek registered the plastic that still bound her.

It was not yet time for him to give up control. Much as he loathed to leave the warmth of her sheath, his slave needed his attention and care. With a tired smile and a look of total contentment on his face, Phillip set the third act of their time together into motion.

Sarah felt the rest of plastic being cut from her body, the cool air giving her a slight chill. Her mind noted the fact as if it were happening to someone else, someone not even related to her in any way. Phillip had sent her into the heavens again and she had come several more times. Sated now, she simply accepted that he was done, contentment stealing into every pore of her body.

Even when he peeled the plastic from her face and gently removed the pads from her eyes, she stirred only enough to murmur, "Thank you, Sir," before he blew out the last remaining candle and scooped her into his arms. Tired and satisfied, she mustered just enough energy to snuggle beside him in bed before sleep took her.

Chapter Three
Wedding bands

ᔓ

Saturday morning dawned rainy and cold. Overnight, the last of the summer weather had fled for the season, leaving harbingers of the coming winter in its stead. Sarah woke to the drumming of rain on the roof and lay listening to it, letting it lull her back into a pleasant dream where Phillip placed a ring of gold around her ankle and called her his.

Why my ankle? The stray thought came from nowhere as she lay suspended between the worlds of the conscious and unconscious mind. *Why would Phillip put a wedding band around my ankle? That doesn't make sense.*

Still sleepy, she rolled over to look at the man she would marry in another few weeks. But her body didn't exactly cooperate. Her ankles moved as one unit. She snuggled into her pillow. Apparently Phillip had tied her cuffs together at some point, though her hands were free. The thought brought a smile to her lips. She loved that he had control over her even as she slept. And she had an answer to her strange dream.

Returning to sleep, however, was no longer an option. She needed to use the bathroom and listening to the rain wasn't helping. Craning her neck to see the clock, she could just make out the red numbers. 6:50 a.m. She sighed and waited.

Nope. No use. She had to go to the bathroom. Pushing the covers back, she pulled her legs from under the sheets and placed them together on the floor. Only a shoelace joined the two rings at her ankles. All she had to do was reach down, untie them, go to the bathroom and come back to bed. Once in bed, she could retie them and Phillip would never know.

Sarah shook her head. Didn't matter whether he knew or not. She would know and that was enough. Untying them would be cheating. Sliding down onto her hands and knees, she was careful not to jiggle the bed too much and wake up her lover and Master.

There was enough play in the shoelace to allow her minimum movement. By throwing her hip out to the side, she could move her knee forward an inch or so, then do the same with the other. She must make quite a sight, she realized, squirming her way across the room like an oversized worm. All the same, it didn't take as long to reach the bathroom as she thought it would.

Getting onto the toilet seat proved interesting. Using the sink to balance herself, she got up onto her knees and then hopped up onto her feet with a fairly loud thud. Thankfully the toilet wasn't more than a small hop away.

Phillip's head poked around the corner. "What are you doing?"

Sarah's heart jumped as it did every time he walked into a room. She stated the obvious answer to his question. "Um…using the facilities?"

He came into the bathroom, not a stitch of clothing on. "Why didn't you untie your ankles first? You could have fallen."

"No, I couldn't. I crawled in here, then only needed one short hop to get to the toilet. I was fine."

"You didn't answer my question." Phillip stooped down in front of her, grabbing the end of the tie and pulling it loose.

"Why didn't I untie myself? Why should I? I figured you wanted me tied, so I just went with it. I'd never undo something you did unless it was an emergency or some such." She gestured to the bathroom. "I needed to go but I managed just fine."

Phillip grinned and shook his head. "I'm sorry. I thought I undid all your bindings last night but must've missed this one when I carried you in to bed. I'm afraid this was an unintentional tie-up." He stood and walked to the door, the shoelace dangling in his fingers. "Finish up, then my turn."

As she later sat on the bed waiting for Phillip to finish his shower, she jingled the locks on her cuffs, idly playing with them as she thought about what he'd said. That the shoelace was just a leftover from the night before. She didn't even remember him tying them together but that didn't matter. Phillip sounded as if he wouldn't have cared if she had undone the lace and left it undone. But she couldn't do that. Didn't he understand that?

Phillip reappeared in the bedroom doorway, toweling his hair. Sarah loved to look at him. Strong shoulders that carried her when she was too exhausted to move, tapered down to a firm, flat stomach. Since he used his towel on his hair, she had a great view below his waist. Even though his cock wasn't active right now, she still loved the sight of it, nestled in its thatch of dark hair. She knew how long it would grow and how the tip could turn a beautiful shade of red-purple when he was close to bursting. She loved the feel of it growing in her hand, the veins rising as she excited him. A wicked little grin raised the sides of her mouth.

"Oh, no, you little minx. Not this morning." Phillip laughed as he turned away from her, rummaging in his drawers for his clothes. "We have errands to run today. Or did you forget we have a few wedding appointments to keep?"

Sarah glanced in panic at the clock. He was right. They had plenty of time but not if they dawdled for sex. "All right." She knew disappointment colored her words but grinned to let him know she didn't really mind. "I need to get into the shower, though."

Holding her hands up to him, she waited as he retrieved the keys and removed the cuffs from her wrists and ankles. Obediently, she held up her hair while he also removed the heavy collar they used for play.

"Off to shower, then, minx." Phillip glanced at the clock. "I'll take you out for breakfast after we meet with the jeweler."

"Sounds good!" Sarah bounced across the room, pausing for one last glance before she shut the door on the sight of his naked ass just being covered with dark slacks.

Phillip laid out the new clothes he'd bought for her during the week. He loved dressing her. He set the clothes on the bed, then stared at the bathroom door a moment as he thought about what life would be like when they married and she moved here full time. A snippet of song came from the shower and he smiled.

Obviously he couldn't dress her every day. In some of his fantasies he thought of her as a real, live doll he could dress up and then play with. But in reality, she was an independent working woman with responsibilities of her own. He picked up one of the cuffs and stared at it, weighing his dream world against the truth. While having a woman to do his every bidding, to play with or put on the shelf—or in a cage—as he saw fit, certainly held a great deal of attraction, the responsibility that came with such control boggled his mind. Having any pet meant taking care of that pet's needs often before his own. He'd had a dog for a few months once but had found a good home for it when the constant need to be walked, fed, petted and bathed just got to be too much.

Of course, he had just been starting up the business then and didn't have a lot of extra time. Now that he was semi-retired and had made enough money to live on for the rest of his life, he had time on his hands.

But he didn't want Sarah to become just a pet. Well, he did, if he was being honest. Only a pet that could bathe herself, except when he felt like bathing her. A pet he didn't need to take for a walk, except when he felt like putting a leash on her. A pet he could do anything he wanted with, except when he was too tired to do anything at all. In other words, a woman who would be his slave-pet combination when he wanted her to be and be a normal wife at all other times.

Selfish, that's what you are, he chided himself. *You want it all. Companion, sex-slave, trophy to show off to your friends.*

But Sarah doesn't seem to mind, another part of his psyche chimed in. *She likes being controlled. You saw that with the stupid shoelace this morning. She's not going to say no to you. To anything you want to do to her or any way you want to treat her.*

He chuckled. Okay, not the last. Although he'd been rough, he'd never been abusive and never would. There was a line there and if he crossed it, Sarah would be out the door in a heartbeat. And he wouldn't blame her. Pushing limits was fun only until he pushed too far. He was determined not to let that happen.

The song and the water stopped. Phillip scooped up the cuffs and put them in the top drawer where they belonged when they weren't being used. With a last look at the clothes on the bed, he sauntered out of the room to get things organized for their errand day.

The outfit on the bed took Sarah's breath away. He had such exquisite taste, she should probably let him choose all her clothes.

Actually, from the waist down, the attire was fairly ordinary for a Saturday of errands. White socks, sneakers and a pair of low-rise jeans with no panties made her feel naughty without giving anything away. But the white demi-cup push-up bra was anything but normal for her. The push-up bra she'd worn for him before had covered her entire breast. This one left very little to the imagination.

The blouse, however, caught her eye. White-on-white embroidery traced a flowing design around the low-cut neckline. The long sleeves belled at the wrists, making her feel like a lady-in-waiting in a fairytale Camelot. She spent a moment preening in front of the long mirror in the bedroom before giving her wet hair a final combing and dancing out to the living room.

Turning a pirouette, she modeled the blouse for Phillip. "Thank you, Sir. This blouse is beautiful!" She flounced the sleeves.

Phillip grinned. "Glad you like it." He tugged it lower on her shoulders, exposing her cleavage.

Sarah's eyebrows rose at the amount of skin she was now showing and resisted the urge to pull the material back up. If Phillip wanted her showing her attributes like this, then show them she would. And proudly.

"I do have one more thing to make that outfit complete." Phillip picked up a small box from the table at the end of the couch. "Something you and I understand but the rest of the world admires in a very different way."

Sarah knew what was in the box. She'd worn it before. Obediently turning around and holding up her hair, she waited as he pulled out the thin strip of leather that was her "going-out" collar.

"I like this," he told her as he tied the ends together. "It's something that reminds you of your slavery but not in an overt way."

Sarah blushed. "It's wonderful." Snug and comfortable, she knew she'd forget all about it after a while and then have its presence come flooding back when she would suddenly remember. The thought caused a minor flood somewhat lower in her body right now, as she was sure Phillip intended.

"I like it very much, Sir. Thank you." She took his hand as they walked to the door, pausing at the small, gilt-framed mirror that hung beside the front door. With the blouse pulled off her shoulders, the choker made her neck look longer and more slender than it already was. "Definitely like this a lot," she murmured, her fingers lightly brushing it as if to make sure it was real.

"I'm glad." Phillip slipped his arms around her, examining her reflection in the mirror. "From now until the wedding, you'll wear this every time you go out instead of just when we go out together on the weekends. Even when you're going to work."

Sarah turned a little so she could look up at him. "And at work, they'll see it as a fashion statement."

"And only you will know otherwise."

She turned back to the mirror and leaned against the broad expanse of his chest, loving the strength and contentment she found there, her mind skipping ahead to Monday when she would walk in wearing a normal suit...and this collar. Her pussy twitched just thinking about it. "Oh, yes," she sighed. "I am definitely going to love this."

Sarah giggled as she slid into the passenger's side of Phillip's winter rat. He'd put the sexy black Corvette in storage for the snowy months and now he escorted her from place to place in an old, but still stylish, Saturn.

"We're stopping so often...are we ever going to go?"

Phillip gave her an evil grin. "Tonight. Tonight we will go so far that you might wish we'd stopped earlier."

She opened her mouth to make a retort but couldn't think of one. Instead, she just narrowed her eyes and gave him a penetrating look as if trying to see through his plans.

Phillip laughed. "No use, slave. You're not going to figure it out until we meet up with everyone."

Sarah shook her head and sat back. "Where are we going now?"

As he drove, Phillip explained that Anberg's had been making one-of-a-kind jewelry for over forty years and that the shop was located in a neighborhood that had seen better days. Sarah shook her head over the abandoned houses and empty storefronts that lined the streets in this part of the city. "Seems to me the city could do something about luring people back here."

"Crime is the number one reason people moved away in the first place."

"Is that why you moved away?"

Phillip shook his head, stopping at a traffic light. "Nah, I just wanted somewhere nice and private so I could bring women back to my place and torture them."

Sarah snorted. "Some torture. Orgasm after orgasm after orgasm?" She gave a mock sigh. "It's a tough life but someone has to do it."

She loved to hear him laugh, his rich baritone rumbling in the car's small space. As the car moved forward again, she gestured to a burnt-out house sitting in the middle of the next block. "Like that one there. And those..." She pointed to a collection of boarded-up houses, one of which had very little roof left and another with a sagging porch. "See those? They look tired. Have pity on them and tear them down and start all over. Maybe put in two houses where there were three. Redesign the entire block." She sat back smugly, then shook her head in dismay. "We're creating donuts out of our cities with everyone moving to the suburbs. People are moving out of the center and leaving great big holes where wonderful downtowns used to be. There's only a finite amount of land and we're wasting some of the best living spaces!"

"Okay," answered Phillip, in his best devil's advocate voice, "you create neighborhoods of bigger houses and more property, they're going to cost more, right?"

Sarah conceded the point.

"And if all these neighborhoods in the city go upscale, then where do those who can't afford the bigger houses go to live?"

Phillip loved the way her brow furrowed when she puzzled out a problem. "People take better care of property they own than property they rent. That's a given."

"Why do you think that?"

She shook her head. "Don't distract me, now. They just do. Probably because they know they'll just have to pay to repair something that breaks rather than call the landlord to deal with it. But my point is, you'd have to get the houses into the hands of people who care and the way to do that is through ownership rather than renting."

"You didn't answer my question."

She grinned. "I know. I'm stalling while I think up a really good answer." She gazed at the postage stamp-sized yards with spaces between the houses no bigger than a single-car driveway. Finally she sighed. "I have no idea. There has to be a way to have all classes live side by side in peace and harmony."

She rolled her eyes. "Okay, I'm sounding like a bad Christmas commercial. I don't have a solution but I know there is one somewhere. Just 'cause I haven't stumbled on it yet doesn't mean I won't."

He glanced at her, bemused. He hadn't seen her so intense about a subject before. Apparently sexual passion wasn't the only emotion she kept bottled up. Well, he'd begun unchaining her sexual desires... Briefly he wondered if he could help her channel her other energies and interests as well.

Phillip turned the corner and pulled up to a yellow brick building. Two shops stood side by side. The sign above the one on the right was cracked and peeled. Yellowed newspaper taped to the windows showed Sarah the store had been vacant since 1983.

The sidewalk in front of the jeweler on the left was freshly swept and the trim around the windows of his storefront had been freshly painted, though the bars on the windows were a testament to the changing times. Even though the awning over the door had faded in the sunlight, no rips or holes marred the stretched fabric. Phillip opened the door for her and a bell tinkled on the handle.

The narrow store stretched back only about twenty feet. To the left, a glass-topped counter ran the length of the store, the dark wooden case well-polished. Sarah peeked through the glass and her breath caught at the beauty of the silver pieces that gleamed up at her. Bracelets, necklaces, rings...all were displayed on artfully draped lengths of black velvet. Each piece was distinctive, yet a similar style pulled them all together. The artist was magnificent.

At the sound of the bell that signaled their entrance, a door quickly opened at the rear of the store and an elderly gentleman entered the shop. With his white hair and slow step, one might be tricked into thinking this was a feeble old man, but when his bright blue eyes lit up upon seeing them, Sarah saw an indomitable spirit that would not be cowed by the slow death of the surrounding neighborhood.

"Phillip, my dear boy! How good it is to see you." He held out his hand to shake Phillip's over the counter. Sarah had the distinct impression that they would have hugged if the glass display case hadn't been between them.

"Hello, Uncle Irv. You're looking great."

His uncle? Sarah resisted the urge to raise an eyebrow. Phillip had somehow forgotten to mention that little tidbit of information.

"And who is the lovely woman at your side?"

Phillip put his arm around her waist as he introduced her. "This is Sarah. She has consented to be my wife."

Even as she extended her hand to Phillip's uncle, Sarah felt the atmosphere change. Was it her imagination or did Mr. Anberg hesitate ever so slightly before taking her hand? But then the moment passed and he was smiling and charming and offering to show them his favorite set of wedding bands. Sarah glanced outside and decided the sudden chill she got must just be from a passing cloud.

Phillip picked a ring from the velvet pad on the counter and held it for Sarah to see. Made of silver, the artist had taken a traditional Celtic knot design and changed the angles slightly, giving the intricate pattern that circled the ring more of an art deco flair.

"And see?" Phillip's uncle pointed to one of the threads of silver that made up the knots. "If you follow that all the way around the ring, you'll discover the entire series of knots is made up from one single line."

"Really?" Sarah reached over and Phillip handed her the ring. She twisted and turned it, her eye following the line as it intersected itself over and over until she had gone around the ring twice.

The old man nodded toward the ring in her fingers. "The symbolism is perfect for a wedding ring. Two lines that seem independent of each other but are truly one life intertwining."

"And you designed this?" Sarah was enchanted. "Mr. Anberg, it's wonderful!"

"You call me Uncle Irv if you're going to be a member of the family."

This time Sarah knew for certain that the atmosphere changed. Mr. Anberg—Uncle Irv—and Phillip exchanged a glance that seemed to communicate some sort of secret message. What were they up to?

"And will you need anything else?" Uncle Irv looked pointedly at Phillip who turned to Sarah.

Phillip pushed a lock of her hair behind her ear, playing with the end in a possessive gesture. Without looking away from Sarah, he answered his uncle. "Yes, Sir. We do."

A huge smile came from the old man. "Good! Good. Come in the back, then and let me get my tape."

Sarah sent a quizzical look at Phillip, who only smiled at her and gestured for her to follow his uncle. Mystified, she did so, trusting that he wasn't leading her into some den of iniquity.

The workshop behind the door looked like any other artist's studio. Tools and scraps of paper covered the workbench where a large, round magnifying glass sat propped on its bent metal arm. Sarah wondered what treasures she would find if she looked through it.

A smaller display case occupied a similar position in the workroom as did the larger one out front. The bracelets here were more of the wide-banded type, although there were several that had small chains connecting the bracelet to a ring that were obviously meant to be worn as a set. She flexed her hand unconsciously as her mind reacted to the confinement such a ring and bracelet could produce.

She looked a little further in the case and saw an assortment of earrings. Sarah shook her head. Why would anyone want to wear an earring with such a huge gold ball on both sides? Looked more like a barbell than an earring. Well, there was no accounting for taste. Although she did rather like the set with the two small hoops and a chain of amethyst hanging from each one. But why the tiny gold chain connecting them? It didn't seem long enough to go under a woman's chin and would look silly across the bridge of her nose. She turned to Phillip to ask about them when Uncle Irv noticed what had her attention.

"Ah, I see my soon-to-be niece has discovered the nipple rings."

Phillip wished he had a camera to capture the look on Sarah's face at his uncle's pronouncement. Her jaw dropped open and the color came up in her cheeks so wonderfully.

"Nipple rings?" Her voice trembled and Phillip hurried to reassure her.

"Perhaps we will purchase a set in the future, Uncle. But Sarah isn't quite ready for those. Yet."

He let the seed be planted. Time would tell him if it would take root or not. He peered over Sarah's shoulder. "That amethyst set is nice, though."

Beside him, Sarah took in a deep breath. "Actually, it's quite pretty." She smiled wanly. "At least now I know where the little gold chain hangs."

Phillip chuckled and turned back to his uncle. "If you have your tape, you can take measurements for her collar."

Sarah darted a glance at him and he smiled down at her. "A silver torc to match our silver wedding rings. One the world will understand, the other…well, the other will only be understood by a small, select group of people."

She let the air out of her lungs as sudden understanding came. "Like Will and Anton and Jill and Mistress Aleshia."

"Yes, among others you haven't met yet."

Sarah looked at Uncle Irv and Phillip grinned. "Uncle Irving has been making specialized jewelry for longer than I've been alive." He gestured around the shop. "And he's very, very good."

Uncle Irv stood by his workbench, a cloth tape measure in his hands. "I taught Phillip how to appreciate women, how to make them feel special with beautiful adornments for the glorious, too-often-hidden parts of their bodies." He gestured for Sarah to come sit on a stool by his bench. With a look at Phillip for support, she did so.

Phillip gathered and lifted Sarah's hair. If he'd thought about it earlier, he would have had her wear it in a ponytail today. He especially liked the exposure of her neck, circled only by the strip of leather she would wear from now until the wedding. The thin brown line accentuated her natural elegance, yet gave her an air of vulnerability at the same time. Standing in his uncle's shop today, Phillip enjoyed the way Sarah's hair felt in his hands, how it fell over his clenched fist to tickle against his knuckles.

Uncle Irv laid the tape flat around her neck. "Here, Phillip? Or do you want the torc to go lower?"

Phillip peeked around the front. The tape lay across the hollow of her neck that he loved to kiss. "A little lower," he told the jeweler, who made the adjustments.

"Yes?"

Phillip looked again. "Perfect."

"Good." Uncle Irv turned to get a pencil and a fresh sheet of paper. "Now you sit like a good girl and don't move. Let me write this down."

Phillip continued to hold up her hair as his uncle took a few more measurements and drew rough sketches on scraps of paper. He let it down only when Uncle Irv stepped back with a satisfied smile. "Done!"

Sarah's smile was a little tight as she took Phillip's hand and rose to stand next to him. Phillip watched her eyes continually rove to the display case. Did she want her nipples pierced? Or was she afraid he was going to ask her to get them done as a part of the marriage ceremony? Silently he cursed himself for not preparing her as to what he had in mind. He'd remedy that soon.

They took their leave, Phillip giving the old man a hug now that the counter wasn't in his way. He was gratified when Sarah did the same. He saw the pleasure that came into the old man's eyes when she kissed him on the cheek and thanked him for his art. When his old uncle nodded and winked at him over her shoulder, Phillip knew Sarah had definitely charmed him. Was it any wonder he loved her?

By the time they left the shop, the sun had come out and the weather was warming. The autumn colors blazed in solo events here in the city, however. Rather than a hillside tapestry of reds and greens and oranges, the city block held spaced splotches of single trees here and there. They still hadn't had a frost inside the city limits, so this couldn't officially be called an Indian summer, but the warmth of the sun promised a pleasant turn to the day.

"That's the first member of your family I've met." Sarah slid into the passenger seat as Phillip held the door for her. She loved that he did that. While she was perfectly capable of getting her own door, and did most of the time, the fact that Phillip cared enough to take the extra steps meant a lot to her.

"Uncle Irv has been a Dom longer than I've been alive." He shut the car door and came around to the driver's side, sliding in and buckling his belt before starting the car. "He was the first one I confided in when I was a young teenager."

"How did you do that? I can't imagine telling anyone about…" She left the sentence unfinished. Heck, she didn't even have the words to express it to Phillip, how could she ever tell a family member she liked to be tied up and dominated?

"I still don't know if it was by accident or design on his part." They pulled away from the shop and Sarah glanced back. Such a lonely building that held such wonderful secrets. She sighed. Like she used to be before she found Phillip.

"I was about fifteen and had just discovered girls," Phillip continued. "Or rather, they had discovered me." He grinned that rakish grin that Sarah suspected had something to do with girls falling all over him.

"My dad was away a lot on business and hard-ons are definitely not something a boy talks to his mother about."

Sarah giggled. "It's hard enough for a girl to talk to her mother about sexual feelings. For a boy it's gotta be downright impossible."

"Uncle Irv and Aunt Tess were my favorite aunt and uncle. They've always lived above the shop and there's a separate entrance in the back. We kids weren't allowed into the store much back then and certainly never in the back room. He sold a lot of other jewelry back then. Stuff he'd buy from a wholesaler and then resell. Once Aunt Tess died, he sold off all that stock and went into semi-retirement. Now he only sells what he makes himself."

"So how did the two of you get to talking about sex?"

"I had walked over to see them—" At Sarah's look of surprise, he smiled. "This neighborhood used to be pretty middle-class. A mixture of cultures, really. Great place to grow up. There were the Steins living next to us, the Washingtons across the street, the Riveras two doors down. The American melting pot right on my own street."

"What happened?" Sarah gestured to the row of abandoned houses they were passing.

"The suburbs." He shrugged. "Upward mobility meant moving out of the crowded city and into identical houses in subdivisions. Everybody left. The donut effect, as you so recently called it. And where there's a void left..."

"Crime moves in," Sarah finished for him, looking out the window.

"One of these days I'd like to do exactly what you said before—buy up an entire block, both sides of the street, and start again."

"Why don't you?"

Phillip looked at her. "Guess I just need the right woman beside me egging me on."

Sarah grinned. "I bet I can find a cattle prod somewhere if you need it."

He laughed out loud. Sarah loved that laugh. So rich and rolling it always made her chuckle in response.

"If you've already found it, I think I need to find a better hiding place!"

She looked at him in mock horror. "You don't really have one, do you?"

He waggled his eyebrows at her but didn't answer as he turned onto the expressway that would take them out of town and back to their cozy nest in the middle of the woods. She changed the subject.

"Okay, back to your story. You walked to your aunt and uncle's and…"

"Uncle Irv was in the store and Aunt Tess was out grocery shopping. With no customers in the store, we shot the breeze for a while, then I asked him about girls. Specifically, I asked him how come they kept calling me, when I knew…when I wanted it to be the other way around. I didn't like it when they called me." Sarah watched him frown over the steering wheel, remembering his early struggles with understanding what he was.

"He and I talked for a bit. I don't know what prompted him but at one point, he stood up and told me to follow him to the back room." Phillip glanced over at her and Sarah glimpsed the little boy's pleasure at being allowed his first look at the adult world.

"It was there he told me about Dominance and submission. About what a Master was and about the responsibilities that went along with the role. He also told me I wasn't really old enough to understand it all and that if I wanted to go out with girls I liked I should take the initiative and make the first call."

He chuckled. "After that, my visits to the back room became more frequent but always controlled by him. I didn't realize it until much later, but in many ways, Uncle Irv was my first mentor. He taught me a great deal about the lifestyle, but in language a boy could understand. I owe him more than I could ever express."

"And so do I." Sarah shyly put her hand on his thigh and gave it a squeeze.

They rode in companionable silence for several miles. Not until they turned onto the country road that led to the cottage did Sarah broach a subject she had been turning over in her mind. She chose to use his title, signaling her train of thought.

"Sir, the torc I was just measured for. You said it would be a symbol to a select group of people that we were wed. What did you mean by that?"

"The civil ceremony we're planning will be the legal one. That's the one that binds us in the eyes of not only the law but by all standards of society."

"Right. Is there another one?"

"By agreeing to be my wife, you agreed to wear my collar."

Sarah nodded. "Yes, but I already do that." She thought about the thick leather collar waiting for her at the cottage. The snick of it locking home always gave her a little thrill. So what purpose did the torc... She turned to him. "Wait, do you mean..."

He pulled in the drive and parked next to the house before turning to her. "Yes, I do mean. The torc I will put around your neck will bind you to me forever, Sarah. We'll have a second ceremony that night. One with fewer guests, yet no less meaningful." He took a deep breath. "Probably more meaningful, really."

"How so?" Sarah wasn't afraid, though her heart was beating hard. She put her hand over his as she faced him in the car.

"We will exchange another set of vows, vows you and I will write together. I will promise my love and fidelity, just like in the civil ceremony, but I'll also promise to protect you and keep you forever."

Sarah began to understand the drift the vows would take. "And to my promise of love and fidelity, I'll be promising to serve you always?"

"Something like that."

She saw doubt in his eyes and with a shock, realized he didn't know if she would agree to this. "Phillip, we probably should have talked about this earlier but to be honest, I want to be with you. Always. I want to serve you and I definitely like being your sex slave." She couldn't keep down the naughty grin that spread across her face. "Saying vows to that effect will only formalize what we already have."

Phillip reached across the car and kissed her. Hard, taking possession of her all over again and Sarah kissed back, giving all that she could. He must never doubt this was what she wanted with all her heart.

Not until their lips parted did Phillip pull back from her, a look on his face like that of a little boy who hadn't told the entire truth about breaking a window. Sarah braced herself, knowing there was something more. But Phillip's words, at first, seemed innocuous.

"The torc will be permanent, Sarah."

She nodded. "Of course it will. Just like the wedding band."

"No, a wedding band can be removed."

Sarah frowned, then sat back as his meaning suddenly dawned. "You mean I'll never be able to take it off?"

"It will be welded on during the ceremony."

"Oh." She sat for a moment, trying to decide how she felt about that. Her pussy twitched. Welded on meant she would be his slave. Forever. She would never be able to remove it. Ever. She swallowed hard, her hand going to her throat, feeling the naked skin and trying to imagine the strip of silver there for always.

Slowly she lowered her hand and looked at Phillip, who sat facing her, his arm up on the steering wheel and a concerned look on his face. She knew that if she objected, he wouldn't press the issue but his disappointment would be palpable. Something irrevocable would change between them if she refused.

Did she want to refuse? After Tom's death, Sarah hadn't known if she could ever find love again. With Phillip, she had discovered not only that she could, but that she could love again tenfold. She glanced at her empty ring finger. When married to Tom, she had never taken her wedding band off. Ever. What would be the difference with the collar?

The difference would be the lack of choice. With the ring, she could wear it or not as it pleased her. With the torc, she would wear it whether she wanted it on or not. She would have no choice.

She smiled softly to herself. That wasn't true. By agreeing to marry Phillip, she'd already made her choice. She looked over at him where he waited anxiously for her answer.

"I would love to have that beautiful torc welded on as a sign of my submissiveness, as a sign of my slavery, Sir."

Chapter Four
Boundaries

℘

Phillip wanted her. Now. The total submission she was agreeing to had hardened his cock and the light of passion in her eyes enflamed him.

"Get out of the car." His voice was a growl as he unlatched the cage of the animal he kept locked inside, cursing himself for dressing her in jeans and not a skirt.

Sarah anticipated his mood, pulling her blouse out of her jeans as she came around the front of the car. A far cry from the night before when he had her undress on the porch. Then she'd been nervous and embarrassed that someone driving by might see. Today, the light in her eyes shone with the feral light of her inner slut. They could rut right here in the broad daylight of the now-mild autumn day and she wouldn't object.

Grabbing her around the waist, Phillip pulled her into his demanding kiss. Eagerly, she obeyed his unspoken command, giving him her submission as he unzipped her jeans even as his kiss devoured her lips. His tongue plundered her willing mouth, tasting her sweetness, feeding on its hunger.

They parted only long enough for her to pull her jeans off and for him to release his cock from the confines of his pants. Already he stood hard and wanting, his cock rigid with desire, the tip darkened with need.

The animal inside him had taken Sarah on the steps one night when Phillip had been unable to keep him in his cage. Today, in the bright sunlight, with the birds singing in the trees, the animal didn't even have the patience to take those few steps. Putting his hands around her waist, Phillip lifted her up onto the hood of his car and spread her legs. White cream glistened in her slit.

"Oh, yes. My slave likes this, doesn't she? She likes to submit to my will, to my whims."

He stepped in close to her, the tip of his cock brushing against that warm wetness. Sliding his hands under her blouse, he pulled her up to him with one hand around her back while mauling her breast with the other. Her eyes closed and a low moan came from the back of her throat as he squeezed her flesh.

"Do you want this, slave? Do you want to be taken out here in the driveway?" He pinched her nipple hard, just to hear her gasp of breath. Before she could respond, he bent and sucked it into his mouth, biting down to hear the wonderful squeal he knew she could make.

She didn't disappoint him. Her hands on the hood behind her supported her and she used them now to try to push her pussy toward him. But his grip on her was too tight and she barely moved down an inch.

"Right here in broad daylight, slave? You know what that makes you?" He leaned down to whisper the word in her ear. "A slut." His cock throbbed. The warmth of her pussy beckoned but he held on, enjoying the sweet torment.

"With all due respect, Sir," Sarah breathed, her eyes slowly opening and revealing the response of her own animal. "Shut up and fuck me."

Her words threw open the cage door and he lost control, slamming his cock into her. She cried under him as he forced his way deeper and deeper, his hand squeezing her breast between his fingers, his mouth claiming her even as his cock slid deep inside. Part of him—a small voice that was all that remained of his sanity—told him he was hurting her but he couldn't stop. The car moved under them in time to his thrusts and still he pumped, slamming himself deep inside. And then her muscles contracted around his cock, pulling him in as she came around him. Her legs wrapped around his waist and pulled him into her with a passion to match his own. Throwing his head back, he growled as he came, his body exploding into hers, pumping his cum deep inside until he had nothing left to give. Desperately he clung to her as he slowed, needing her embrace to tame him. The beast—sated—slunk back into its cage. Gulping down a big breath, he let it out slowly as his body finally relaxed.

Sarah felt his muscles relax and she pulled him to her as she lay back on the hood, not ready to move yet. Turning her head, she looked at the porch steps. He'd lost control like this only once before, right over there. She smiled up at the treetops. Must be something about this particular part of the property.

He didn't stir for several minutes and she lifted her head to look down on him. A slight breeze lifted his hair a little and he shivered. Slowly he rose onto his hands and looked at her.

"What you do to me, woman…"

"No more than you do to me on a regular basis, my dear Sir."

He stepped back and she slid off the hood and onto her knees before him. Before he could tuck his cock away, she leaned forward, capturing it in her lips. Looking up at him for permission, she waited.

When he nodded, she cleaned him with her tongue, wiping away all traces of their activity. Only when she was satisfied did she reach up and tuck his cock back into his pants and help him zip them up. She saw her own jeans draped over a bush where she—he?—had thrown them. In her passion, she had ripped them off but had he taken them from her or had she flung them all the way over there? Waltzing over to retrieve them, she made sure he got a good look at her swaying ass.

Phillip put his arm around her when she returned, drawing her close as they covered the short distance to the house. "If I hadn't just come, I'd take you again, you minx." He bussed her nose, then yawned as they climbed the steps.

"I do believe I've worn you out, Sir," she teased.

He grinned and opened the door for her, bowing her in. "You did, slave. You most certainly did. Into the bedroom with you." He yawned again and Sarah grinned.

She helped him undress and slide under the covers, then undressed herself the rest of the way and slid in beside him. His eyes were already closed but he still snuggled in, using her breasts as his pillow. Sarah lay there, holding him in her arms, content to just listen to him breathe. Bending down, she kissed the top of his head, his hair soft against her lips. "Sleep now, my dear Master," she whispered. "You deserve a rest after that."

Sarah dozed in and out for the next half hour while Phillip slept on. In truth, sex like that often invigorated her. Finally, unable to lie still any longer, she slid out from under Phillip and got up to go to the bathroom.

When she came back, she studied him in the late afternoon light. He had rolled over on his back, one arm thrown up over his head, the other across his belly. A stray sunbeam slanted through the window to land right straight on the mound of his cock and Sarah chuckled. Only him.

She sighed and looked around the room, pursing her lips. So what was she supposed to do now? Without Phillip to command her, she was restless and unsure.

Wandering out to the kitchen, she looked around for signs of what Phillip wanted for dinner. Last time this had happened she'd found meat marinating in the fridge and had taken it upon herself to cook dinner. She'd been concerned that he wouldn't like the fact that she had gotten up and taken the initiative but that hadn't been the case. He'd explained he wasn't looking for an unthinking doormat but a partner—a woman who had a mind and wasn't afraid to use it.

Quietly she shut the door to the refrigerator. Nothing in there to give her a clue. The sun went behind a cloud and Sarah glanced out the back door. Off to the west the sky had an ominous look. Mentally she ran through all the rooms, determining which windows would probably need to be shut when the rain came. A breeze came in through the open door that was decidedly cool. The temperature was dropping again.

Idly she walked from room to room. *Come on, Sarah. Think. What would you be doing if you were home at your apartment?* That was easy. She'd be dusting, vacuuming, packing. She ran a finger over the mantelpiece in the living room. No dust. Only area rugs on the floor and they looked clean. So did the wood floors. Kitchen floor didn't need to be mopped.

Damn. My crocheting is home. So is my book. Should've brought them with me. Hey! She looked at the front door. How could she have forgotten? Her trunk was filled with things she was bringing to Phillip's. Not too many, as most of her stuff was going into storage until she could decide what to do with it all. But she had brought her albums and CDs, intending to mesh her collection with Phillip's.

Despite the fact that they had just had sex on the hood of Phillip's car, Sarah still hesitated in the doorway. Being naked and in the throes of passion was one thing. But going out in the cold light of day wearing nothing but her birthday suit just to get a few boxes out of the back of her car was something else. She remembered that pickup truck roaring down the road last night when Phillip had her undress on the porch.

She chickened out. Grabbing a jacket from the closet just inside the door, Sarah slipped her arms through and hurried out to her car. The hem just covered her rear end, until she bent over the back to pick up the first box. Even though no one was around, she blushed and hurried back to the safety of the house.

By the time she brought the third box to the porch, the rain had started. Big drops spattered the drive as she slammed the trunk shut and hurried up the steps. She made it just inside the door when the heavens opened. Shrugging off the jacket, she hung it up and was just turning around when she felt Phillip's hands on her waist.

"What a sight to come out to," he murmured into her hair and Sarah snuggled into his arms.

"I couldn't sleep, so decided to go get these few boxes I brought with me. Figured it would be easier to bring a few each time rather than have to deal with a whole lot after the wedding."

"Show me what you've got?"

Sarah laughed as she bent down and hefted the smallest of the boxes. "I think you've mostly seen what I've got."

Phillip picked up the largest box with ease and hefted it to his shoulder, his grin turning to a frown. "You carried this all by yourself? Sarah, call me next time. I don't want you lifting things this heavy."

She stopped at the archway to the living room. "It wasn't that heavy. I'm not some wimpy little pretty girl, you know."

He arched an eyebrow at her and she realized her tone had been a little snippy. "I'm sorry, Phillip. But I'm perfectly capable of knowing what I can and can't carry. If it had been too much for me, I would have waited until you could get it for me."

Sarah led the way into the living room and set her box down on the small trunk that served for a coffee table. Phillip set his down on the floor and she stood, waiting for him to sit on the couch.

Except he didn't. He simply stood beside her as if waiting. Sarah wasn't sure what he wanted and feeling a bit like a girl who had just been scolded for doing something good, she grudgingly put her hands behind her back, spread her feet apart and took a stance of submissiveness.

Phillip's fingers under her chin forced her to look up at him.

"I never said this was going to be easy. Nor did I mean to impugn your judgment. You must learn that you do not need to do everything yourself."

Sarah took a deep breath. "I'm used to doing for myself. Even when Tom was alive. Being in the military meant he was away a lot. After he died, well, for a while it just felt as if he were out on maneuvers for a really, really long time." Her eyes dropped, though he kept her chin up. After a moment, she looked up at him again. "I'm sorry I snapped at you. I guess I'm just a little frustrated by not knowing what I'm allowed to do on my own."

Phillip nodded and sat on the couch, gesturing for her to sit by his side. "Doing this twenty-four/seven is much different than doing it only on the weekends, isn't it?"

She nodded, then looked up at him as he put his arm around her shoulders. "I almost feel like we need a code or something. On the weekends it's easy." She nodded toward the front door. "I come through that door and leave my other life outside. I'm not expected to do anything but serve you, mostly sexually but I don't mind serving in other ways either." Sarah looked up at him. "My role is clear when I'm here only on weekends. It's exactly where I want to be."

"But this weekend you find yourself slipping out of that role."

She nodded. "I do. And I don't know why."

He brushed a stray lock of hair from her cheek. "I do."

"Then what is it?"

"Do you remember when I told you part of what I was doing to you was training your body? That the world had taught you that being tied up and controlled was a bad thing, but it isn't?"

"Yes, I remember."

"Your body has responded, hasn't it?"

Sarah blushed, remembering how wanton she felt out on the hood of the car. Who would have thought she would ever not only agree to such a thing but want it with all her heart? "Yes," she whispered. "My body likes what you do it. A lot."

Phillip chuckled. "Your mind, however, still gives you trouble, doesn't it?"

Sarah made a face. "All the time. I mean, part of my mind is fine. It accepts submission on a very logical level. That part understands not only that it can't be in charge all the time but that it doesn't want to be."

"And the other part?"

"The other part screams bloody murder at me for giving up my rights to free will. Loudly. And I don't know where the line is between them. Even though I know they're not, both sides feel right."

"Both sides *are* right." Phillip turned her around so he could take both her hands in his. "Both sides are right," he repeated, emphasizing his point. "You spoke before of a code, that when you come here on the weekend, the door serves as a physical boundary between one part of your life and the other."

Sarah nodded. Phillip was leading her somewhere and Sarah followed willingly, being open and honest with him.

"But isn't that also the boundary between both parts of your brain? In this cottage, you listen to only one side. Only when you leave again on Monday does the other side become predominant."

"So why am I having trouble this weekend?"

"Because in a few weeks' time, my dear, that door will no longer be your boundary and your mind knows that."

Sarah thought about that for a moment, then sighed. "So it looks like I need a new boundary, Sir. A way of knowing when I'm Sarah Independent and when I'm Sarah slave."

"In time, the front door will become the boundary again and you will totally submit to me when you come home each night. But you're right. There needs to be an in-between time for the two of us. A time for us to get to know and anticipate each other's needs." He paused, looking out over the room as he considered. "Let me think about this some," he finally told her. "Tonight we have other activities." His grin was wicked and Sarah's stomach fluttered.

"We do?" He raised an eyebrow. "I mean, we do, Sir?"

"Yes and you need to dress. We're meeting Master Will and Lady Aleshia for dinner."

Sarah smiled. "And Jill and Anton too, Sir?"

Phillip took on an imperious tone. "I do believe they are bringing their slaves with them." He looked down at her, all mirth gone from his gaze. "As I am."

Well, there was a boundary if ever she saw one. Shutting Sarah Independent back into her closet, slave Sarah slid to her knees before her Master. "Yes, Sir, you are."

"Then go take a shower, slave. Your clothes will be on the bed when you finish."

* * * * *

Combing out her wet hair, Sarah eyed the clothes with some misgivings. So far, every outfit he'd chosen for her had shown excellent taste. This one, too, was tasteful, though skimpy. She hadn't worn a skirt that short since high school. The push-up bra she was getting used to but the plunge of the zippered blouse left little to the imagination. No stockings were on the bed and no panties. Just the skirt, the blouse and the bra. Lace-up heeled sandals sat at the foot of the bed.

Once dressed, she stood before the full-length mirror at the foot of the bed. The skirt flared out just below her hips, the hem coming to just above her knees. Not as bad as she had feared when she'd seen it on the bed. *At least it's not a miniskirt*, she mused. The blouse, however, lived up to all her expectations. With the white push-up bra underneath, its demi-cups barely hidden by the fabric of the blouse, there was no doubt where men's eyes would be. Deciding the outfit made her look naughty but not slutty, she went to find Phillip.

At his wolf whistle when she walked into the living room, Sarah slung out her hip and put her hand high up on the archway frame. "Hey, big boy, looking for a good time?" she joked.

He unfolded his lanky frame from the couch, standing and giving her a once-over. Making a gesture with his hand, he instructed her, "Turn around and let me see it all."

Throwing her hair over her shoulder in what she hoped was a sexy move, Sarah turned and modeled the outfit. When she faced him again, she leaned forward and shimmied.

"Just like a true vamp," he laughed. "Here. Let me retie this and we'll be ready to go." Phillip gestured to her leather going-out collar that now hung a bit loose. Turning around and lifting her hair, she waited patiently while he fixed it so that it lay snug against her skin. Would she still wear it when her permanent collar was attached? Permanent collar. The words gave her a shiver.

"Cold, slave?" Phillip's hands ran down along her arms.

"No, Sir." Sarah shook her head. "Just thinking."

"Naughty thoughts? Or misgivings?"

Phillip gestured toward the door and Sarah sauntered toward it, her hips swaying provocatively. "Naughty thoughts, of course."

Phillip stood back a bit, watching her walk out the front door before following her and locking up the cottage. Did the woman have any idea how innately erotic she was? All the clothes did was accentuate what she already held deep inside—a wish to be sexy. She looked every inch of what she was becoming—a woman comfortable with her own sexuality. A true rarity in Phillip's experience.

Of course, Sarah hadn't been comfortable when he had first met her and yet he'd seen something in her that had gotten his hopes up. And then that first night, when he had brought her back to the cottage and showed his true dominant nature? Not only had she not run away but she had challenged his ideas, making him a better Dom than he'd ever been.

Helping her into the car now, Phillip noticed how she kept her knees together like a lady should, picking up her feet together to swing around and sit comfortably in the front seat. He liked that demureness that promised so much more. He also liked toying with it, pushing her to show more than she intended.

"So where are we going?" she asked as he pulled out of the driveway and headed toward the city. He noted her surreptitiously checking her cleavage. Was she making sure it was straight? Or was she nervous about showing so much? Too bad if it was the latter. He was counting on Andy to not be able to take his eyes off her tits all night long.

Mentally he ticked off the people who would be gathering at the restaurant. Master William and his slave, Jillean, for sure. Lady Aleshia and Anton, her slave. The five of them, Will and Jill and Aleshia and Anton and he, had been friends for years. In fact, when Phillip had first acknowledged his need to dominate women sexually, Will was the person he had turned to. Over the years, Will had mentored Phillip in more ways than one, even though he was only a few years older. Will and his slave, his wife of many years, had seen him through not only the two failed relationships but several other false starts. Now the two were happy for him that he'd finally found the woman of his dreams. Jill and Sarah had met a few times for lunch and Phillip was glad the two were becoming friends.

But there would be others at the restaurant she hadn't yet met, including Andy, who styled himself "Master Andrew" and had yet to even play the role of Top with a woman, much less Master. They tolerated him because these were open meetings and Will always felt it better to include the clueless and attempt to teach them something than to exclude them and release them on the unsuspecting. Andy's lewd comments

84

had gotten him in trouble with the female members of the group more than once. Tonight, Phillip counted on the fact that Andy hadn't learned his lesson.

All told, there were twelve who would make up the participants in tonight's bunch. Just a gathering of friends who shared a common interest. Not much to differentiate between the gathered and any other group that got together to socialize over dinner. Andy would leer but otherwise the conversation would remain on neutral topics all through dinner.

No, dinner would be pleasant. Phillip grinned in the darkness of the car. It was the after-dinner get-together with Master Will and his slave-wife where he intended to expose Sarah to a deeper and darker level of submission.

Sarah sat demurely, murmuring polite hellos to the people she didn't know and smiling more broadly at those she did. Shy by nature, these types of events always made her a little nervous. At least here she could fall back on the role of slave to keep her from having to hold up a conversation with total strangers.

One man, however, didn't want to stay a stranger. Phillip introduced him as Master Andrew but it was pretty obvious even to her untrained eye that he didn't fit in with the rest of the crowd. For one thing, he didn't take his eyes off her boobs. Even when Phillip was standing right beside her outside the restaurant, the man's gaze had been fixed. She could have sworn he was almost drooling.

It wasn't as if she was the only one with cleavage showing. Jill's blouse was cut fairly low, though granted, not as low as hers. Lady Aleshia wore a beautiful sweater that clung to her figure but showed no skin. And Tammy, the only other woman of the group, wore a low-cut tank top with a long-sleeved see-through blouse. So why was this guy fixated on her?

The restaurant was one of the chains that catered to noisy crowds. The maître d' led them to a large, round table in the corner with a booth along two sides and chairs for the rest along the outside. Phillip leaned in to whisper in her ear as she prepared to slide into the center of the booth. "Lift your skirt before you sit down, slave. I want your bare ass on the vinyl."

Blushing, Sarah glanced around the table to make sure no one heard him. In the bustle of getting seats, no one paid any attention to them. Sarah slid along the seat, dismayed to see Andrew sliding in from the other side. Glancing at Phillip, her eyebrows asked if she really had to. His stern gaze gave her the answer.

Trying to be unnoticeable, she lifted her rear end from the seat and pulled her skirt up quickly. She sat again, realizing the hem was still partly under her. Another shift and the skirt came clear, allowing her ass to meet the seat with no interference. Her cheeks a bright red, she chanced a glance sideways to see if Andrew noticed, fervently hoping he hadn't.

He had. His eyes glittered with lust as he made a pointed effort to try to see what the fall of the skirt still hid. Just knowing that only a small scrap of fabric covered her lap and prevented his gaze from seeing everything she owned made her pussy flood. Damn. And the evidence would be all over the seat when she got up. Clenching her legs together, she quickly unrolled her silverware from the cloth napkin and covered her lap.

It took until the meal was delivered for her to forget about her naked skin on the vinyl seat. The food was delicious and the conversation fun. No mention was made of bondage or slavery throughout the entire meal and Sarah found herself forgetting all about their lifestyle choices. But then she'd get a glimpse of Andrew's leer and she'd be reminded all over again. At one point, he reached across her for the salt, being sure to get his face good and close to her breasts. Sarah gritted her teeth and glared at Phillip, who didn't notice. He was listening to Lady Aleshia tell a funny story and hadn't seen the man practically drool down her cleavage. By the end of dinner Sarah was about ready to take the ice water the waitress had refreshed for her and pour it all over his lap. A decided bulge had been under his napkin all night and she was done with it.

Getting out of the booth at the end of the meal turned out to be a sticky situation—literally. Phillip slid out his end and held out his hand to her. But when Sarah went to take it, she realized her skin was sticking to the vinyl, just like the backs of her legs did in the summer when she wore shorts. Being as unobtrusive as possible, she first lifted one cheek and then the other, her napkin in hand to wipe the seat as she left. The fact that Andrew's eyes never left her ass during this entire process wasn't lost on her.

If anyone else noticed her discomfiture, they pretended not to, for which Sarah was grateful. If Phillip asked her, she knew she'd submit to Master Will or even Lady Aleshia or the nice Master Robert who'd joined them partway through dinner. They all held the same...presence that Phillip had. But Andrew just gave her the creeps. She made a point of taking Phillip's arm as they walked out of the restaurant, giving Andrew the cold shoulder as she passed.

Phillip handed her into the car, then went around to speak to Will for a moment before joining her. She watched Andrew out her window and sure enough, he was taking his sweet time passing the car, pausing by her window to try to see down her blouse. The temptation to open the door into his groin was a hard one to resist but resist it she did. Instead, she simply folded her hands demurely on her lap and stared straight ahead.

Chapter Five
Caught

છ

Phillip pulled Will aside. "Let Sarah's performance tonight be Andrew's parting gift."

Will nodded. "Oh, he's definitely not invited to any more of these gatherings. He was over the top tonight, and this after repeated warnings. Why didn't you say anything to him?"

"I wanted Sarah to see the wannabes of the world for what they are. Figured at the least this guy isn't dangerous. He'd look his fill but I knew he wouldn't touch her."

"Something tells me that woman of yours could take on men like Andrew. When she was done with him, he'd wonder just where his balls had gotten to."

Phillip laughed. "Making her show her ass to a guy like that, a guy she'd normally ignore, was also part of my lesson for her tonight."

"Evening's lesson number two coming up at my house?" Will grinned. "Jill and I cleaned all day getting the place ready for the two of you."

"Then after I take care of a few details, we'll be right over."

Sarah obviously had questions for him when he got in the car. Her first one, however, surprised him.

"Would you ever share me with a man like Andrew?"

The question threw him. Every time he thought he had her pegged, Sarah managed to break out of the mold he tried to fit her into. He grinned. It was one of the reasons he had fallen in love with her.

"You're smiling. Does that mean yes?"

"No, it…" he paused to start the car as he decided how far to push her. "I was smiling because I didn't expect you to hit the heart of the matter so quickly."

"What do you mean?"

Phillip pulled the car out of the restaurant lot, stopping to let Andrew, in his car, exit first. Nodding toward the man who'd ogled his wife-to-be all night, he explained. "As your Master, I have the right to share you with anyone I want."

Sarah nodded, her fingers laced so tightly together, he could see the whites of her knuckles. He decided to push a little further.

"In fact, Andrew is not the first to ask me for permission to use you."

Although he kept his eyes on the road, he stayed very aware of the tenseness in the woman beside him. If he played this right, she would come right here in the car from his words alone. He would also plant a seed that would start a longing blossoming in her soul.

"He asked permission to use me?"

Her voice sounded very small and he glanced at Sarah's face. Her lower lip trembled a little, the only outward sign of the roiling he knew was going on inside.

"He did."

She was silent for an entire block.

"And what did you tell him?"

"Does it matter?"

The question hung in the air between them as Sarah considered it. Did it matter? As his slave, he could do with her what he wanted. She had given him permission a dozen times over. Hadn't she proven that when she'd shown that slimebucket her ass tonight? Could she go farther, however, and let the leering Andrew actually play with her? She shivered.

"Maybe someday it won't matter, Master. But right now? Yes, it does matter."

She watched Phillip's smile deepen. "Good answer, slave. I like it when you're honest with me."

"So did you? Give Andrew permission?" Sarah felt her nails dig into the skin of her hands, she clenched them so hard, but she couldn't stop. She had to know.

"I did not. You are worth far more than a man like that could ever offer you."

A flush of pleasure rose into her cheeks. While the thought of being shared certainly aroused her, even with a lech like Andrew, knowing Phillip thought so highly of her made her feel like she was someone special. And damn it, she was! Her feminism leapt to the fore at Phillip's recognition of her worth and she grinned even as Phillip eased the car to the side of the road.

"Why are we stopping?" She hadn't really been paying attention to where Phillip was driving. Looking around the neighborhood now, she realized she didn't know where they were.

"Several members of the group are getting together tonight. We are invited."

The light of a nearby streetlamp lit the interior of the car, though the light did not travel up far enough to illuminate his face. Still, Sarah heard the unmistakable deeper tone his voice got when he was her Master. "And everyone there will know I'm your slave, right?"

"Yes."

"Thank you for telling me, Sir." He didn't have to, she realized. And yet, this was a part of the dance—taking steps toward the future as they both found comfortable positions in their relationship. He could have just driven there and expected her to follow along without question. The fact that he'd stopped and was now informing her, gave her an opportunity to object if she didn't want to. "I'm ready if you are," she told him.

Phillip nodded once and reached into the back, pulling out a small bag from behind her seat. "I don't want you to see where we are going, so I want you to wear this."

Sarah realized it wasn't a bag he was holding but rather a black leather hood, straps dangling from it at odd angles. "Of course. I'd be happy to wear it." All the same, her stomach gave a little flip. "How does it go on?"

"Turn around."

She faced the door and he lifted the hood over her head, settling the closed face over her eyes and cheeks and mouth. He smoothed down her hair, then zipped it closed in the back. Sarah felt him buckle the straps and when he was done, she heard his muffled voice. "Can you breathe all right?"

She tried to open her mouth to reply but discovered the straps held her mouth closed tightly. With no sight, no ability to talk and barely able to hear, her world shrank in an instant.

But she could still nod her head. Were there holes where her nose was? The air she was breathing felt warm. If there were holes, they were small ones. She sat still, her hands on her lap as Phillip ran his hand over her encased head.

Cold metal touched her wrists and she jumped. Handcuffs, she realized. Even through the leather she could hear the snick as he locked them around her wrists. The car moved forward and Sarah sat back, trying to gather information from her blunted senses.

Phillip made several turns, forcing her body to sway first right, then left, then right again. A short acceleration later, it felt as if they were flying down the highway. It was possible — there was an expressway that encircled the city in two different loops.

She thought she heard Phillip mutter something but wasn't sure. The car started slowing down very quickly and Sarah's heart started thumping when she heard a siren right behind them. When the car came to a stop and Phillip leaned over her, a whimper forced itself through her closed mouth.

"Don't worry, Sarah. I just need to get my registration. You're going to be all right."

All right? she thought to herself. They'd been pulled over by the police, how on earth was she going to be all right? She was about to die of embarrassment. Under the hood, her face became very hot. Forcing herself to remain calm, she took in deep breaths and concentrated on making herself very small. If she pretended she wasn't here, maybe the officer wouldn't see her.

"May I see your license and registration, sir?"

Her eyes tightly shut behind the hood, Sarah didn't move. Silence stretched into silence. What was happening? *Just breathe and pretend everything is normal,* she repeated over and over, quieting the turmoil in her mind.

"Would you step out of the car, sir? Slowly."

The car shifted as Phillip opened the door and left her alone. Keeping her hands tightly clasped, she fought the urge to reach out to him as he left. *Don't bring any attention to yourself. He won't notice you if you don't move.*

In fact, the trooper had already noticed her. Pulling over a car for a routine traffic stop had never before given the young man such a shock. Drugs, guns—those he found on a semi-routine basis. A hooded woman with handcuffed wrists? That was a first.

"Ma'am? Are you all right?"

She started, her bound hands flying to her heart but then nodded. The trooper sought to reassure her. "Don't worry. You're going to be just fine now." Turning to the tall man looking impatient by the hood of the car, he kept his voice level and calm.

"Turn around and put your hands on the hood."

Clearly the man wanted to talk back to him. Instead, he swallowed his anger and turned around, deliberately putting both palms wide on the hood of the car. Kicking the perp's feet wider, he did a quick search, finding no concealed weapons. For good measure, the trooper decided this guy would be safer if he were handcuffed. Then he could rescue the woman without needing to worry about the man who had obviously kidnapped her.

Phillip saw the trooper reaching for his wrist and knew what was coming next. Torn between lashing out with indignant anger and swallowing the officer's mistake until Sarah was unmasked, he decided discretion was the better course. He had done nothing wrong and the trooper would be apologizing to him soon. Phillip made no moves that could be interpreted as threatening to the man and simply allowed himself to be handcuffed. When the trooper started to steer him toward the patrol car, however, Phillip complained.

"Is this really necessary, officer? When you take off her hood, you're going to be very embarrassed. There is no crime here."

"Into the car." The trooper gave him no choice. With a sigh, Phillip got into the backseat of the patrol car and watched as the cop moved around to the passenger side of the Saturn. A brief surge of jealousy flashed through him and dark thoughts filled him. Sarah was unprotected. With the mask and handcuffs on her, this guy could do anything and she wouldn't know what was going on. Sure, most cops were honest but was this one? Glaring, he watched him open the door and stoop down next to her. With the windows closed, he couldn't hear what the trooper was saying, which only frustrated him more.

When the door opened beside her, Sarah jumped again. What was happening? Where was Phillip?

"It's all right, ma'am. You're safe now."

Safe now? What was he talking about? She'd been safe before.

She felt his hands slide around the hood, searching for and finding the buckles that kept it in place. He released them, unzipped the back and gently pulled it off her face. The bright interior light of the car blinded her and she blinked as her eyes watered and adjusted.

"Here, let me get those cuffs off you." He reached for her hands and Sarah pulled them back.

"No..." Her voice cracked and she cleared her throat. "No, thank you. I mean...where's Phillip?"

"He's in the back of my car. He won't hurt you."

"Of course he won't hurt me. He's my fiancé." The truth of what the officer suspected suddenly hit home. "Oh, no! You think...that he... Officer, it isn't like that at all!"

The young man didn't say a word, only raised his eyebrows in skepticism. "Then what is this like, ma'am?"

Damn, that word made her feel old. Her eyes, more focused now, took a good look at the trooper and she realized he really wasn't that much younger than she was. But his question needed an answer and she didn't have time for stray thoughts. Phillip was on the verge of being arrested. "We...that is...I...like bondage games. We just went out for a ride and the destination is a surprise, so Phillip put the hood on me so I couldn't see. That's all."

Her cheeks were flaming. She knew it. She couldn't even look the trooper in the eye as she made her admission of guilt. What must he think of her that she liked to be handcuffed?

"Ma'am, if he's forced you to do this, you have a right to press charges."

Sarah shook her head, swallowing hard and remaining resolute as she confessed her deepest secrets to this officer. "He's not forcing me. I'm here willingly and I'm not going to press charges."

The officer shook his head and stood up. He went back to the patrol car and Sarah saw him sit in the driver's side and speak into the microphone. A car went by and in the headlights, she saw Phillip's silhouette in the backseat. How terrible for him to be there! She ran over the short conversation again. Should she have let the trooper take off her cuffs? Would that have convinced him she told the truth?

An eternity passed as she waited, unsure what to do. No, that wasn't true. She knew what she wanted to do...she wanted to jump out of the car and give that trooper a piece of her mind. The longer she sat waiting, the more ticked off she got. Why had he pulled them over in the first place? Phillip occasionally pushed the speed limit but she doubted he would have done so with her in such a getup tonight. Blushing, Sarah remembered she wore nothing under the skirt.

Before she could follow that line of thought, the trooper put away the mic and opened Phillip's door. She watched as the officer helped him out, then turned him around and undid the handcuffs. Her sigh of relief was explosive.

The trooper handed Phillip a piece of paper, then gestured to the car. Phillip gave a terse response and held out his hand. With reluctance, the trooper put the hood into Phillip's hand, then watched as Phillip came back to her. Before he was even all the way in the car, his concern came out in his first question. "Sarah, are you all right?"

"I'm fine but what about you? Did he arrest you?" She wanted to touch him, to smother him with kisses but the trooper's headlights still shone in through the back window. Instead, she contented herself with putting a hand on his arm.

Phillip let his breath out in a rush and pulled her to him. "No, my dearest, sweet, sweet love." He kissed her hair, her temple, her cheek. "He didn't arrest me. I'm so sorry I put you in danger."

In the light, she looked up at him, puzzled. "Danger? I could have died from embarrassment but that was all. And I'm over that. I don't really care what that guy thinks." She stopped. "Phillip, you're shaking."

"When I was sitting in the back of that car, I suddenly realized what kind of predicament you were in. A stranger coming to you while you were bound and helpless? And me locked up and unable to protect you. I swear, I will never let such a thing happen again, Sarah. I swear."

She sat back, considering. "Phillip, I knew we'd been pulled over by the police. I heard the siren and heard him tell you to get out of the car. You weren't fighting, so I knew it was the law." She shook her head. "I know, not all cops are good cops. And I wasn't totally helpless, you know." A wicked grin spread across her face and she opened her hands. Clenched inside was a small screwdriver.

"The glove compartment!" Phillip looked at her in astonishment.

"Yep. I could feel it still open against my knee, so I rooted around inside it for something I could use as a weapon just in case. I found this, then closed the glove box so the light wouldn't shine on me. I do have a brain, you know."

Phillip pulled her to him, ignoring the light and the watching cop. "I love your brain." He kissed her hard, relief flooding him. He would not be so stupid again.

And when the kiss ended, Sarah took the hood from his hand. "I believe we were on our way somewhere?" Very deliberately and making sure the cop could see, she awkwardly pulled it over her own head. But with her hands bound together, she couldn't zip it shut. Turning, she angled herself so Phillip could take care of that and then re-buckle the straps.

She heard him start the car, then felt him reach over and check the seat belt that was still around her. His fingers rested over hers, still handcuffed together. He tapped the screwdriver she held.

"Hang on to that for a while, slave. Just remember to leave it in the car when we get to where we're going."

The car moved forward and she sat back, grinning behind her leather hood.

Chapter Six
Submission

൫

By the time they got to Will's, Phillip was back in control. They spoke little, Sarah because she couldn't and Phillip because his thoughts replayed the incident over and over. How could he have put her in such danger?

Both Will and Jill knew immediately that something was wrong. Phillip had fastened a collar and leash around Sarah's neck and led her up to and inside the house. But Phillip was distracted, something Will hadn't seen in his friend in a long while. He took the leash from the man he'd mentored and gestured for Jill to take him into the other room. Leading Sarah to the room they'd set up for tonight's activities, he helped her to sit on a straight-back chair.

"Put your feet and knees together, slave of Master Phillip. Do not move until he instructs you."

Sarah folded her hands together, the handcuffs not really letting her do much else and waited. Master William left the room, she was pretty sure, but was she alone? Straining her ears, she tried to pick up any sound. With the hood muffling so much, she couldn't tell if there was anyone nearby or not. Determined to make Phillip proud of her, whether eyes watched her or not, she remained silent and still.

Jill was giving Phillip a shoulder rub when Will walked into the kitchen. "Okay, what's going on?"

In a few short sentences, Phillip filled them in. "And you want to know the kicker?" He stood up and pulled the ticket out of his pocket. "Why I got pulled over in the first place? A burnt-out taillight!"

Will and Jill exchanged glances. Phillip had just about shaken off the incident but was still more rattled than Will was comfortable with. "I'm thinkin' we ought to have a quiet night playing cards instead of...what we had planned."

The disappointment in Will's voice came through loud and clear to Phillip, even though his friend tried to hide it. He stretched his shoulders and shook his head. "No, I'm fine. And really, so is Sarah. I don't think it's really hit her what could have happened if he'd been a crooked cop." The smile he gave held a growing mischievousness as Phillip settled down and began looking forward to their long-planned evening. "In fact, she's been alone with her thoughts under that hood for quite some time now. She doesn't know where she is, either. Obviously she's figured out you two are here but we could be in some warehouse for all she knows."

A soft knock on the front door caught their attention. Jill stepped out to answer it and Phillip heard her greet Lady Aleshia in respectful tones. She ushered them into the kitchen as well and Phillip repeated what had happened on their way between the restaurant and Will and Jill's house.

"Sarah doesn't know where she is," he finished up. "And she has some concerns about being shared. You all must remain silent in order for what I have in mind to work. She can't know who you are...or how many of you there are."

Were those footsteps? Sarah tried to focus on where the noise had come from but not a whisper got through the leather. From several feet away, Phillip's voice made her jump.

"Slave. You are doing well. My friends like what they see. You are very well-behaved."

So she wasn't alone. Relief flooded her that she had done what Will had told her. She would never want to shame Phillip or cause him to lose face.

"I want them to see more."

His voice was closer and she didn't jump when he picked up the end of her leash, pulling her to a standing position. Her steps coming in from the car had been tentative over uneven ground. Yet this smooth floor, hardwood she thought by the sound her heels made on it, wasn't hard to walk on at all. She followed where Phillip led with confidence and pride in her step.

He stopped her, however, after only going a few steps. Taking her shoulders, he turned her around, moving her back a step and against something solid. The wall? Some contraption? She waited patiently, knowing she was in good hands—hands that now caressed her face through the hood. She felt Phillip's lips close over hers and even though the leather stood between them, she responded, pressing back with ardor.

He unlocked her wrists from the handcuffs and she resisted the urge to rub them. The cuffs hadn't been tight but the reaction was instinctual. Letting her hands drop to her sides, Sarah was fairly certain they wouldn't remain unbound very long. She was right, though not in the way she expected. She remained free only long enough for the hands that caressed her to unzip her blouse and push it off her shoulders. In the darkness of her hood, her shock was audible. Phillip unveiled her to myriad eyes she couldn't see but knew were there. Her heart beat harder, yet she could not deny the warmth that spread upward from her pussy.

She thought he'd stop there, with her blouse. After all, when she had been caged and on display before, she'd been still dressed in her underwear. But when his fingers undid the clasp of her bra and pulled it off her quickly, her breath quickened and her mind reeled. And when four hands grabbed her wrists from either side of her and raised them over her head to fasten them wide apart, she had to beat down the urge to fight them. He had half stripped her before strangers. How many were there?

Desperately she struggled to hear a sound that would tell her who was in the room. Were these strangers she was half-naked for? She knew Master William was here...or at least had led her into the room. That meant Jill was probably here too. She'd seen and spoken to both of them not an hour before at the restaurant but neither one had given her any indication that they would be getting together again tonight. How many others from the restaurant were here? Was Andrew out there too? Leering at her now-exposed breasts? Where had Phillip brought her?

She pulled down on her wrists but they were tightly strapped in by heavy cuffs that almost entirely covered her hand. Forced onto her toes by the height of the cuffs that held her, she felt stretched like a string pulled taut.

"Remove her skirt."

That definitely wasn't Phillip's voice. She fought panic as hands again reached around her, this time unzipping her skirt and letting it fall. Someone picked up first one, then the other foot and the skirt was gone. She was on display for all to see wearing nothing but her sandals.

Where was Phillip? He had to be here. Why was he letting them do this to her?

The memory of being on display before, in the familiar location of Phillip's living room, flashed into her mind again. Then the cage had been almost a comfort she could draw around her. The bars served as a blanket of protection as the others had looked their fill.

She squirmed, remembering her initial reaction to being shown off in such a way.

Shown off. That was what Phillip was doing now. He had put her here, naked and stretched tall, because he wanted to show off his prized possession.

Finding her courage, she raised her chin, unable to see who stared at her. If Phillip thought enough of her to put her on display like this, then she would be proud of her body and let them look their fill.

Her heart quickened, however, as she felt a change in the atmosphere around her. No noise gave her a clue, yet she was sure someone stood very close to her—one on either side. Attuning every sense to the space around her, she still jumped a little when someone's warm hand cupped her right breast, the thumb circling around and over her nipple, bringing it to hardness.

A second hand cupped her other breast. A separate person. She'd never been touched this way by two at once. And she wasn't very good at hiding her reaction. The hands that held her must be able to feel her beating heart and faster breathing.

A third hand caressed her cheek, sliding down to circle her neck and plunge into the crevice between her breasts. Something wasn't right, though. The hand was flat against her skin. No one who held her breasts could possibly run their hand against her like that. Her heart fluttered. Three people touched her.

More hands now, caressing her thighs, her calves, working down to her feet. They slipped her sandals off, one, then the other, pulling her legs apart and fastening them, spreading her body into an X that hung suspended for their pleasure. Sarah's head fell back, finding rest against a chest that rose and fell. There was no wall behind her. What was she bound to?

The hands roamed over her skin, massaging, caressing, coming close but never touching the spot between her legs that tingled in anticipation. Moaning in her darkness, she longed for someone to touch her there that she might explode in pleasure.

As quickly as the touches began, they stopped. The sudden lack made her gasp and pull her head up. She didn't lean back again. He wouldn't be there now.

A set of hands grabbed her right breast, strong hands that roughly squeezed, mauling the flesh between his fingers, pinching the nipple and digging his nails into her skin. She bore it, letting this stranger's familiarity with her body fuel the need growing between her spread legs.

He hefted her breast as if weighing it. Because of her hood, she didn't see him raise his hand and so was unprepared for the slap he delivered. The leather didn't permit her to open her mouth but the grunt that filled the room was clear. Another slap and her head fell forward, trying to suck in the pain that so quickly turned to pleasure.

He held her breast up by the nipple, pulling it outward until she groaned again. The pain shot through her, yet there was nothing she could do. Helpless, she moaned and he dropped it, letting the weight bounce and turn the pain to tingles.

He slapped the other one now, first one side and then the other, turning the skin pink. She was defenseless against the onslaught. His fingers burned on her skin and her pussy flooded, jealously desiring attention down below.

Something circled her breast and tightened, noose-like, around it. The sudden constriction made her pussy twitch and for a moment, Sarah rode a wave of pleasure she thought might take her over the edge.

But that was not to be. Not yet. The wave lessened, like the sea that crests far away and then gently laps against the shore. Her other breast was encircled as well and then she was left alone again.

Her own breath did the work this time…pressing her breasts hard against their bindings each time she took a breath. A drop of white cream escaped her nether lips and slowly slid along her skin and down to her thigh.

A noise pierced the silence of her hood. So slight, she almost missed it in her burgeoning arousal. Tension coiled in her body, she listened hard.

There it was again! A slight whoosh, as of a blunted sword cutting the air or a bat swung hard at a missed pitch. Close by. She cocked her head, trying to figure it out...and it landed. A sharp strike against her bound breasts that sent a streak of pain shocking through her system.

Taken by surprise, she couldn't breathe. One second, two, then the pain faded and her breasts heaved as air rushed back into her lungs. What was that? Sarah's mind reeled. Even as she struggled with what was happening, another blow fell.

Her body arched and she cried out, the sound more a moan because of the restricting hood. Stinging pain arced across both breasts, caused by a stripe of skin that burned for several seconds before fading into memory. She needed to come. Her pussy, a throbbing arousal pulsing with every heartbeat, ached for release. A third hard strike across her breasts made her scream, tears of frustration flowing into the leather hood.

Phillip watched Sarah's body writhe on the crossbeams that formed a giant X. Known as a Saint Andrew's cross, the structure stood independent at one end of the room. With the two planks crossed at such an angle, her body was effectively spread-eagled and available, her arms stretched to their limit and her toes barely reaching the floor.

Phillip made a motion and Will moved away from Sarah, putting the short cane back in the rack on the wall. Motioning for Anton to take his turn, Phillip went to stand behind her, letting her head rest on his chest again. He didn't intend for this to be a respite, however. His slave needed to come and he intended to give her what she wanted.

Using only his fingernails, he lightly brushed against her bound and beaten breasts. She stiffened and moaned and he knew his nails felt like razorblades against her sensitive skin. Quickly he checked the temperature of her skin, stretched taut by the rope pulled tight at the base of her breasts. There was plenty of time yet before he needed to release them.

Anton had taken his position in front of Sarah, kneeling between her legs. Phillip had instructed the male slave to take his time...to tease her softly. By juxtaposing Will's harsh cane with Anton's soft touch, he knew her agony would be exquisite.

Hot. Hot air warmed her pussy, pulling her attention away from the torment of her breasts. Through the fog of her mind, Sarah tried to focus but couldn't. Too many sensations assaulted her. She couldn't concentrate on any of them. She could only let them happen to her and follow where they led her. Her pussy gaped wide open—wanting, needing to be filled, but all she could do was hang in her bindings, completely at the mercy of those who watched.

The razors mutilating her breasts disappeared. Someone fastened a belt around her waist that shortened her breath and held her tighter against the wood. The constriction, rather than further exciting her, served to center her, to give her a focal point. Leaning against the solid chest of the man behind her, Sarah took several measured breaths, isolating and enjoying each separate sensation. From the stretched muscles of her arms and torso and legs, to the hot moistness of her pussy, to her bound breasts, straining against their bindings with every deep breath, each one pushed her farther and farther into the realm of subspace.

Someone's fingers now...one hand...circling around her thighs...over her shaved mound...down along the valley where hip and thigh met...circling...light touches...lulling her...

One finger dipping, sliding between her lips, plunging along her slit, then sliding up, dragging her wetness with it to circle a nipple, tightening it, making the risen nub harden in response.

Dipping again, the touch harder now. More insistent. Pulling her wetness from its warm birthplace to harden her other nipple. Pinching, tweaking first one, then the other

105

before returning. Fingers that searched now, searched to find the spots to make her squirm.

Instinctively, her arm muscles tensed, wanting to bring her hand down and guide the fingers. But the bindings prevented her and a whimper of frustration whispered in her throat as two fingers plunged into her. Her pussy responded, relaxing to welcome the incursion even as her spirit soared.

Phillip held Sarah's body, listening intently to every sound she made under the hood, feeling the way her body alternately tensed and relaxed under Anton's skillful fingers. From where he stood behind her, Phillip couldn't see exactly what Lady Aleshia's slave was doing, though he was sure the man wouldn't deviate from the instructions he'd been given. When Anton glanced up at him, he must've seen the concern on Phillip's face, for he paused, holding up his left hand with four fingers raised.

Phillip nodded. Sarah's mind had long since reached the state where they could do anything to her that they wanted and she wouldn't say no. He'd chosen Anton for this particular task, since he had the smallest hands of all the men in the room. Maybe someday Sarah wouldn't mind being fisted by a woman but he didn't think she was ready for that quite yet. Even if she didn't have a clue whose hand invaded her now, he was certain she would assume it to be a man's.

Her head lolled on his chest as Anton's fingers worked deeper into her pussy. Using his own hands to hold her waist, Phillip let his touch keep her grounded. With her mind floating free as it was now, she would need some way of returning when they were done with her.

Anton's face was a study in concentration as he pushed gently against the muscles that tried to keep him out. He worked slowly and with great patience. Lady Aleshia stood to one side, occasionally oozing oil out of a plastic jar to help lubricate his hand as her slave gave pleasure to Sarah. Phillip felt grateful not only that Anton loved giving pleasure to women in general but also that his mistress didn't mind sharing. Several times Sarah had mentioned being fisted as one of her fantasies, yet Phillip knew his own hands were much too large.

Will reclined on a small settee pushed against one wall of their dungeon, Jill kneeling before him, her mouth around his cock. Phillip's own cock responded to the sight, seeing the naked slave servicing her Master just as Sarah now serviced him in a way she had yet to understand. Someday she would come to realize these things he did to her aroused him in a way he couldn't always explain. She gave her body to him, trusted him to do her no harm and in return, he played her body like a fine instrument. Would she ever realize how erotic it was to see her like this? Totally at his mercy, being shared with his friends who knew him better than anyone in the world? And to know she not only agreed to this but enjoyed it as well made it all the sweeter.

"I'm in."

Anton's voice, quiet in the dimly lit room, sent a thrill straight to his cock. Nodding to Lady Aleshia, he watched her pick up a digital camera from a nearby table. Apparently finding several good angles, Phillip let her take over a dozen shots of Anton's hand buried inside Sarah's body before they moved to the last stage of what they had planned.

Time had stopped in Sarah's mind. She hung from her wrists, her knees barely able to support her slender frame, her legs spread wide, her body invaded by a hand so large she could thought she would split in two.

And yet, he had been so patient, worked so slowly, her body not only accepted him but welcomed his persistence, swallowing his fist whole and closing behind, encasing his wrist like a lover's hug. The part of her mind that still worked concentrated on her shallow breathing, letting the air fill the small space allowed by the constricting belt before expelling it slowly so as to not expel the wonder inside her body at the same time.

The person behind her moved away, taking care that her head should not drop backward. She was sorry to feel him go—his steadying presence had been welcome. The fist inside her didn't move now. The two of them hung suspended in time and she just waited, accepting whatever they wanted to do to her.

Something small and cold and hard rubbed against her clit, slick, engorging that tiny organ even further. Far off, she thought she heard a low murmur but was past caring. Inside her, the hand moved, the fingers slowly opening like a flower in the rays of the sun. Her breathing, still shallow, quickened in pace.

Phillip knelt beside Anton, the long vibrator with the tiny head ready in his hand. "Tell me every time she comes," he instructed quietly to the slave, careful to pitch his voice so Sarah wouldn't hear him. Not that she would anyway, in the state they'd put her into. Her body simply waited for his touch.

Without turning the power on, he rubbed the vibe against the slickness of her clit. Already engorged from Anton's touch, he watched it respond anew to the smooth ball at the end of the toy. He turned to the slave. "Open your hand."

He gave Sarah a moment to adjust to the movement inside her before turning the toy on low. Lightly he skimmed it over her shaven pussy, letting the soft vibrations seep into her consciousness. Lady Aleshia now moved behind Sarah, supporting her head against her shoulder as the bound slave once again moaned in her ecstasy.

Phillip turned the vibrations up and centered the small round head right on top of her clit. Sarah's reaction was immediate. Anton winced even as he grinned. "She's coming, and coming hard."

Phillip did not relent. He kept the vibe right where it was, prolonging her orgasm, wanting to push the limit of her endurance. How long could she come? "Still?" he asked Anton.

"Still." The slave shifted his position to get a more comfortable angle for himself. Sarah's pussy lips contracted around his wrist, alternately pulling him deeper and trying to push him out.

Sarah's muffled screams had the attention of both Will and Jill now. They watched her sweat-covered body writhe on the crossed beams, totally at the mercy of the man who guided the toy and the slave who invaded her body. Jill's lips were parted and her breathing quick. Will leaned down and whispered in her ear, "You may come as well, slave."

Not needing a second invitation, Jill's hand slipped between her legs and she rubbed her clit, coming gently in counterpoint to Sarah's violence.

Phillip turned the setting on the vibrator again, this time pushing it to full strength. The loud hum filled the room and Sarah's whimpering changed in response. No longer dark and feral, she now whimpered loudly in high-pitched tones as her body continued to orgasm, wave after wave plunging through her body. Phillip worked a finger in beside Anton's wrist and reveled in the contractions.

A full three minutes had passed from the first moment of her orgasm and Phillip decided he'd pushed Sarah enough. He lowered the setting on the vibe gradually, letting her down easy. Knowing her clit would be either supersensitive or deadened by now, he pulled his finger from her pussy and slid it over the hood of that delicate organ, testing to see which it was. She didn't appear to notice and that confirmed it. She was ready to come back to earth.

He leaned back on his heels, watching as Anton carefully pulled his hand from her pussy. Sarah's body spasmed on the beams but Phillip knew they were simply leftovers as her body recovered.

He untied the foot closest to him, signaling to Will to untie the other, not surprised when she didn't even make an attempt to stand up.

While Anton went to wash, Phillip took the belt from around her waist, standing close and holding her as Jill and Lady Aleshia released her arms.

"I'm here, Sarah. Can you hear me?"

The nod against his chest was weak but it was a nod. Picking her up in his arms, he carried her to the couch and laid her down. Unbuckling the hood, he unzipped it and turned the bottom up so that fresh air caressed the lower half of her face but he did not yet pull it off.

Not until everyone had left the room, blowing out all the candles as they went, did he remove it the rest of the way. The room was dark and no light would hurt her eyes, or give her a clue as to where they were. Phillip turned the mask inside out to dry a little before he would make her wear it home. The night was magical to her because she didn't know where she was. He wouldn't take that away from her.

There wasn't enough room for him to lie beside her, so he gathered her into his arms, letting his warmth comfort her while he spoke soothing words to ease the transition that reunited her soul with her body and mind.

She shivered and he pulled a blanket off the back of the couch, tucking it carefully around her body. "I love you, Sarah-my-slave," he murmured, holding her again.

Her reply, softly whispered into the darkness, drifted up as she curled into the warmth of his arms. "I love you too, Phillip-my-Master."

Gently kissing her forehead, he knelt by her side, cradling her, gently rocking her to blissful sleep, his soul resting with a peacefulness he had not known for a very long time.

Chapter Seven
Marks

℘

Rolling over and stretching, Sarah's mind woke as slowly as her body. Sighing as the last remnant of sleep faded away, she opened her eyes and focused on Phillip's bedroom, frowning as she tried to remember how she had gotten there. The memory of being stretched on some sort of vertical rack and played with like the toy she was flashed through her, waking her completely.

Her head snapped to the pillow beside her. Phillip lay on his side, propped up on one arm, watching her, dark circles showing under his eyes.

"Good morning, slave. How do you feel?"

A wicked grin crossed her face. "Naughty." She breathed deep. "And alive."

"Glad to hear it. You went sailing pretty high last night."

"I don't even have the words to describe it. To be used like that, shared with so many other people? And I couldn't even see their faces so I didn't know who they were or even whether they were men or women. And being on display and then being *used*? And fisted! Oh, my glory, Master, it was more than wonderful, more than incredible! Even better than fantastic!"

Phillip laughed, his rich baritone filling the room. "So you had a good time, then?"

Sarah giggled. "It was okay."

"I watched you all night long."

She turned on her side to face him. "What do you mean?"

"You were pretty out of it by the time we finished with you last night. Do you remember me bringing you home?"

Sarah considered a moment, then shook her head. "I remember you putting the mask back on me and that it was cold and wet and I didn't really want it back on. And I have a vague memory of climbing into bed."

"You didn't so much climb as collapse. And the mask was wet from your own sweat, so you can't complain there."

"Do you mean you didn't get any sleep? That you watched over me all night long?"

Phillip rolled onto his back. "Yep."

A slow smile crept over her face. No one had ever done that before. Not even her husband when she'd been really sick that one time. He'd said he would but then had fallen asleep not long after his usual bedtime. But Phillip had stayed awake. The dark circles made sense now.

"Did you get to come last night?" She still couldn't ask that question without feeling just a little embarrassed at saying the word "come".

He yawned. "No. But that was all right. The night was for you."

"Then if last night was mine, this morning is yours." She pushed off the sheet that covered them both and slid down so she was mouth-level with his cock. Even unexcited, his size was impressive. And once she was done, she knew he'd reach his full length—long and powerful.

Moving so she crouched between his legs, she kissed the tender flesh between his hip and his thigh, letting her hair brush against his cock with its soft caress. He responded, shifting so he could better enjoy her ministrations. His cock stirred.

She felt the movement against her cheek and turned to kiss the shaft. A chaste kiss that only hinted of what was to come. Lifting her head, she let her hair tumble over and around his cock as he grew harder.

Knowing he was tired, she decided not to tease too much this morning. Opening her lips wide, she bent down and took all of him into her warmth. Her tongue flicked over his shaft and around the tip, leaving no spot untouched. She loved how he grew in her mouth, filling her and forcing her to retreat.

But she wouldn't surrender. Keeping the velvety soft tip in her mouth, she only paused before plunging down over the ridge and covering him again. Using her hand, she wrapped her fingers around the base she could no longer reach with her throat at this angle and started a slow, methodical pumping. Phillip settled deeper into the bed and she had to fight away the smile.

He was so good to her, taking her into places her fantasies had gone for years but her mind had told her were something to be ashamed of at best, dirty at worst. He had taught her to accept those fantasies for what they were—expressions of deeply held desires that held no shame, that weren't dirty, but simple sexual needs shared by millions of people.

Fully hard now, she admired the beauty of his cock as she picked up the pace. Lines of purple traced intricate designs under his skin where the blood raised the veins along the ridge. The whiteness of his skin turned to burgundy at the end where the pre-cum formed in the cloven tip. Slipping her tongue along the underside, she scooped up that cum, loving his salty taste.

Moving faster now, she kept her lips tight against his hardness as his body moved in tandem with her hand. Over the ridge and back again, she gave him no choice but to come in her mouth.

With an explosion of warmth, his cum spurted out, quiet moans of pleasure filling the room. Bent over as she was, she found it difficult to swallow his gift, yet she managed to get most of it. Slowing her movements, she glanced up, hoping for his approval.

"Thank you, slave."

She beamed. "I'll be right back." Since she hadn't swallowed all his cum, his cock gleamed in the morning light. So did her hand. Being careful not to get any on the sheets, she climbed out of bed and went into the bathroom to wash up. Wetting a cloth with warm water, she returned to do the same for him. He didn't move as she cleaned him, his wonderful cock already shrinking back to a more comfortable size.

"There you go, Master. All washed and ready to go." She stood by the side of the bed, the cloth in her hand. "Master?"

A gentle snore was all the answer she got.

Standing in the shower a few minutes later, Sarah rubbed the washcloth over her body, washing away all traces of her recent activities. When she scrubbed her breasts however, she frowned and looked down. Three red stripes lay across the top, marking her. Gently rubbing with the cloth, she experimented with how they felt. Sore but not painful, she decided. No, not even sore, more like an already fading two-day-old bruise.

With a start, she realized what had struck her last night. She'd seen pictures on the web of a woman's ass that looked much the same as her breasts did now. Those marks had been made by a thin cane. That meant someone had caned her breasts last night. Flushing as she remembered the stinging blows against her lightly bound breasts, she washed her pussy again, fully aware that the thought had aroused her. She didn't know if Phillip's hand had wielded the instrument that left these lines or if someone else had, but both ideas excited her.

Someone had caned her last night. She giggled as she turned off the water. What a little slut she was becoming. Such a far cry from the prim and proper innocent she'd been just a few short months ago.

Drying and combing out her hair, she glanced at the clock and froze in momentary panic. Every Sunday morning since spending her weekends with Phillip, he had taken her to his church for their Sunday service. If the two of them were going to go this Sunday, they needed to leave within the hour.

Phillip, however, hadn't slept at all the night before for watching over her. She felt gloriously alive today, with the energy of a dynamo. Last night's activities had energized her and she felt she could take on the world.

So should she wake him or let him sleep? Where was the slavery line here?

The digital number on the bathroom clock rearranged itself, marking the change of a full minute. Sarah turned away. Being a slave was supposed to simplify her life, not complicate it. By turning over most of the decisions to Phillip, she had thought she'd have no worries left in life. She would be content to simply sail along at his side, bringing her own opinions into the discussion, of course, but never having to make the final, harder choices.

And yet here she was, faced with whether she should wake him for church or not and she was frozen like the proverbial deer in the headlights. For crying out loud, this wasn't even an earth-shattering decision. Leaving the bath, she went in to look at the man she loved more than anything as he lay sleeping, his hair tousled, the trace of his beard just shadowing his chin.

Another minute passed as she watched him breathe, the sheet silently rising and falling in an even, regular pattern. "Silly," she muttered to herself as she turned on her heel and left the room. "Stand here long enough and the decision's taken out of your hands. The clock will run down and then there won't be enough time to get to church."

Okay. She was deciding. He needed sleep. If he didn't like that decision, too bad. He might choose to discipline her for making the wrong one. Well, so be it. At least she'd know for the next time. This time around, she was letting him sleep. So there.

A few items lay in the bottom of one last box she had brought with her from her apartment. The others they had dealt with yesterday, putting away and tucking things here and there as she moved, bit by bit, into his life. If she didn't like the location of his cottage so much and all the privacy, combined with the easy distance to the nearest mall sprawl, she probably would have suggested getting rid of both their places and building something together.

But wasn't that what they were doing? She lifted a frame out of the box and took it to the mantel. This was her favorite picture of her parents. Just an old black-and-white picture with a wide white edge, it showed a young couple entwined in each other's arms and smiling broadly at the camera. The woman held her hand up in such a way as to show off her new engagement ring. Sarah'd had the picture framed when she had moved far from home so she would never forget the wonderful models they were.

What would they think of her becoming Phillip's slave? Sarah snorted as she put the photo on the mantel and stepped back. Her father never quite got out of the late Fifties, early Sixties husband-as-breadwinner philosophy. He had taken care of his family because that was what men did. They worked hard, played hard and protected their own. In that, he and Phillip were very much alike.

And yet, she doubted she had ever met men so different in so many ways. Her dad tended to be gregarious, making friends easily and quickly. He also tended to anger quickly but let go of it just as fast. She never worried when her dad blew up at something, knowing he would let off his steam and be done with it. "No grudges, no punches" he always said.

And her mom? Sarah remembered seeing a copy of *The Feminine Mystique* when she was little and thinking it said, *The Feminine Mysteries*. For years she had thought it was an adult version of a Nancy Drew detective novel. Only later did she realize the importance of that seminal work. Her mom had never worked out of the house until the kids were all in college. And then she'd only gotten a job because she had been bored sitting at home all day. Many times her mother had told her, "I am *not* going to sit in this house and shrivel into some old lady. I've got a lot of living to do yet!" So her mom had gotten a job as a cashier in the local supermarket and loved it. Everyone in the neighborhood passed through there and she had managed to get the latest gossip on everyone.

Yeah, her parents made quite the pair. And would they understand her relationship with Phillip? In some aspects, yes, they already did. Her father approved of the fact that Phillip would keep her in comfort and the romantic in her mother loved the fact that Sarah had found true love not once but twice in her life.

Several other pictures remained in the bottom of the box and she took them around the house, setting them in different places. Breaking down the cardboard box so it lay flat, she stacked it with the others for recycling and went to check on Phillip, her stomach growling.

She felt odd walking around the house without her cuffs on. When had they become so much a part of her? Phillip kept them in the top drawer of his bureau but going digging around in there without permission felt...funny. Like she would be invading his privacy. She felt the same way about the dungeon. He had never forbidden her to go in there without him but she would never think of doing such a thing.

He rolled over onto his back when she pulled the blanket up to cover him and she stood a moment, looking her fill. Even at rest, the smooth muscles of his chest caught her eye, the strong lines leading her eye like an artist's paintbrush to a focal point much lower on his body.

She didn't get more than a glimpse at his cock, however, before he rolled over again, this time opening one eye, then two as his hand groped for the sheet Sarah still held. He looked in the general direction of the clock but his eyes didn't seem to focus on it.

"What time is it?"

"I'm afraid we missed church, Sir. It's a little after eleven."

Yawning, Phillip stretched, giving Sarah a good, long look at those muscles in action. She loved the way they slid under the surface of his skin, hiding his strength until he was ready to use it.

"You didn't wake me."

"Nope. I didn't wake you." Kneeling beside the bed, she took her familiar submissive stance, knees slightly spread, hands clasped behind her back, chin out straight. "You needed the sleep, Sir. After watching over me all night long? Punish me if you will but I stand...erm...kneel by my decision."

Try as she might to remain serious, a little smile kept trying to peep through. Nothing could bring her down today.

Phillip studied the slave kneeling beside his bed in still-sleepy mock sternness. In truth, he loved the fact that she had made the decision on her own. Almost as much as he loved the fact that she wasn't going to back away from it. The way her eyes sparkled, he knew her euphoria from last night reigned.

He pulled himself up, leaning against the pillows, teasing her. "I suppose you think I'm still going to take you out for breakfast?"

She cocked her head to look at him and he liked the way the sunlight brought out the red in the strand of hair that fell across her cheek. "You only got two hours' sleep, so we can go later, although we did talk about trying that new diner in the city, over by Maple Avenue."

He noted the hopeful tone of her voice. The rest had invigorated him and when his stomach growled, he gave in. "Yes, I suppose we did. Let me take my shower and think about it."

Phillip threw back the covers and climbed out of bed, her eyes watching his every move. Although not a vain man, he preened in his nudity, since she was such an appreciative audience. Taking his time, he sauntered to the bathroom. At the door, he turned...her eyes had been riveted to his ass.

Clearing his throat to move her attention to his face, he smiled. "While I'm showering, why don't *you* pick out something for *me* to wear?"

As he lathered up and then rinsed, Phillip's mind turned over the conundrum of owning a slave. On the one hand, he wanted her to make her own decisions and not bother him with details. On the other, he wanted her dependent on him for everything. There was something very empowering about having a person hang on your every word and appreciate every nuance of your physique.

But there was something exhausting in it as well. Yes, he kept in shape, and yes, he loved the way her eyes devoured him. But sooner or later he was going to leave his socks in the living room or forget to put the toilet seat down. And she'd think it cute at first, picking up after him like a good slave should.

And later, when the novelty wore off? What then? The sock smelling up the couch cushion would become an irritant, the forgotten toilet seat a blow to her self-esteem—didn't he think enough of her to be considerate? In time, the love and devotion she held now would turn to dislike and if he was lucky, boredom instead of hatred.

Slashing at the thought, he slammed open the shower door harder than he intended. The door clanged to the side so hard he had to look twice to be sure he hadn't broken it. But the noise brought him back to his senses. These were exactly the issues Sarah had brought up Friday night and he had dismissed with his "this is a journey we'll take together" speech. And it was. He just needed to understand she wasn't the only one who was struggling to find a balance in the roles. Sarah used her intelligence and he intended to encourage her to use it at every opportunity. Deciding not to go to church today was a decision she had made and he would support. And together, they'd find the equation that would work for them.

* * * * *

Not until later in the afternoon, after they'd returned from their breakfast out and Sarah once more stood naked before her Master did she finally ask the question that had been on her mind all day.

"Phillip...Sir..." Shaking her head, she threw the names aside. "I want to ask about the red, well, pink lines on the tops of my breasts."

Phillip made himself comfortable on the couch, patting the cushion next to him. Sarah snuggled in, holding one of her breasts up so they could both see the marks she referred to.

"What was it that gave me these?" She knew, or suspected, but wanted confirmation.

"A cane."

Her eyebrows shot up. She was right!

"A very thin, very short one, made from bamboo, I believe."

Sarah smiled. "I thought so. I saw some pictures..." She stopped at Phillip's surprised look.

"So my slave has been looking at dirty pictures on the web, has she?"

Color seeping into her cheeks, Sarah defended her actions. "I'm not sure you'd call them dirty. I just wanted to see..." She faltered. Just what was it she had wanted to see? The pictures of the woman's caned ass had excited her so much she'd slipped her hand into her jeans and come right there at the computer.

Phillip nodded knowingly. "Yes, slave. I see very well. Someone has discovered that those pictures, while mostly meant for men's fantasies, can also fuel a woman's dreams."

"Oh, they definitely did that, Sir." She ducked her head in embarrassment.

Phillip pulled her head up. "It's okay to be excited by those pictures, Sarah. They serve a purpose." His eyes narrowed a little. "In fact, I think I'll send you a few from my own collection."

Now it was Sarah's turn to feel a little shocked. "Collection? You have an entire collection of those pictures?"

He laughed and she bounced against his chest where she snuggled against him. "I have enough. Where do you think I get some of my best ideas?"

She chuckled. "Well, when you put it like that..." She shifted and found a more comfortable position to cuddle into his arms. Phillip pointed to the stripes on her breast.

"How do they feel?"

She blushed. "Actually, they feel sexy. I mean, when I run my finger over them just the right way, I get...um...aroused." Not believing she'd just made that admission, she ducked her head again. This certainly was a morning for confessions. Phillip pulled her chin back up.

"Good. If you'd like, you can have more of them." He traced one of the lines with his finger, leaving his other hand to rest on her bare thigh.

Sarah cocked her head at him. "Did you give me these?"

For answer, he only raised an eyebrow and gave her an I'm-not-telling look. She acquiesced. "Yes, Sir, I know. It doesn't matter."

And in truth, it didn't. In fact, if he hadn't given them to her, all the better. She was sure it was his chest her head had leaned against, his arms holding her body to the earth so her soul could fly as it had. Nor did she know whose fist had been up her vagina. Just remembering it made her squirm on the couch. Never had she felt quite so physically filled.

"I liked the fisting too." She squeezed his arm. "It didn't hurt, like I was afraid it would."

"So it lived up to your expectations?"

"It did. I was worried I'd built the fantasy up in my head so much that actually doing it would be anticlimactic. But it wasn't." Her eyes twinkled. "Not at all."

"Then you wouldn't mind someone fisting you again someday."

Just the word made her shiver and her pussy gape. "I wouldn't mind at all, Sir."

"So you've discovered a little pain can be arousing and you've discovered you like being blindfolded and fondled by several people at once. Being used as their toy."

Sarah knew her cheeks turned an even deeper shade of red. Her voice wasn't above a whisper. "Yes, Sir."

Phillip kissed her then, his lips a soft caress against hers. She savored his taste, let herself wallow in the sexual freedom he was letting her experience. She wasn't naughty, she wasn't a slut. She was a woman with worth not only in the workplace and at home, but in the bedroom as well. Hot damn! Sarah felt as if she could take on the world today. She relaxed into his kiss, reveling in the power he wielded.

The kiss ended abruptly when Phillip pulled away and stood up. Sarah almost fell over, he had taken her so by surprise. "Come on, then, slave. Let's put your newfound discoveries to the test, shall we?"

Even though her cheeks still burned, she stood up and put her hand in his outstretched one. The thought of being used again thrilled her. Their talk aroused her but it was his dominance she craved.

Phillip turned her hand over. "You seem to be missing your cuffs, slave."

"I am, Sir."

"Wait here."

He stepped into the bedroom, retuning a moment later with the four strips of leather and their respective locks. Would she ever tire of having him fasten them on her?

The locks on her cuffs jingled as the she crossed the living room to Phillip, making a music of their own. She could have danced to it.

Phillip led her directly into the dungeon, not stopping until they crossed the length of it and stood before a low, rectangular box, currently covered with a blue velvet cloth. With a twist of his hand, Phillip threw back the covering, revealing the small cage underneath. Never letting go of her hand, he unlatched the door at one end, then pulled her down as he gave his instructions. "Back in, slave. I'm going to keep you here while I get some things ready."

Obediently, Sarah faced away from the cage and backed in. There was just enough room for her to fit on all fours. Phillip reached in and locked her wrists to the corners of the cage, then shut the door and pulled the velvet covering back over the cage. She was enclosed in a world of blue.

Shifting her weight, Sarah made herself as comfortable as she could. He'd only used a quick-release catch to attach the D rings of her cuffs to the wire sides of the cage but they might as well have been welded on for all the good it did her. She remained on all fours, trying not to wiggle too much and show off her impatience. One thing she had learned, the more eager she was for something to happen, the longer Phillip tended to draw it out. Yes, her arousal would increase but at the moment, she was already so aroused she could have fucked a fencepost. She giggled at the thought. What a bad girl she was becoming!

Phillip saw the cage vibrate and heard her little giggle. The little minx was enjoying herself? Not for the first time did he send a prayer heavenward to whatever force had put her in his life. After years of failures, to find someone who shared his interests with a passion to rival his own? Life was very good.

Peeling back the cloth that covered his toy table, as Sarah had taken to calling it, his eye roved over the various implements of sexual torture he kept there. Each one had its own special spot, arranged by type. He knew other Doms who kept everything on a pegboard, each item hanging from its own hook. But he preferred the table with the length of blue cloth that kept the dust off. He liked to keep her guessing about what was underneath. Picking up a slender rod, he held it in both hands, his gaze going from the cage to the cane, wondering if this was what Sarah thought she was ready for.

Well, there was only one way to find out. He knew she would hate him for what he was about to inflict on her but would she find it as arousing as he did? Or would he be destroying the cane tomorrow based on her response to it today?

Uncovering the extra long massage table he'd built, he double-checked the eyebolts and ran a hand over the leather as he did before every session. He considered adding a few straps, then decided against it. Her muscles would need room to react—within limits, of course.

Satisfied that the equipment was safe, he picked up a new gag he'd found and set it at the head of the table, pulled the blue cloth back over the toys behind him and slid the cane under so that just one end peeked out. Only then did he bend down in front of the cage.

"Slave?"

"Yes, Master?" Sarah's voice, muffled by the velvet, came through low and sexy. Phillip grinned.

"I want to use you, slave."

"Yes, Master. Please do."

"I might hurt you, slave." Phillip knew the cane would sting when he struck her ass, giving her the same marks she currently enjoyed on her breasts.

"Hurt me, Master. Let me feel your touch."

There was a definite begging tone in her voice that triggered the animal inside Phillip. His cock stirred in response. Flipping the cover back, he looked his fill at the woman locked inside the cage.

A lock of golden brown had fallen from her ponytail, hiding one eye from him. Hunger shone from the other as she rocked back and forth on her hands and knees. A low growl came from the back of her throat. Phillip had locked mild-mannered, almost shy Sarah into the cage—the Master would take out a wild slave, her sex fully awakened and ripe for his cane. His eyes hardened in response and his cock came fully erect, straining against the fabric of his pants. This slave needed attention. She would get more than she bargained for.

Slowly, deliberately, he took his time with the locks, making her wait and increasing her anticipation as well as his own. He didn't speak to her but kept his eyes locked on hers, letting the hunger build. An extra leash lay beside the cage. He clipped it to her collar and stood, pulling her out roughly. On her hands and knees, she left the cage and followed where he led.

He held dominion over her and gloried in it. She did as she was told, even as the fires consumed her. He could see it in her eyes. If given choices, she would take charge, pushing him onto the floor and mounting him like the wild animal she was.

But he had tamed her, taught her. It had been his touch that even allowed her permission to acknowledge the feral being that lived inside her. She owed him her allegiance, her servitude, her body. Bringing their circuitous route to an end at the table, he reached down and grabbed the leash close to the collar, pulling her up and forcing her onto her feet. Her hands reached for him but he was ready. Turning her to face the table, he pushed her down, grabbing her hands and pulling her along the tabletop until her arms were stretched and she was off balance. In seconds, he fastened first one wrist, then the other. She cried out, not in pain but frustration and his smile was wicked.

Her feet still touched the floor at the side of the table, her body bent and struggling. With a single movement, he scooped her up, laying her legs flat along the length of the table and coming around to fasten them down. Only once she was caught and could not escape did he step back and take a look at his squirming slave.

More hair had escaped the ponytail to hang about her face, giving her a wild look that fit her. Her slender form, now stretched, showed off muscles he normally didn't notice, making the curves of her body even more sensuous. He could touch her anywhere and she could do nothing to prevent him.

She fought now, the animal inside her out of control. He let her rage, knowing that animal could never be in her control because she had given it to him. He held power over it. His touch awakened it. His touch could calm it.

A single hand on her back. He rested his palm at the base of her spine, quietly asserting command. The effect was almost immediate. She tensed, as if she expected something more. He would give her more. Just not yet. She wasn't ready yet.

Slowly, he pushed his hand up along her spine, letting his dominion flow through his palm and into her muscles. Strong muscles, muscles not afraid of hard work. He liked that. She quieted under his hand.

Her head rested on the leather, her hair covering her face. He gathered it, redoing her ponytail so he could see the light in her eyes. Fear mingled with gratitude and he understood. The feral animal that she could be still scared her, as did the fact that he could control it and that she had given that animal to him.

Picking up the gag, he held it before her. Dutifully, she opened her mouth and he put it inside. For this, he had chosen a penis-shaped gag, a small one, one that would keep her mouth filled. He would fill her pussy later. After he had striped her ass with his cane.

She was ready. Her body lay before him like a canvas for his brush. All that remained was for the artist to prepare himself. Stripping off his shirt, Phillip laid it over the cage he would not use again today. He took off his belt and dropped it beside his shirt, leaving his pants on. His erection under control, he liked the way his partially clothed body reinforced his role as Master over his slave's naked and bound body.

Pulling the cane from its hiding place, he laid it gently against her skin. Lifting the cane only a little, he bounced it lightly against her butt cheeks.

When the bounces produced no reaction, he gave a quick, light snap to get her attention. Her head flew up, her eyes wide. That was more like it. He snapped again, careful not to land in the same spot. A thin pink line appeared on the white skin of her ass.

Phillip tapped the cane lightly all over her upper thighs and the fleshy mounds of her ass, knowing the continuous barrage would sensitize her skin, much as one tenderized a piece of meat. Tapping over and over, he didn't stop until her body protested, trying to move away from the touch of the cane.

He ran his palm over her smooth skin, testing the warmth. Too cool and she would need more to get her to the state he wanted. Too warm would mean he'd gone too far. But like Little Bear, her skin was just right. Phillip grinned. His Goldilocks had a lot more courage than the girl in the fairy tale.

"This is going to sting, slave. Take the pain and direct it to your pussy. Let it feed your need."

Her eyes were shut tight, her mind already working to do as he commanded. To help her along, he ran a finger along her slit, rubbing the white cream already oozing there up to moisten her pussy lips. He heard a bubble of breath blow out from around the penis gag, and knew she was right where he wanted her to be.

Lifting the cane, he aimed his blow. Once, twice—not hitting her either time but only resting it on the spot he intended to hit. Only when he was satisfied the cane would land straight across her ass did he put force behind it, snapping it hard against her ass.

She practically leapt off the table. A short cry of surprise, strangled by the gag, turned quickly into fast breaths as he rubbed the spot with the palm of his hand, easing the pain into arousal. He dipped his finger again, arrowing the sensation where he wanted it to go. She didn't disappoint him. Fresh cream oozed from her pussy.

The earlier pink marks had already faded into the general pink of her ass. Now one red stripe, bright and angry, swelled and stretched across both ass cheeks. His cock hardened.

Again he took aim, carefully placing the cane twice to make sure he did not hit the same spot. He also didn't want the cane to wrap and cause damage to her side. His touch wasn't perfect, he knew. Not enough practice. But he had studied under good Masters and knew the dangers he had to avoid.

Thwack! Her head popped up again, the cry less of surprise this time and more of protest against the invasion of pain. "Master it, slave. Put it where it belongs."

She listened to his demand, her body attempting to arch and bend as she fought for control. Her hands splayed out, then suddenly clenched into fists as she won the battle.

One more. Three stripes and he was out. Carefully setting the cane right where he wanted the last mark to go, he lifted and set, lifted and set, making sure his aim would be true. Cutting the air with his blow, he let it smack against her skin no harder, no softer, than the two blows before.

Again her body arched, again she made that beautiful cry through the gag. Tears formed unbidden in her eyes and Phillip quickly released her ankles and wrists, pulling her body half off the table even as he unsnapped his pants. His cock throbbed at the sounds she made. The stripes across her rear—placed there at his hand—excited him. He needed her…now.

He knew he was being rough. Grabbing her hands, he pulled them behind her, forcing her to bend over the table.

Holding her down with one hand, he tore off his pants and tossed them to the side. His arm brushed the fresh stripes and a soft cry came from the back of her throat as he kicked her legs wide, her whimpers egging him on. The red stripes beckoned and he obliged, rubbing his cock along her slit.

She was soaked with need. She struggled under his hands, opening for him, wanting him to take her from behind. Aiming his cock, he thrust deep inside her in one strong push. Her body arched and she cried out at the sudden intrusion, her head whipping from side to side even as her body pushed back, wanting him to fill her. Pulling out, he thrust in again, knowing from the way she jerked that he had hit her G-spot. Taking aim, he pulled almost all the way out, then hit it again.

Sarah screamed and fought as the slut broke the last lock on her cage with a vengeance. Her mind screamed, *Fuck me!* but the words came out garbled and sounding more like a cry around the gag. Tears streamed down her face at his thrusts, each one pressing his body against her sore ass, the stinging driving her need to come higher with each thrust. The muscles of her pussy tightened around his cock, pulling him in deeper, trying to hold him inside even as he pulled away from her only to slam inside her again, pushing the air out of her lungs and making her gasp for breath.

She came. Loudly. Her body contracted and she gave in, letting go of all her control, letting her body milk every drop of its beauty. Behind her, Phillip thrust in again, prolonging the sweet agony. His thrusts increased in tempo and she rode them, her body welcoming him, wanting him. She longed to hear his groans as he emptied himself inside her.

But he wanted more from her. Roughly he pulled her arms, forcing her body to arch as he pounded into her. She was nothing more than a puppet in his hands. She had no power...she was only a vessel for him to fuck. Sarah couldn't help herself. She came again. An object to be used. The thought echoed in her head as Phillip groaned and came with her, their bodies taken over by the animals they no longer controlled. She howled, an eternal, feral cry that came from the depths of her soul and filled the air. He answered, his growl deep and dark and dominating.

Together their animals fought, not wanting to give in to civility as passion took her leave and their bodies slowed. The growls grew weaker and contentment stole over them both, leaving their minds numb and their bodies sated.

Sarah shivered on the table where Phillip had placed her, his cock still buried deep inside her warmth. His animal made a last lunge at freedom and with an oath, Phillip pulled out, turned her around, pulled her close and held her tight.

Shaking all over, Sarah grabbed on to Phillip's steadiness. He held her, murmuring soft sounds in her ear. His grip around her, so tight she almost couldn't breathe, gave her comfort. He wouldn't let her fall. He would protect her. He accepted her, even if she was ashamed that the pain almost made her come. How could she be such a slut as to like that? In his arms, the wild animal inside her didn't matter. He loved her and he held her and that was all her world right now.

How long she clung to him, she didn't know but her breathing slowed as the pain ebbed into memory. With a final shake, she raised her head to him, wishing she could kiss him. The gag, however, served as another comfort. Something to bite down on, something he had given her to help. Yet when he unfastened it, taking it out and putting it on the table beside her, she didn't complain.

"Shall we go to bed?"

Sarah nodded, not trusting her voice. Snuggling under his arm, she stood, her ass sore and aching, a wonderful memory of a wonderful weekend. And when he removed the heavy collar so she could lie comfortably beside him, she fell asleep in his arms, counting down the days until he would weld a permanent silver collar around her neck.

Chapter Eight
The Accident

~

Driving down the road like a maniac, Phillip forced himself to calm down before he ended up in an accident, too. His heart pounded in his chest and he had to keep swallowing hard to force down the taste of fear. Pulling up to the stop sign just a mile down the road, he took in details even as he searched for Sarah. She'd called him on her cell phone, barely able to talk. He knew immediately that something was wrong and was halfway out to his car before she managed to tell him she'd been in an accident not too far down the road on her way to work. Why she was calling him and not 911 was beyond him, but he kept his head and got her to hand over the phone to someone else.

Two cars at odd angles sat in the middle of the intersection and some guy stood in front of him directing the increasing traffic to an alternate route. Phillip parked and ran toward Sarah's car, ignoring the protests of the makeshift traffic cop.

Someone had already pulled her out of the wreck. He spared only a glance at the compact car she drove. The driver's side of the front end was all pushed in and the door hung almost off its hinges. Broken glass littered the area. His heart jumped into his throat and he had to stop and close his eyes, taking a deep breath before rushing over to the figure lying so pathetically on the grass.

Please let her be alive. He didn't know what he would do if she weren't. Kneeling beside her in the cold grass, he took in her condition even as his voice cracked trying to talk to her.

"Sarah, it's Phillip. Can you hear me?" A gash in her forehead oozed blood, matting her beautiful hair. The daytime collar she wore, the one he had tied around her neck only half an hour before, had turned a darker shade, colored by the blood that ran down her neck from the gash at her temple. Her left arm lay beside her at an odd angle, totally out of joint at the shoulder.

"Keep talkin' to her, buddy. I've brought a blanket to keep her warm. We need to keep her from goin' into shock."

Phillip didn't even look at the speaker as he helped to tuck the plaid blanket around her injured arm. "Sarah, look at me. If you hear me, look at me."

Slowly her eyes turned and found his face. He read the fear in them. And the pain. Not the kind that aroused, but the kind that terrified. At least, it terrified him.

But he couldn't let her see that terror. If there was ever a time she needed him to be strong for her, this was it. Forcing a smile and pulling his shirt out of his pants, he used the tail to wipe at the blood that seeped down her temple. "Keep looking at me, Sarah. Don't close your eyes." She probably had a concussion and staying awake was the only first aid he could remember about blows to the head. "Don't go to sleep on me, Sarah. Stay focused on me. Listen to my voice and know I'm here. You're going to be all right. I'm here, Sarah."

Repeating her name not only helped to keep her focused, it helped him to focus as well. Where were the damn paramedics?

"Okay, sir, we need you to step aside."

A man in a light blue shirt with an insignia on the sleeve knelt beside him. *Ask and ye shall receive*, Phillip thought, moving aside so the emergency personnel could do their jobs. He circled around to Sarah's good side, still talking to her. The paramedic nodded. "She's listening to you. Keep up the patter. Keep her focused on you."

Phillip didn't know what to say anymore and found himself repeating the words he'd already said. He supposed it didn't really matter what the words were. As long as she could hear his voice and stay conscious.

Time no longer existed. It both stopped and stretched as he watched the paramedics work to save Sarah, right there on the ground. Not until they finally wheeled her stretcher to the ambulance did he look at his watch. Only ten minutes since he'd pulled up to the accident? Only eighteen minutes since she had called? His life had turned upside down in just over a quarter of an hour. How was that possible?

"I'm sorry, sir, you can't ride in the ambulance unless you're a relative."

The words only partially registered. His response was automatic. "I'm her fiancé."

The doors to the ambulance were already shutting, metal and glass barriers to the love of his life. He took a step forward, but a policeman's hand stopped him.

"Let them get her to the hospital, sir. Come on, you can follow right behind."

Later, he wouldn't be able to remember that ride in. His mind had gone into some automatic mode that drove the car, keeping the ambulance in front of him and the police car behind him all in a row as they made their way to the hospital. He parked...somewhere, running to her just as the paramedics were dropping the legs on the stretcher.

Phillip held Sarah's hand, forcing himself not to let her see how worried he was. His long legs strode beside the stretcher as the paramedics hurried along the corridors of the hospital. He schooled his face and did not let her see the alarm behind his eyes...that she was conscious at all was a miracle in itself.

Twin doors blocked the corridor. A woman in a paisley shirt and white pants stood in his way. The paramedics never slowed but the nurse put out her hand to prevent Phillip from following.

"You cannot come in here, sir. You must wait out there." Her tone was kind and understanding, yet firm. It was never easy for loved ones to wait and she often wondered who had the harder time of it—the one in the emergency room or the one who waited for news.

Phillip swallowed hard again and watched the stretcher until it turned a corner and Sarah disappeared from his sight. He knew he couldn't follow her. He knew he should go to the little room specifically prepared for those who waited and paced. But he couldn't move. His unfocused eyes stared at the floor as he tried to breathe. This should be a dream. This shouldn't be real. This was the stuff of nightmares.

"She's in good hands, sir. C'mon, let me take you to the lounge." Dimly Phillip felt an aide touch his arm and he allowed her to maneuver him the short distance to a small, well-lit room only a few steps from those fateful doors.

"Let me bring you something to drink, sir." The aide eyed the tall man carefully. She imagined he was normally well-dressed but now his white shirt, streaked with blood across the front, spoke of the horror he was going through. She'd overheard his curt exchange with the nurses who had run to meet the paramedics. The blood obviously belonged to the woman whose side he hadn't wanted to leave. His wife? Girlfriend? She eyed him critically. Shock oftentimes set in among rescuers as the tensions eased and the reality of what they'd witnessed hit them upside the head. No doubt about it, this one needed watching.

Phillip mumbled something—what had the woman asked him? Used to taking command, even in crisis situations, his brain now felt wrapped in cotton and he just couldn't think. All he could see was Sarah's body, bruised and bloody as it lay on that stretcher.

Pacing in the waiting room now, he glanced down at his shirt. The front flap was sticky with blood. Her blood. Phillip ran to the men's room and threw up.

He emerged a different man. Years of self-discipline kicked into action after he'd emptied his stomach. He was no good to Sarah if he couldn't hold his act together. If there was ever a time she needed him to be strong, it was now. He would not fail her.

As he came out into the hall, he took a look around. To his right lay the double doors. Sarah was back there somewhere. A small office was to his left and a little behind him, and directly across the hall, was what passed for a waiting room, a rather large open space with typical orange vinyl seats stretching along the white walls.

He couldn't sit there. And he couldn't go through the doors. He turned to the nurse's station.

But the man who sat behind the desk had no information. "What is your relation to the patient?" he asked Phillip.

"She's my fiancée. We're getting married in three weeks."

"Sorry, sir. I cannot give you any information at this time."

Phillip wanted to slam something. He couldn't just stand here, impotent. The muscles of his neck strained with his effort to contain his frustration.

The double doors, now on his left, swung open and a nurse paused in the opening. "Sir? Are you the one who came in with the accident victim? A woman with light brown hair?"

His heart pounding, Phillip strode toward her. "Yes."

"Will you come with me, sir? We need some information."

Grateful to be doing something at last, Phillip followed her through the doors into sterile surroundings. Small rooms led off a wide corridor that circled around a central medical station. Smocks of every color hurried from place to place, giving one the impression of a well-organized beehive. Every worker had a place to be and a job to do.

Not all the rooms were occupied, Phillip realized as the nurse led him past two that were dark, their metallic arms and locked cabinets waiting their turn to serve. The third room, however, proved to be a major source of the center's activity. They waited as a man, carrying a tray of blood samples, exited the room. Phillip knew that was more of Sarah's blood. How much did she have left?

"She's been calling for you. Well, she's been calling for someone she calls 'Sir'." The nurse shook her head. "At first we thought she was trying to talk to one of the doctors but then realized she wanted someone else. One of the paramedics," she paused to nod at a young man filling out paperwork at the curved central desk, "remembered you had followed them in. We're taking a chance that she'll settle down after she speaks to you."

Phillip listened, trying to get a glimpse of Sarah through the throng of people in the room. How many people did she need working on her? He nodded at the nurse. "She's my fiancée." He looked back through the glass. "Is she...I mean...?"

The nurse put her hand on his arm. "She'll be fine as soon as she settles and lets them take a look at her. She has a broken collarbone and a very nasty cut on her forehead. But she won't let us set the bone until she speaks to 'Sir'."

Phillip took a deep breath, centering himself and relaxing his face into a look of calm. A second breath to calm his heartbeat and take the tremor out of his voice and he was ready. The nurse nodded approvingly and led him into the controlled bedlam.

Sarah lay on the bed, her eyes barely focusing on her surroundings. Even though the wound at her temple had been cleaned, the sight of the bone gleaming through the gap in her skin made him want to throw up again. He didn't. She needed his strength and he bent his full will on her now.

"Sarah, it's me, Phillip. Can you see me?"

He waited until her eyes found him. The spark of recognition thrilled through him. She tried to speak but he put a finger on her lips.

"I'm here. The doctors need to set your shoulder and stitch up your head. They're going to give you something for the pain." This last was just as much a directive to the doctors as it was an attempt to comfort the woman he loved. "You have to let them do this, Sarah. Do you hear me?"

She whispered something and Phillip had to bend down to hear her.

"Tom died. I don't want to die."

With a start, Phillip stood up. "Is that what this is about? Sarah, you're not going to die." His voice took on a softer tone and he bent down, bringing his face close to hers. "You have a broken collarbone and a dislocated shoulder. You also have a cut on your head that's going to need stitches. That's all. Let them fix it. You'll be up and around in no time."

"Promise?"

"I promise. I'm here, Sarah. It took me years to find you. I'm not going to let anything like a little car accident take you away from me." He smiled as he said it, even as he fervently prayed it was true.

She nodded, closing her eyes, trusting him. From where he was, Phillip looked up at the doctor across from him.

"We'll take it from here. Why don't you wait outside?"

Phillip shook his head and stood, keeping Sarah's hand firmly in his. "No, I'll stay. She needs to feel me here."

"Then at least sit down so when you faint you don't have so far to fall."

Someone kicked a rolling stool at him and Phillip hooked it with his foot. He would sit down. Not because he might faint—he knew he wouldn't, no matter what. He was in control now. But because by sitting, he'd be out of the way of the people who worked to help Sarah. His ego didn't need him to be front and center. It only needed him to be there.

* * * * *

Will listened to his friend's strained voice, trying to hear over the phone what Phillip wasn't telling him. "Will, she's hurt and I can't help her."

"Is she in surgery?"

"She is now. They let me stay while they prepped her in the emergency room and then walk with her all the way to the operating room. She was out of it by then. They'd given her some drugs to make her sleep so they can set her shoulder. She's still there."

Will was already closing down his computer at work, mentally going through the instructions he would leave his secretary. "Phillip, I'm on my way. You don't need to wait alone."

"Thanks, Will."

Relief, palpable in Phillip's voice, gave away the state of his worry. Will hung up his phone, decided the papers on his desk could stay right where they were and threw on his suit jacket, already dialing Jill on his cell phone. He gave her the news, trusting that she would call Aleshia. Did Sarah have any family in the area who should be notified? He'd have to ask Phillip when he got to the hospital.

Thirty minutes later he found Phillip pacing like a caged lion in the surgical waiting room.

"What's the word?" He handed Phillip a cup of hot chocolate he'd picked up along the way. Will would never understand his friend's dislike of the rich, brown coffee that sustained the majority of Americans, himself included. Phillip took the large paper cup, setting it absentmindedly on one of the small tables at the end of the row of chairs no one sat in.

"No word. She's been there for over an hour now. What's taking so long?"

Will shook his head and picked up the cocoa, putting the cup in Phillip's hand again, this time steering him toward a seat. "Sit down before you wear a groove in the linoleum and tell me what happened."

Phillip filled him in about how Sarah had dressed that morning for work, just like every other Monday morning, then gotten in her car and driven off. Except this time there had been one difference—they'd had their first ever almost-argument. Phillip had mentioned to Sarah that he would be going shopping today to buy her some outfits he would like her to wear to work and she had quickly put the kibosh on the idea. When he'd reminded her of her upcoming vows, she had shaken her head and told him she wasn't budging on this. What she wore to work was her prerogative.

"It was a silly argument, really," Phillip tried to explain. "At some point in the discussion, she accused me of wanting her to be independent but not giving her clear boundaries of where she could and couldn't be."

"Are you?" Will's voice remained neutral.

Phillip shook his head. "Maybe not. I don't know. We agreed we'd discuss it later, since trying to talk about it five minutes before she left for work wasn't really the time."

"Did you kiss and make up?"

For the first time since entering the hospital, Phillip smiled. He thought his face would crack it hurt so much. "Yes. Like I said, it wasn't really an argument—it was more of a…heated discussion."

"Mr. Townsend?"

The two looked up. A man in clean scrubs stood in the doorway. Phillip stood, his heart suddenly beating so loudly he could hear it in his ears. "Yes?"

"Mr. Townsend, I'm Dr. Riley. We have some questions to ask you."

From behind the doctor, a uniformed police officer stepped into the room.

"What's the matter?" Phillip looked from one to the other, a small unease settling into the pit of his stomach. "Is Sarah all right? What's going on?"

The doctor held up his hand. "She's still in surgery. There was more damage to the shoulder than we anticipated. Mr. Townsend, according to the information you gave the admitting nurse downstairs, Mrs. Simpson-Parker is your fiancée, is that correct?"

"Yes."

Will stood up and came to stand beside Phillip, a frown on his face.

"And the two of you are living together?"

"No. I don't see what our living arrangement has to do with her injury, Doctor." Phillip tried to keep the sarcasm out of his voice and knew he was only partially successful.

"Was Mrs. Simpson-Parker coming from your house this morning, Mr. Townsend?"

Will stepped forward. "I don't think Mr. Townsend is going to answer any more questions until you tell us what this is all about."

The police officer spoke for the first time. "Mrs. Simpson has some marks on her body that are not consistent with a car accident. We'd like to know where those marks came from, Mr. Townsend."

Phillip opened his mouth but again Will intervened. "Are you asking Mr. Townsend if he beat up on his girlfriend?"

The officer nodded, irritation puffing him up. "That's exactly what I'm asking him."

"Sarah is going to be my wife. I love her. And you stand there and accuse me of beating her up?" Phillip's head swam. He had beaten her. In addition to Will's marks across the tops of her breasts, his three red stripes across her bottom would give her something to remember for the better part of the day. He'd teased her about it just before she had gotten in the car, giving her a little swat and watching her turn red as she realized how sitting all day was going to feel. Will and the cop were arguing about something…what were they saying? Mastering himself, Phillip caught just the end of Will's tirade.

"…and what goes on between two consenting adults is none of your business, buster."

The officer narrowed his eyes and pulled out his handcuffs. "You're under arrest, Mr. Townsend."

"What for?"

"Domestic abuse. And if the doctor finds out you fucked your wife-to-be in the ass, I'm throwin' sodomy charges in as well."

"You can't arrest a man for—" The officer's Miranda rights recitation cut off Will's protest.

None-too-gently, the cop turned Phillip around, pushing him to the wall and spreading his legs wide. His rights went in one ear and out the other as the officer brought back first one, then the other wrist, cuffing them behind his back. Not until the cop started to push him out the door did he protest. "No, I can't. I have to stay here. My…she needs me."

"Yeah, she needs you like she needs another accident. Out, mister. You're going down."

"Will…"

"I'll take care of it."

Anger mixed with hopelessness prevented Phillip from seeing the stares as he walked through the corridors of the hospital, handcuffed and under arrest. It wasn't true what he'd told the cop. Sarah didn't need him by her side right now. He needed her.

Chapter Nine
Charges

ஐ

Breathing. The first thing Sarah was aware of was her own breathing. For some time now, she'd been taking small breaths. Slowly, deliberately, she drew in air, filling her lungs, letting the fresh air blow away the dust and cobwebs in her brain.

But the deep breath made her shoulder ache. Why did her shoulder hurt?

Sounds filtered into her consciousness. Muffled at first, she gradually distinguished voices. A man's and a woman's. They sounded troubled. She'd heard them before, somewhere. In some other life, maybe.

With an effort, she opened her eyes. White. And green. White above her, green to the sides. Dim. Where was the light? Why wasn't she in her own bedroom? At least, she didn't think this was her bedroom.

"Sarah, thank God you're awake."

A woman she didn't recognize stood beside her bed. She was beautiful, with a radiant smile. Sarah wanted to smile back at her but it just seemed like so much effort.

"They've been keeping you pretty heavily sedated. I've called for the nurse. She'll be right here."

Another woman came from around the green curtain at the side of the bed. Funny how she could come through a curtain. Where were the walls?

"Oh, look! You're awake. What pretty brown eyes you have."

The nurse checked a tall pole at Sarah's side. Lights blinked and several lines wormed across a screen, making no sense to Sarah. She felt wrapped in soft cotton. Pulling in another long, slow breath, she closed her eyes and went back to sleep.

The next time she awoke, her head felt clearer. Sound still came several seconds after awareness. She was lying flat, the pillow under her head not doing much to give her head any lift. As a result, she could really only see the white ceiling above her. If she turned her head a little to the right, she could see the IV monitor. She knew what that was now, even if the numbers and squiggly lines still didn't make any sense to her. A light green curtain hung at the window, pulled shut against the night. Above her, somewhere behind, a small light illuminated the room.

This was definitely a hospital. She blinked several times as her mind focused. Now what was she doing here? She looked left at the long green curtain that cut off her view of the door. Only then did she notice the bandages and casting of her left arm. The dull ache in her collarbone began to throb.

Fumbling on the blanket, her hand located a remote control. Was this for the TV that hung just at the edge of her vision? Or would she move the bed up and down if she pushed the buttons? Blinking and bringing the remote closer, then moving it farther away, she tried to clear the remnants of her sleep so she could read the icons beside the buttons.

Deciding that the most worn button must be the one for the nurse, she pushed it. Nothing happened. No bell went off, no alarm. At least her bed didn't move. She wasn't sure she liked lying flat but she was pretty sure she didn't want to sit up with her shoulder aching like this. She pushed the button again.

"Nice to see you awake and alert this time. How are we doing?" A rather short, plump woman in a bright purple print shirt hovered into view.

"I'm thirsty."

The words surprised Sarah on two counts. First, until she spoke the words, she hadn't realized how parched she was. And second, her voice didn't sound like hers at all. Wispy and gravelly at the same time. She tried to clear her throat but found she was too dry.

The nurse checked a clipboard she'd gotten from somewhere. "You can have a few ice chips. That'll help. Be right back."

Just a minute later, the nurse returned. "By the way, my name is Jody. I'm your night nurse. Here. Let's get one of these into you and then I'll need some information." Using a spoon, she fished a small ice chunk out of the plastic glass she held. Waiting until Sarah opened her lips, she set it carefully so that Sarah could pull it into her mouth and suck on it.

The ice chip was so tiny, it melted quickly. Sarah opened her mouth for another and Jody complied. But then she set the glass on the long table by the side of the bed and picked up the clipboard again.

"Do you know today's date?"

Sarah shook her head and immediately decided not to do that again. "Monday. I know it was Monday but I can't remember the date."

"Can you remember the month?"

"November."

"Good." Jody made a notation on her clipboard. "And your name is?"

"Sarah Marie Simpson–Parker."

"What do you remember about your accident, Sarah?"

She closed her eyes and sighed. "Nothing," she finally admitted.

"What's the last thing you do remember?"

Phillip's cane. His hugs afterward. Snuggling into his arms in bed. Nothing of the morning at all. Nothing of getting up, showering, dressing—all things she supposed she did simply because she did them every morning. Her last memory was of lying safe in Phillip's arms.

"I remember going to bed but not getting up this morning" was all she answered. "Was I in an accident?"

Jody nodded and Sarah wished she would sit down. It was hard to look up at her at this angle. She closed her eyes.

"Just a few more questions, Sarah, then I'm going to give you something for the pain and you can go to sleep again."

Forcing her eyes open, Sarah nodded slowly, keeping her movements gentle.

"Do you know a William and Jillean Danton?"

Sarah nodded. "Yes." Her voice was sounding raspy again.

Jody fished out another ice chip for Sarah as she asked her last question. "Do you give permission for them to visit you and to know your condition?"

"Yes." Opening her mouth, Sarah gratefully accepted the ice, letting its coolness ease away some of her discomfort.

"There you go. You're allowed a pain reliever in your IV drip. Would you like it now?"

She nodded. The throbbing in her shoulder was taking over her thoughts.

"Be right back, then."

Again Jody disappeared around the green curtain and again she was back sooner than Sarah expected her. She carried a small bottle in her hand, from which she withdrew a clear liquid into a hypodermic needle. Flipping open a cap on part of the IV tube and slowly depressing the plunger, Jody let the painkiller mix with whatever else they were feeding into her arm. She really didn't care what they were giving her as long as it made the pain go away.

Jody turned to smile at her but once again, Sarah was finding it too much effort to smile back. She sighed, turned her head and fell asleep.

"C'mon, sleepyhead, time to wake up. C'mon, Sarah. Up and at 'em."

Sarah opened one eye and stared balefully at Beth, who poked her good arm, prodding her into wakefulness. "I'm awake, I'm awake." Her bed still lay flat and Beth bent over and waved at her like she was a two-year-old. "What're y'doin'?"

"Just making sure you're really awake. You gotta wake up, Sarah. There're important doings going on and you're sleeping right through 'em."

Taking a deep breath to clear her mind, Sarah blinked several times, using her good hand to rub away the last of her sleep. Then she grinned. Her head was a lot clearer this time than the last time she'd been awake. And her shoulder, while achy, didn't throb. Her stomach growled. Loudly.

"I'm starved."

"It's about time. Let's get some food into you and put you on the road to recovery, girl."

Sarah's best friend bustled around the room, calling for the nurse, adjusting the blankets over Sarah, opening the curtains and letting light into the room as she talked. "You've been sleeping long enough. Now you need to get up and get moving, get some life back into you. Paul's been by to see you and a couple of friends I guess you know from Phillip, everybody was real worried there for a while."

Sarah detected a faint note of disapproval when Beth mentioned Phillip's friends but lying as she was, she found it hard to get a word in edgewise. The nurse entered and Sarah thought she'd seen her before—a short, plump woman with dark hair and a friendly smile.

"The doctor was in to see you about an hour ago and took you off the pain meds you've been on. Said when you woke up, you should try sitting up."

Sarah nodded. In her brief lucid moments over the past several hours, the white ceiling and glimpses of the walls had been all she could see. With Beth assisting by holding down the button and the nurse supporting Sarah's back and injured arm, the head of the bed rose, allowing her to get a better view of the room that was her current world. Cool green walls, their color meant to be soothing, were broken only by a window on her right, a corkboard at the foot of her bed, another at the foot of the bed next to her and then the door on her left. The other bed in the room remained empty and Sarah sent up a thank you to whoever was watching over her for that small favor.

The small corkboard had several unopened cards pinned to it. One side of the board, separated by a thick black line, held a photocopied sheet with squiggles all over it Sarah couldn't read from her bed. The nurse gave a final check to her IV tube once she was sitting and went over to add to the arcane marks on the page.

"I'm hungry."

"Good," the nurse called over her shoulder. "I'll get something sent up for you, since you missed breakfast. We'll start you out on liquids this morning, then, if those stay down, we'll move up the food chain. Keep everything in its place and you'll be on real food by the end of the day."

She left and Sarah wondered if she carried the same purposeful bustle with her wherever she went. Taking a deep breath and finding it didn't hurt her shoulder, she took another, then gave Beth a wry smile.

"So you want to tell me what happened and how come I'm here in the hospital?"

"You were in a car accident."

"Yeah, I know that. The nurse told me that..." She frowned. "I don't remember it." She gestured toward the door.

"She said I missed breakfast but I distinctly remember those curtains…" She paused to gesture with her good hand to the window now streaming sunlight across her lap. "Those curtains were pulled and it was dark. How long was I out?"

Beth pulled a large chair from the corner of the room up to the bed and made herself comfortable. "Just a day. A guy ran a red light and hit you on the way to work yesterday morning. He's fine but you broke your collarbone and smashed up your shoulder…and you have a concussion, they think from hitting your head on the door window. Doctors did a CAT scan to make sure you didn't have any problems in your head but didn't find anything."

Sarah grinned. "You tellin' me my head is empty?"

Beth laughed. "Yep. Nothing there to damage."

Sarah didn't want to ask the question that really was on her mind, almost afraid to know the answer. But she had to know. Unconsciously picking at the blanket that covered her lower body, she tried to remain casual as she asked, "Where's Phillip?"

Beth's face darkened. "Where he belongs." She leaned forward, taking Sarah's hand. "Why didn't you tell me? I'm your best friend. I would have stopped him. You don't need to put up with that bullshit."

"What are you talking about? Tell you what?" Even as she pretended ignorance, Sarah's heart pounded harder. The machine at her side gave her away as her pulse rate quickened. She looked away, suddenly afraid Beth knew all about her kinky side.

"Sarah, that bastard's been abusing you—physically abusing you—and you didn't tell anyone!" Beth's tone accused Sarah right along with Phillip.

"No, he wasn't!" Sarah's voice rose, along with her blood pressure. The machines beside her started beeping. "He wasn't abusing me. It's not like that at all."

"Here, here, now. What's all this?" The plump nurse hurried back in, one hand going to Sarah, resting on her forearm where it lay in its sling, the other quickly resetting the monitors. Turning a stern eye on Beth, she scolded both of them. "You cannot be upsetting her that way. And you..." she turned to Sarah. "You cannot be going off like that. I'll have the doctor put you right back on sedatives and keep you still." With quick professionalism, she checked Sarah's bindings. "Almost time to change that bandage anyway."

With a tone that brooked no discussion, she looked straight at Beth. "Say your goodbyes while I go get what I need to redress that. It won't take me more than two minutes."

Turning on her heel, she stalked out of the room. The two friends were left with a heavy silence between them.

"I'm sorry, Sarah. I didn't mean to upset you." A stiff formality remained in Beth's posture and voice.

"He didn't beat me, Beth. It's not what you think."

"Fine. He didn't beat you. You got those bruises from falling down the stairs. Think up some more good lies, Sarah. I've got to go to work." With a vengeance, Beth pushed the chair back into the corner and gathered up her jacket and purse.

"Beth, don't be like that." Sarah watched, feeling helpless. A headache pounded in her skull and she found it difficult to focus. "Beth?"

Halfway to the door, Beth stopped, turned around and came over to her bad side. "Sarah, I don't know why you're protecting him, but know I will protect you. You're my friend and I support you."

"Thank you, Beth. I appreciate your support. If you give me a chance, I will explain it all..." The entrance of the nurse prevented Sarah from saying more. Telling Beth about her sexual preferences was going to be hard enough, she didn't need strangers knowing too.

"I'll be back after work to see how you're doing." Beth squeezed her hand and was gone.

Sarah sighed. Why did life have to be so complicated? And where was Phillip?

"Multiple contusions, a broken clavicle, a broken arm and a dislocated shoulder." The doctor slammed shut the metal clipboard and pulled a penlight out of his pocket, taking aim at Sarah's eyes. "Don't turn your head, just follow the light with your eyes," he instructed.

Sarah did so, feeling irritated for no reason she could fathom. The little hand on the clock opposite her bed crawled toward three o'clock in the afternoon and Phillip still hadn't come to see her. Of course, they still weren't letting her look at herself in a mirror, either, so maybe he just didn't want to see her when she was so ugly and bruised. Although, if they were going to get married, didn't this fall in the "in sickness and in health" section of the marriage vows? Where was he?

"On a scale from one to ten, ten being the worst pain you've ever felt, where would you put your shoulder?"

Sarah set aside her unease about Phillip's absence and concentrated on the doctor's abrupt bedside manner. "About a seven, I guess. The headache is really what's bothering me."

"And the headache is what's keeping you here. You have a grade three concussion." He flipped open his chart and glanced at it. "Although you've kept down both clear liquids and some light food today." He gave her an appraising look. "That's a good sign."

"So what does a grade three concussion mean? I've been sent back to grammar school?"

Jenny, her afternoon nurse, giggled, quickly stifling it when the doctor didn't laugh. Sarah looked him over in his staid white coat, the pens protruding from his breast pocket, the stethoscope draped over his shoulders. She guessed his age to be close to her own—somewhere in his mid-thirties, maybe?

If he didn't wear the perpetual grave look, she might have considered him handsome, though she didn't really go for the brush cut and dark-rimmed glasses. Still, if one had to choose a doctor, she guessed she'd rather have a nerd who graduated top of his class to someone suave and sophisticated and not nearly as smart.

"Your brain rides in a cushion of fluid that protects it from slamming against your skull when you trip or when you turn suddenly." The doctor pushed his glasses more firmly up onto the bridge of his nose and continued his pedantic tone. "There are three levels to what we call concussions—the first grade occurs with a mild slap, if you will, of the brain against the bone of the skull. Second grade concussions are more of a jar against the skull, in effect bruising it, although lasting damage is rare. With a grade three, the brain has been violently slammed against the skull. The damage again is usually temporary, though the headaches are stronger and often last for quite some time."

"So what does one do for a concussion?"

"Take two aspirin and call me in the morning." Dr. Johns grinned, obviously enjoying his own joke.

"And what should I call you?" Sarah played along, even though her head was starting to pound just trying to take in all he was telling her.

Dr. Johns looked at her as if she'd grown a third eye. "Beg pardon?"

"You said, 'call me in the morning', and I said, 'what should I call you?' Get it? It was another joke."

"Hmm… Yes. I see." Obviously not seeing at all, the doctor made a note on her chart and Sarah wondered if he thought she had sustained more brain damage than the tests showed.

"Well, I think we're going to keep you one more day. I want to watch that headache."

"But I'm keeping my food down." While being waited on hand and foot certainly had its attractions, Sarah didn't really want to stay in the hospital any longer than she had to.

"But your headache still isn't fading. One more day." He shut the clipboard with finality.

She sighed as the doctor left the room, turning to Jenny once he was out of earshot. "A bit abrupt, isn't he?"

"Yep. Much as I hate to admit it, though, he's also one of the best doctors I've ever worked with. He's a nerd even among the other doctors."

Sarah laughed, then winced when the movement jarred her shoulder. "I guess I'd rather have a smart, nerdy doctor than someone who can charm the pants off me but graduated last in his class."

Jenny adjusted the covers and helped Sarah sit more comfortably. "You do have another visitor waiting outside if you're up for more company."

"Is it..?" Sarah caught herself, not wanting the nurse to see how anxious she was to see Phillip, or how worried she was that he hadn't come to visit her yet. It just wasn't what she had expected from him. She kept her voice neutral. "I mean…is it Phillip?"

Jenny clucked her tongue in what Sarah was sure was disapproval. "No, a young woman. She was here last night. Seemed real nice. Jill, she said her name was."

Relief flooded through her. At last! Someone who could give her real answers. "Oh, yes. Please send her in. I really need to talk to her."

Jill came in shortly after Jenny left. Sarah thought she looked drawn and tired, a look she covered up quickly with a look of concern for Sarah.

"How're you doin', sweetie?" The willowy blonde came right over and gave Sarah a gentle hug.

"I'm going to be fine. The doc just left. Not much on bedside manner but good on medical advice, I hear. He's keeping me one more day 'cause he wants to watch my headache."

"Another day?" Jill frowned. "I'll let Detective Hassini know that. He'll want to talk to you."

"Who's Detective Hassini?"

Jill arranged the flowers she'd brought on the windowsill so Sarah could see them. "He's the one doing the investigation. He's a little rough but I know his heart's in the right place. I'm pretty sure he believes us but the hospital staff has already made statements that have him pretty concerned about you."

"Jill, what are you talking about? Concerned about me for what? It was an accident...I think. Beth told me a little about what happened. The guy didn't see the light and went straight on through the intersection and plowed into me. He walked away, I'm here in the hospital. What's to investigate? Don't they have his license and phone number and stuff?"

Jill shook her head, sitting down on the side of the bed. She picked up Sarah's good hand and held it a moment before explaining.

"You and Phillip must've had one hell of a session Sunday night."

Sarah blushed. "We did. He used the..." She paused, finding it difficult to share such an intimacy even with a fellow slave. If there was anyone who would understand, it would be Jill. Rolling her eyes at her own foolishness, she blurted it out. "He used the cane. It was the most incredible feeling I'd ever felt. Hurt, yet the orgasm afterward was..."

She had no words to describe it. Jill grinned and squeezed her hand. "I know. You feel helpless and the pain, sharp at the moment of impact, courses through every vein, even out to your fingertips. You can't breathe and when you do, you gulp in big breaths of air as your body goes haywire. And just as you get control again and the pain eases, the cane descends again and the tension between your legs becomes almost unbearable."

"That's it exactly!" Sarah grinned back. "That's exactly what it felt like. It was wonderful." She let out air she hadn't even realized she'd been holding. "I don't think I'd like it as a daily meal but as a treat now and again? Oh, yeah..."

Jill's face became serious. "Yeah, well...there you've hit the point. Sarah, when you were brought in, the doctors checked you over...all of you."

Sarah shrugged her good shoulder. "So?"

"All over, Sarah, even your tush."

Color seeped into Sarah's cheeks as Jill's words registered. "You mean...they found..."

"Three cane stripes across your ass. Yes."

Sarah looked away. "Oh, my glory. What must they think of me?" Her eyes went wide and she pulled at the hospital gown, looking down at her breasts. Barely visible pink lines still showed against the whiteness of her skin. In panic, she looked up at Jill.

"Yep. They found those too. And the fingerprint bruises on your upper arms."

"Fingerprint bruises?" For a moment, Sarah had no idea what her fellow slave was talking about. Then she remembered. Saturday night, when she was blindfolded and at the mercy of the hands that caressed her. One man had stepped between her spread legs, his hands tightly gripping her bound upper arms. It hadn't been Phillip. The Master who had pressed against her had had an aura of cruelty in him. The fabric of his pants had brushed against her mound, his hardened cock taunting her. Dominance and brutality had oozed from his touch.

But then he had stepped away and hands more soothing and caressing had taken his place. In the wake of so many touches, so many sensations, she had forgotten him.

Now Sarah turned to Jill. "There was a man Saturday night who held me hard. I didn't realize he'd given me bruises but that's the only place I could've gotten them.

"Will and I decided that as well." An explosive sigh came from her. "Look, I have no idea what Phillip has told the police. Will and I have managed to say very little so far because really it's you who has to call the shots on this one."

"On what one? Jill, I still don't even know what we're talking about."

"You came in with marks of a beating, Sarah. Marks you couldn't possibly have gotten in a car accident. Phillip was right there, pacing, pestering the desk nurse about you. What were they going to think?" She snorted, disgusted. "You weren't even out of surgery when they arrested him on suspicion of domestic battery."

Sarah sat straight up, ignoring the shooting pain that sliced through her shoulder. "Arrested? Phillip? Is that why he hasn't been here?"

Jill looked at her like she'd grown another head. "You didn't know?"

"How could I? I've been doped up and stuck to this bed."

"But Beth was here earlier, wasn't she? I thought that was who the nurse told me…"

"Yeah, Beth was here." It registered and Sarah's voice dropped. "You mean Beth knew Phillip's sitting in jail somewhere and she didn't tell me?"

"Beth knows Phillip was arrested on suspicion of battery, yes?" Jill shook her head. "Maybe she just didn't think you were ready to hear the news, though."

"I'll be asking her that question. In the meantime, get that detective down here. I have a few choice words for him."

Jill stood and grabbed her coat from the chair. "You got it, babe. But be warned—the police don't look kindly on our activities. Not all of those who were there Saturday night want to be ratted out to the police."

Sarah's mind flashed to the man who'd gripped her arms and leaned his body so possessively against hers. That was a man who definitely wouldn't want to be ratted out, even if it meant Phillip sat there for years. "I can tell him we played with others but remember…" Her mouth turned up in a wry grin but there was no mirth in her eyes. "I was hooded the entire night. I have no idea who was there and who wasn't." Although, from the look on Jill's face, it was pretty obvious she and Will had been two of those in attendance. Sarah could make some educated guesses about the others but decided to keep that information to her herself.

The interview with the police did not go well. Sarah's headache had blossomed and the food she'd eaten earlier roiled in her stomach. She tried to tell the nurses it was just because her fiancé had been arrested for no reason but they wouldn't listen to her. As a result, she found it difficult to concentrate on the detective's questions and knew her answers rambled. She remained adamant, however. There were no charges to press and they had no reason at all to keep Phillip in jail.

"I'm afraid that isn't your call, Mrs. Simpson–Parker," the detective informed her. "In these cases, the state can step in and make an arrest. He's already been charged."

Sarah stared at the middle-aged man who stood beside her bed, his staid complacency frustrating the hell out of her. A few strands of gray colored his temples but other than that, he still looked like he was a force to be reckoned with. Built like a quarterback, his sturdy frame had undoubtedly been in more than one altercation. He'd introduced himself as Detective Hassini. Sarah wondered if he were Greek or Middle Eastern. But then he'd started talking, the news just getting worse and worse as he informed her about "the man she was involved with" and Sarah decided she didn't care what his heritage was, the man was nothing more than a block for her to beat her head against.

"Because he had a recent previous incident with the police, I suspect the judge will set quite a high bail for Mr. Townsend at his hearing this afternoon."

"Bail? He's got to post bail? Why did you arrest him? I didn't ask you to. I didn't need you to. I'm fine. He's not beating me." Sarah punched the mattress beside her with her good fist. The other still lay bound to her side, just one more frustration.

The detective sighed. "In cases where domestic abuse is suspected, the officer at the scene can make the arrest for the state. Often the person abused is too frightened to post the charges herself, so the state gave that right to the police a long time ago. As I already told you, Mrs. Simpson-Parker, the charges are already brought against him. Now he goes to a hearing, bail is determined and if he can pay the bail, he'll be out on the streets again until his trial. If he can't make bail, he'll stay in jail until the trial."

Sarah shook her head absently, wishing Will were here. She had so many questions she just couldn't ask about the law. What they did was consensual. Was she going to have to testify to that in a court of law? "Please stop calling me 'Mrs. Simpson-Parker'. Mrs. Parker all by itself will do fine."

"What I need from you is a statement about those bruises."

"No. I'm not going to say anything. You can't make me, either. Isn't there some double indemnity thing between spouses?" She was feeling decidedly grumpy and didn't feel like being pleasant. She forced herself to remain civil, however. Phillip's life hung in the balance.

The detective chuckled. "I'm not sure that holds here, Mrs. Parker. But I also wanted to inform you that you have the right to an order of protection if you want it. The judges in this county usually give an automatic order of three weeks unless the victim asks for a longer period."

"Three weeks?" Her voice rose to a shrill shriek. "I don't want any order of protection, do you hear me? Not three weeks, not three days! What I want, Detective, is to see the man I love." Her voice cracked and tears filled her eyes. "I don't want him in jail, I want him here, in my arms. We're going to be married..." A vision of her wedding day flashed through her mind. Only the ceremony wasn't being held in city hall but in the city jail. She didn't finish the thought.

Detective Hassini pulled a tissue from the box beside the bed and handed it to the woman. He'd seen hundreds of cases like this over the years but he had to admit, this one did seem different. Her bruises didn't look like any other beating he'd ever seen. Three thin stripes across her breasts, another three across her ass. No accident put them there, however, and he was inclined to err on the side of the woman's safety, whether she wanted it or not.

He checked his watch. "The hearing's going on right now, if everything's on time over there. Which means the judge will use his or her own judgment about the length of the order. I'm just offering you the chance to lengthen it, which," he added quickly, "I understand you do not wish to do at this time."

Pulling a card from the notebook he had been consulting, he held it out to the woman. He had to admit, she was stronger than she looked. Those tears had formed but only one had fallen before she had herself under control again. "If you have any questions or decide you do want that order of protection extended, just give me a call, all right?"

Sarah took the man's card, realizing it wasn't right to hate the messenger. He hadn't been the one to arrest Phillip. "Thank you for your concern, Detective, but let me make it plain. I do not want an order of protection at all, let alone extended."

Her head hurt. She closed her eyes and rested her throbbing head against the pillows, turning the card into her palm, almost as if she wanted it to disappear. With a few more banalities, the officer finally left the room and Sarah allowed her tears, held back far too long, to course down her cheeks.

Chapter Ten
Expiation

ॐ

"Just stay away from her. Right now, that's your best course of action."

Phillip looked at his lawyer as if he'd grown a third head. "The wedding is only two weeks away. How am I supposed to stay away from Sarah and marry her at the same time?" He balled his hands into fists as the two of them hurried down the courthouse steps, alternately wanting to punch something or hurl useless obscenities into the air.

The expensive lawyer put his hand out, stopping Phillip. "Look, the courts don't care about that. They don't care about anything except the fact that Sarah Simpson-Parker was beaten and they think, by you. Don't jeopardize your bail or your trial by making stupid mistakes. Stay away from her."

Taking a deep breath and forcing his hands to relax, Phillip finally nodded. "All right. I'll send her a letter instead."

"No!" Exasperation sounded in the lawyer's voice. "Don't you get it? No contact. Period. None. No visits, no letters, no emails. Nothing. Nada. Zilch. You have to act as if she doesn't exist. For three weeks." He turned and threw up his hand. "Then you two can do whatever the hell you want." The lawyer stopped two steps down. "But until then...nothing."

Out of the corner of his eye, Phillip saw Will waving to him from across the street. "All right, Ray. You're the boss. No contact of any sort for three weeks."

The lawyer's eyes narrowed. "Wait a minute. Why are you suddenly so compliant?"

Phillip clapped him on the back as they reached the sidewalk. "Let's just say you're persuasive. That's what I pay you the big bucks for, isn't it? To persuade people to our causes?"

A taxi waited at the curb and Phillip opened the door, ushering the counselor inside before he could protest. Shutting the door, he waved as the cab pulled away from the curb. Will came up beside him and watched the taxi disappear into traffic.

"So what's the verdict?"

"It wasn't a trial, just a hearing to set bail."

"I tried to get here faster but as you can see..." Will gestured to the street before them, packed with rush-hour vehicles. "And the accident over at the corner of Seventh and Elmcrest just made things worse." He looked his friend over and decided the man needed a drink. "Come on, we're going over to Maxi's and you're filling me in."

* * * * *

Phillip sat back and sighed. He hadn't been to Maxi's Gentlemen's in months...ever since he and Sarah had started dating. The dark oak paneling, the color deepened on the ceiling from years of cigarette and cigar smoke, surrounded him, enclosing him in a manly embrace. Looking more like a library reading room than a bar, the plush leather armchairs and thick-piled Orientals on the floor gave comfort to the soul. Life might have wild swings but Maxi's would always be a place for the relaxation of men of elegance and class. Phillip's eye caught an ornate oak door off to the side of the fireplace and his lips curled in a nasty smile. If the courts ever found out what happened on the other side of that door or found out that he had, on occasion, participated in the events that took place on the other side of that door, they would put him away for sure.

"Here. Whiskey, straight up." Will took a chair beside Phillip's, setting two glasses on the low table between them.

Phillip picked up the shot glass and downed it in one gulp. He looked around. Even as the liquid fire burned his throat, he wanted another. "You only brought me one?"

"One is all you need right now. I see that look in your eyes."

"What look?" Phillip frowned.

"The look that says, 'I'm pissed off and just want to get drunk'."

"I am pissed off. And I do want to get drunk."

"But you're not going because I'm your friend and I'm going to keep you out of jail so you can get your girl back."

"Sarah's never going to want me back. Not after what she's going to go through."

"What are you talking about?"

Phillip motioned to one of the unobtrusive waiters. "Another whiskey." He saw the look on Will's face and added, "A double this time."

"They brought up my traffic ticket. Damn cop who gave it to me showed up at the hearing and told them all about her being hooded and how she seemed scared." He slammed his palms on the arms of the chair. "Of course she was scared! I was locked up in the back of the damn police car and wouldn't have been able to protect her if he'd tried anything with her. Stupid!"

"Is that word for you or the cop?"

Phillip shook his head. "Both." He looked around. "Where's that drink?"

"Just because you needed one drink doesn't mean you need more."

Phillip waved his hand dismissively. He closed his eyes and let his head fall back against the cushioned chair. "If Sarah never speaks to me again, I don't blame her."

"That's the whiskey talking. Sarah loves you and is very concerned."

"Sarah hasn't been awake enough to be concerned." He sat up, his voice rising unconsciously. "I should be there, Will. Not here, not sitting in some damn jail cell. I want to be with her."

"And you will be. In three weeks."

"Shit." Phillip got up and marched over to the bar. "Another." He slammed the shot glass down, not missing the glance the bartender shot at Will before pouring the single shot. Still standing at the bar, Phillip tilted the glass, again downing the entire contents in one swallow. He savored the burn this time, letting the fire punish him for his sins.

His gaze landed on that arched oak door again and he came to a decision. Determined, Phillip pushed away from the bar and started across the room. The expiation of his sins lay on the other side of that door. Will's hand on his arm was but a small deterrent. He brushed of his friend's protests as if they were gnats that buzzed around his head and opened the door.

An empty anteroom, lit only by a table lamp, glimmered in tones of burgundy and cream. On the far wall, a small sliding panel at face height reminded Phillip of a confessional. Exactly what he looked for right now. To the right of it, another arched doorway with no handle. The only way through was by permission. Permission he would willingly beg for right about now.

The two shots of whiskey buzzed in his head as he knocked on the sliding panel. It slid open, revealing blackness. A grillwork, designed to make it difficult to see through, added to the feeling that one was in a church, a holy place where all problems could be solved if one prayed hard enough.

"What is it you seek?"

The voice, soft and promising comfort, was neither male nor female. Or maybe it was both. Phillip dropped his head. "I seek forgiveness."

"Have you committed a crime?"

"No."

"Then what is the sin you have done?"

"By hooding my slave, I put her in jeopardy. By marking her, the law has forced us apart."

"Neither is a sin, my son."

"I need forgiveness." His voice, hard as steel, threatened to break.

He lifted his chin defiantly at the long pause from the other side. Finally, it spoke again.

"You feel guilt because you gave your slave six small marks. Society at large sees that as beating, we see it...differently. Why do you seek expiation from us?"

"Because only you know how to give it properly." Phillip didn't ask how the speaker knew the cause of his guilt. It didn't matter. All that mattered was the fact that here he could get what he needed.

"And you are prepared to take whatever punishment we deem appropriate?"

"I am." The steel was back in his voice.

"Enter."

The panel slid shut at the same moment the door snicked open. Another hooded figure stood on the other side, holding the door for him. His eyes glittering, Phillip stepped through.

A second small room met him. He'd been here only once before but then he'd come as the Master and had walked straight through this tiny area. This was for slaves, and today it was fitting that he be here. The robed figure shut the door. The only way now, was forward.

"Stand still."

Phillip did as he was told, the glory he felt in dominion a tarnished memory. He deserved to be ordered about, deserved to be treated as a common object.

Light blazed on from above and he put his hand up to shield his eyes.

"Hands down!"

With an effort, and still blinking in the sudden brightness, Phillip put his hands at his sides. The voice of this figure, while unfamiliar, definitely belonged to a man used to being obeyed. A bit of the rebel blossomed inside Phillip. Taking orders from a woman would be easier today than from another man. He clenched his fists but kept them at his sides.

The figure circled behind him and Phillip fought the urge to turn and watch him. He chose, instead, a spot on the far door—the door that led to his punishment—and he stared at it as if his glance could drill a hole through the oak to reveal what awaited him.

Even when the man's rough hands reached out and tore off his shirt, sending buttons flying in every direction. He kept his gaze fixed as the man's hands invaded his privacy, caressing his ass and circling around to cup his cock through Phillip's pants.

He remained still when the hands unbuckled his belt, drawing it slowly through the loops the same way Phillip did when he was teasing Sarah. Only today, there was no tease. The belt came free and in one fluid motion, fell across his shoulders with a loud snap and heavy sting.

Phillip hadn't been braced for the blow, though afterward he wasn't sure why he hadn't expected it. The surprise forced him a half step forward before he caught himself and returned to his original position.

"That will cost you, big man. You move only when you've been given permission. And were you given permission?"

"No, Sir." Phillip gritted his teeth to keep his temper. He wanted forgiveness, didn't he? So why did he feel like punching this guy's lights out?

As if sensing he'd pushed Phillip to a limit, the man said nothing more as he unzipped Phillip's pants and pushed them down to his ankles. Instructing him to lift first one, then the other foot, the pants were gone and Phillip didn't care if he ever got them back. His briefs were taken off in a similar manner.

"You have nothing. You are nothing. Not a man, not even a dog."

A swift blow to the back of his knees sent Phillip crashing to the floor on all fours. "Crawl, slave. Crawl through the door like the penitent you claim to be."

They were testing him, he understood that now. Testing his resolve. He wanted punishment—did he have the courage to accept what he'd asked for?

Setting one determined hand before the next, Phillip crawled to the still-closed door. It opened only when he was close enough to reach forward and touch it, although he kept his hands firmly planted on the ground beneath him.

He couldn't see much of the room on the other side in the position he held. A wooden floor...also oak, he thought...lay in his line of sight. And a pair of shapely female legs, her feet encased in dark, heeled boots that stretched to her knees. What was higher, he didn't dare look up to see.

"What do we have here?"

Phillip knew that sultry voice. Mistress Clare and he had punished slaves together in the past. That she should be the one to greet him today had a poetic justice that fit.

The figure behind Phillip spoke up. "A slave who needs use, Mistress."

"He needs more than just use, from what I understand." The toe of her boot touched him under the chin, forcing his face up. "You have put your slave in danger, then gotten yourself arrested for beating her up, is that correct?"

"Yes, Mistress." The words came strangled out of his mouth, his head tilted back at an extreme angle.

"And now you wish for the beating you never gave her."

"Yes, Mistress."

"Why?"

The word momentarily confused him. Wasn't it obvious?

"Did you want to beat her black and blue?" Mistress Clare pressed the issue. "That's what you're afraid of, isn't it, Phillip? That you will one day lose control again and actually perform that which you're only accused of now?"

"Yes." The word tore at his soul.

"You know the accusation is false. This time. But it wouldn't have been false in the past, would it, Phillip?"

He remembered Tamara, his first slave. They'd both been new to the lifestyle then and he'd pushed her too far, too fast. She'd left him after a scene had gotten out of hand and he'd lost control of the beast inside him. Mistress Clare knew that. How had she known he'd never forgiven himself for that, even if he'd managed to put it out of his memory for longer and longer periods of time?

"No, it wouldn't have been false. Before."

She dropped his chin and turned away. "Tie him to the post."

Two men lifted him and half dragged him to a post in the center of the room. Now that he was upright, Phillip could see little had changed since the last time he was here. Of course, his perspective had been different then. A tall wooden post in the middle of the room had a large ring suspended from the top. Cuffs were locked onto his wrists. Threading a chain through the two rings, one man stood on a small stepladder while the other handed the chain up. The length of cold steel was pulled through the hoop and then brought down again, forcing Phillip onto his toes. They fastened the chain on the other side, Phillip's memory filling in how. He knew the hooks on the far side of the pole and how they locked down tight, making it impossible for the person suspended to get free.

Mistress Clare approached him now, running her hand along the tightened muscles of his back, reaching down to cup his ass in a familiar gesture. "You've kept in shape, I see."

Phillip didn't answer, her touch inflaming him in a way he did not expect. Her low chuckle made him realize he would never be able to keep anything from her. He never could.

"You love this one in a way that frightens you, even as you embrace your demon." Her hand shifted as she slid a finger along the division that separated his ass cheeks. He shifted on his toes, unsure whether he wanted her to explore more...or leave him alone.

She made the decision for him, bringing her hand up to entwine her fingers in his hair. With a sudden gesture, she pulled his head back, forcing him to look up at the ceiling—a surface decorated with dozens of hooks, chains and cages that dangled down. All of them empty, he realized. Mistress Clare ruled this dungeon with an iron fist, a fist that now pulled his hair painfully as he stretched backward as far as the chains would let him.

"You seek to expiate your sins, both real and perceived, at the end of my whip."

Even had he wanted to nod, he couldn't, not with her hand in control of his head. But she was right. He wanted to feel the pain of the lash, to let the pain ease away his guilt.

She let go as suddenly as she had grabbed him. The relief, he knew, would be short-lived. Clare understood what he was after and he knew she wouldn't shy away from the delivery.

He heard the whoosh of air behind him. From the sound, she'd chosen a thin leather that would leave a sting and a mark every time it landed. Phillip took a deep breath and bowed his head, forcing his muscles not to tense. He wanted this and he wanted the sting.

When it came, however, it was worse than he remembered. Mistress Clare had taught him everything he knew about whips and floggers, oftentimes using his skin so he'd remember the differences. The slicing heat felt like it tore through his skin and even though he knew it only raised a welt, he still felt as if he should feel the blood coursing along his back.

Another crack across his back, again across his shoulders and his hands balled into fists as he fought to control the pain. She didn't give him time, however, slicing a third, a fourth and a fifth blow in quick succession.

"Each caress of the whip excises a little bit of the sin, Phillip. How much do you want removed?"

Through gritted teeth, Phillip answered. "All of it, Clare. Take it all away."

From her pause, he knew she was only changing whips. She wasn't one to get squeamish.

The pain this time tore through several layers of skin. He thought he shouted but wasn't sure. His back felt ripped open from shoulder to shoulder. With a word, he could stop her but wasn't this what he'd come for? Phillip thought of Sarah, alone in the hospital—apart, separated from him where he was not allowed to go.

Another crack as the multi-tailed whip landed on his back. Each thong dug deep into his soul, pulling out the guilt and filling the gap with pain. Pain he welcomed, pain he deserved. He lost count how many times Clare snapped the whip. The world became red behind his eyes and he sank deep into the darkness.

Will stood off to the side, admiring the way the woman handled first the single-tail, then the five-thonged bullwhip. Under her blows, Phillip's back turned bright red, with several welts crisscrossing across his shoulders. From experience, Will knew the welts would sting for days, eventually fading to nothing. But for the next twenty-four hours, Phillip would be one sore puppy.

Clare let her arm fall to her side, throwing Will a glance that told him Phillip had had enough. She hung the whip on the wall, then with a nod to Will, came to stand beside Phillip. Will accompanied her, ready to be her accomplice.

Phillip hung in his bindings, his strength depleted by the beating. His breathing was even and his head hung down between his arms. Nodding to Clare, Will grabbed his friend by the waist as she released the chains from the other side. Phillip sagged into his arms and Will lowered him gently to the floor.

At a motion from Clare, the two men who'd accompanied her earlier now came and picked Phillip up as if he weighed nothing at all. A curtained alcove off to one side hid a comfortable double bed and they deposited him there. Will watched Phillip curl into a fetal position and knew his healing was only partially complete.

Clare joined him at the entrance to the alcove and put her hand on his arm. "I'll take care of him. Come back after dinner. If he's awake, you can take him home then."

Will nodded. "Thank you, Clare. For everything."

She looked at the shaking figure on the bed. "He's carried so much for so long. Things he buried and never dealt with are now coming to the surface. You were right to bring him to me."

With a bow, Will took one last look at Phillip, then turned on his heel and left.

Clare held out her arms and her attendants undressed her, removing her loose bustier, unlacing her boots and helping her out of them. When she was naked, she stepped into the room, motioning the men to cover them as she spooned Phillip's body into hers. After lighting the two oil lamps that spilled their light from either side of the bed, the two left, drawing the curtains closed behind them.

* * * * *

Phillip's first thought was one of confusion. This wasn't his bed and those weren't Sarah's arms wrapped around him. He shifted and memory flooded back along with the pain in his shoulders. Stifling a groan, he lay on the whip marks, letting the pain waken him the rest of the way.

Clare shifted as well, rolling onto her back and arching an eyebrow at him. "Feeling better?"

Stretching his arms toward the ceiling, Phillip tested the limits of his endurance. "Actually, much."

And it was true. Clare's whip had done exactly what he'd hoped. The anger and frustration were manageable once more, the demon back under control. He sighed and twisted his shoulders, a grimace of pain crossing his face.

Clare rolled over and leaned her head on one hand. "That's gonna hurt worse than a really bad sunburn for a few days, you know."

"I know. Clare…" Phillip looked up at her, uncertainty in his voice. "I don't remember being put to bed last night. Did we…?"

She smiled, a genuine smile that Phillip knew she didn't show very often. Not much moved Mistress Clare. "No, Phillip, we didn't. You needed care afterward, just cuddling and acceptance."

He closed his eyes as the memory of his breakdown flooded back. He'd sobbed in her arms last night. Not just a few tears of frustration but cries from the heart. He'd reached back and poured out years and years in his sobs, totally unable to control himself.

And now he felt…cleansed.

Reaching over, he took Clare's hand in his. "Thank you."

She squeezed his hand. "Next time, don't wait so many years before you have a breakdown. Not really good for the body, you know. Or the heart."

Clare tapped his chest with her finger, then stood. "It's three in the morning, you know."

Phillip admired her lithe body, a body she kept active by swimming, tennis, skiing—you name the sport, Clare did it. They'd met years ago and had had some good times together but the timing had never seemed right for romance. As a result, their friendship had deepened into something stronger. He remembered a night when he had held her much the same as she had just done for him. He flexed and winced.

"How does this look?" He turned so she could see, though the oil lamps, still burning, didn't give much light. There were no windows and the heavy curtains that separated them from the other room didn't let any light in. The alcove had definitely been designed for maximum privacy.

Clare picked up one of the lamps and brought it closer, running her cool hand over his welts. "You'll live," she pronounced. "General pinkness and about a dozen stripes that are pretty swollen. I hit you hard last night."

"I wanted you to."

"I know." She pulled two charcoal gray robes from a peg and threw one toward him, slipping the other one over her arms and belting it. "So what are you going to do?"

Phillip put the robe on, easing it over his sore muscles and sat on the edge of the bed. "I don't know, Clare. I want to see her so much, to hold her in my arms and tell her how much I love her, but I can't. If I do, I'll go back to jail."

"Will can carry a message for you."

"I know. He already has been to see her. So has Jill. And Aleshia said she'd stop in today."

Clare sat on the edge of the bed and took his hand again. "You need to find the silver lining here."

Phillip chuckled, although there was little mirth. "Yeah, right."

"I'm not kidding, Phillip. I don't care if you call it God's Will or Fate, Karma or some other damn thing, the reality is, things happen for reasons. You escaped it once when the cop let you go Sunday night. But you can't run from destiny, Phillip. It'll find you no matter what."

Phillip shook his head, a wry grin on his face. "Clare, you are good for my soul, you know that? We haven't seen each other in years and yet you don't get mad when I drop in and want my ass kicked. You let me sob it all out and then you top the entire surreal experience with a healthy dose of philosophy." He brushed her cheek with a kiss. "Silver lining, hmm?"

"Silver lining, boy-o. There is one. You just need to find it." She dropped his hand and stood. "In the meantime...out. It's now three-thirty in the morning and I'm going home."

"I'll drive you."

"Can't. You came with Will. If I'm not mistaken, we're going to find him sound asleep in one of the other alcoves, all alone and snoring. Wanna bet?"

Phillip laughed outright for the first time since Sarah's accident. "No way. I'm thinkin' you're too right."

They found Will by the sound as soon as Clare opened the drapes. The room was lined with little alcoves, at the moment all empty save one. Will hadn't drawn the curtains and the sounds of his slumber filled the room.

"Will, wake up. You need to take Clare and me home."

"Right. I'm not asleep, I was just resting my eyes." Will blinked like an owl several times as he struggled upright.

"Yeah, we could tell."

Clare touched Phillip's arm. "While he wakes up, I'm going to go change. You're going to have to go home in the robe. Your pants are being laundered, I'm sure. Your shirt, however..."

172

"Thanks, Clare. I'll get him going and meet you out front."

* * * * *

Phillip waved to Will's disappearing taillights and turned toward the empty cottage. He hadn't been here since Monday and today was what? Wednesday? He'd totally lost track of days. Each one had seemed an eternity.

But he was home. And Sarah was safe, even if he couldn't see her. It would have to be enough.

Chapter Eleven
Together

ဆာ

"Thank God your three-week separation is almost up. I swear I can't take one more day!"

Will sat in his kitchen watching Phillip pace the floor from the back door, past the table, over to the dining room door and back again.

"You've paced that same spot so many times before dinner these past..." Will did a quick figuring in his head, "twenty days. I'm gonna have to replace the tile!"

Jill came in the front door and Phillip held himself back, even though he wanted to dash to her and get the latest on how Sarah was doing. For the past week and a half, Jill had been driving Sarah to and from work since she couldn't drive with her arm still immobilized with a sling. Impatiently, he waited for Jill to enter the kitchen, then take forever to set down her stuff and kiss Will hello. She turned toward Phillip and gave him a casual greeting but then saw his distress and took pity.

"First of all, Sarah's fine. Her stumble last night did no damage."

The force of air out of Phillip's lungs pushed a lock of Jill's hair into her eyes. With a grimace, she tucked it back behind her ear and shook her head.

"She really shouldn't be staying in that apartment all alone. I've said that over and over." Phillip loved Sarah's independence, though he thought this time she took it too far. "I wish she had come here to stay with you two."

Will got up and checked the soup on the stove. "She's doing fine on her own, Phillip. Besides which, *you* come here every day."

"Well, I wouldn't if she were here."

"Phillip, be a dear and open this jar for me?"

Phillip took the jar from Jill and absently tapped it on the corner of the counter before popping the top. He didn't even look at it as he handed it back to her.

"She could've tripped going to the bathroom in the middle of the night here too, you know. Or at the cottage." Will tasted the soup. "Perfect." He gestured to Phillip. "This is a make-your-own sandwich and grab-a-bowl-of-soup dinner. Last of the garden vegetables!"

Phillip grabbed three bowls from the cupboard, as at home here as he was in his own home. "Yes, but at both those places, there would have been someone to help her. She wouldn't have been alone."

"I don't know who's more grateful today's the last day of the court order, you or her," Jill told him while piloting him over to the counter with the bowls to get him out of her way.

"She misses me?"

Jill rolled her eyes at Phillip's insecurities. She hadn't seen him when Tamara left but from what Will had told her, it had been a messy breakup. Jill had met Phillip only a few years ago and in all that time he'd been a polite, pleasant and mostly cheerful person. Occasionally, however, she had caught glimpses of the loneliness he hid. She didn't see it much when he was visiting them. No, she saw it almost always when there were couples involved. He'd get a sad look in his eyes when he thought no one was watching or those magnificent shoulders of his would droop a little as he turned away.

Since he'd met Sarah, however, she hadn't seen any of that occasional black cloud. And the night at his cottage when the whole gang had gotten together? Jill hid her smile as she remembered the show they'd put on for Sarah and how Phillip had beamed all night.

Now, however, he fretted and it was just about driving her crazy. He wandered from their place to Lady Aleshia and Anton's like a lost puppy. It was almost as if he didn't want to face being alone without her. Jill understood. Keeping busy kept the demons at bay.

"Yes, you big lout. She misses you. I told her you'd pick her up after work tomorrow, since she's not driving yet."

Phillip held the bowls as Will ladled the vegetable soup. "You expect me to wait until five o'clock?"

Jill shook her head. Men. Did they have to be so dense? "Of course not. I expect that you'll be over to her apartment at 12:01 tonight. Well, tomorrow morning..."

She didn't expect the sudden kiss she got from Phillip. He bussed her right on the mouth. "Jill, you're a genius!"

Will laughed and Jill gave him a "come-hither" smile. "It isn't rocket science. Sarah told me to make sure you're there right at 12:01. She doesn't want to be kept waiting one more minute than she has to."

"I'd say that means she missed you," chimed in Will, enjoying Phillip's sudden animation. "And I'm thinking you might want to take a nap after dinner, since I'm pretty sure you're not going to get much sleep tonight..."

* * * * *

Once back at the cottage, Phillip tried to nap but found his mind racing. Would Sarah look any different? How many changes can a person go through in three weeks' time? The last time he'd seen her, she was bruised and bloody. That image haunted him and he had nothing to replace it with. He tried to remember how she felt when he held her or the sight of her naked and in cuffs but each time the image was quickly supplanted by his last view of her in the emergency room.

By eleven o'clock, he couldn't stand it anymore. Although tempted to throw on a pair of jeans and a sweatshirt, he decided he wanted Sarah's first impression of him after three weeks to be one of self-control. He might be coming unglued in the privacy of his own home but he didn't need to show that to the rest of the world. If he had realized how much Will and Jill had seen, he would have been mortified.

Blissfully unaware of his friends' perceptive natures, Phillip mastered himself, forcing himself not to speed down the country roads on his way to the city expressway that would take him within blocks of Sarah's apartment. This was not the time to be getting another ticket.

She lived in an old two-story brick building with not much in the way of parking. Sarah's space was open and Phillip knew her car would never occupy it again. He slid his winter rat into her spot and checked his watch. Five minutes and not a cop in sight. Chuckling, he got out of the car, knowing the courts and law enforcement weren't really watching him and wouldn't care about him being early.

He bounded up the stairs, taking them two at a time and knocked only once on her door before it flew open and she stood there.

For several seconds, he stood drinking in the sight of her like a thirsting man gulps water. Her hair, always at shoulder length, seemed a bit shorter. Her face, still pixie-like and beautiful, glowed with hope. Her left arm, protected in a white sling, hung across her naked body. Phillip chuckled.

"Good thing it's me at the door. Or were you expecting someone else?" He gestured to her lack of clothing.

She laughed and Phillip knew he'd never heard anything sweeter. "Get in here before I lose my nerve entirely!"

He stepped over her threshold, shutting the door and twisting the lock. Prolonging the torment, he lifted the chain and put it in place before turning back to her. She looked so vulnerable, so alone. Phillip stepped forward and scooped her into his arms, picking her up and holding her tightly to him, being careful of her arm and shoulder. How long they stood there, he didn't care. His arms felt filled again.

Phillip had only been in Sarah's apartment a few times to help her move out some boxes but he remembered the way to the bedroom. She weighed nothing as he carried her along the short corridor.

Because Sarah had been packing for the move to his place, the room held only a double bed and an almost-bare dresser. Scattered boxes, some of them open with clothes hanging out the sides, were a testament to her efficiency. Before the accident, she'd packed everything with an eye toward moving within two weeks. Three weeks later, the boxes had been reopened and the clothes worn. He kicked one out of the way and set Sarah gently on the bed.

"I missed you," she murmured against his chest, not willing to let go. Her arms ached from the need to hold him. He slid next to her, keeping her close and she put her face up, wanting his kiss.

Phillip saw the unshed tears in her eyes and brushed her hair back from her face. "I missed you too." Her lips beckoned and he bent down to claim what was his.

He took his time, savoring every nuance. It had been so long. A mixture of spices filled his nose and he drew in a gentle yet deep breath, memories of her stretched body beneath his awakened by her perfume. Her lips, soft and pliant, opened and he took her invitation to taste deeper, his tongue swirling around hers in a dance of desire.

Sarah felt herself relaxing for the first time since leaving his cottage that fateful Monday morning. Phillip was here. He would take care of everything. She broke the kiss, the words tumbling out of her like water falling off a cliffside. "I missed you so much," she said again, only this time it sounded like a cry of loneliness. "You can't know how it is to have someone in your life all day and all night and then suddenly have him not there. You do all these things together, make decisions together and then you have to do it all yourself. And you know you can. You have to, you don't have any other choices. Well, you do but curling up into a ball and wailing is only allowed for a little while."

She couldn't stop the words and didn't even realize the tears had escaped and now cascaded down her cheeks. "So you go on. You get yourself up every morning and you force yourself to go to work. And you find every excuse not to come home at night because you can't stop thinking at night. There's no one but you and four walls and insanity."

She took a breath to sniffle and Phillip caught her chin in his hands, tilting her head up toward his. "Insanity. Exactly."

He understood. She should have known he would. With a sob, she threw herself into his arms and let the pent-up tears fall. Soaking his shirt, she didn't stop until every last ounce of tension had released.

"You've been holding that in all this time, haven't you?" He handed her a tissue from the box on the floor.

Sarah nodded. "Three weeks. I don't see how you can sit there, so calm and self-assured while I fall to pieces. It isn't fair." She looked at him with a hint of petulance. "And it isn't because I'm a woman and you're some macho kind of man."

Although tempted to tease her, Phillip didn't. He couldn't. Not after his own breakdown at Maxi's. Everyone needed a knight-protector sometimes. His had given him welts of forgiveness.

But that wasn't what Sarah needed. He pulled her close, the softness of her body as it melted into his reminding him how long it had been since he'd felt her skin next to his.

Laying her back on the pillows, Phillip looked down at his injured slave. He wanted her and he would take her tonight. Beneath him, she looked so fragile with her broken arm no longer in a cast, but still bound with an elastic bandage and encased in a sling. Above her, he unbuttoned his shirt, his eyes never leaving hers as he prepared to make this a night she would never forget.

She loved watching his shoulder muscles ripple as he took off his shirt. God, how she'd missed him. Having cried out her frustrations, his presence filled the empty spot in her life that had been there for the past few weeks. It wasn't that she needed someone to take care of her but now that he was here, for the first time in far too long, she felt whole once more.

Her eyes drifted down as he unzipped his pants, smiling as she realized he hadn't even taken the time to put on underwear. His cock, semi-hard already, poked out from the dark hair surrounding it. Soon it would grow and she would reap the benefits. Grinning in anticipation, she squirmed up onto the pillows, pushing down the covers with her one good hand.

No grin answered hers. "Here, let me get those." Phillip took the sheet and blankets from her and pulled them all the way to the bottom. "I want nothing in the way between you and me."

His dark eyes smoldered and Sarah shivered. For ten days after her accident, she had been a good girl, stifling all erotic thoughts as her body healed. After that, without Phillip to guide or fulfill her, she had depended on her own fingers, the one unpacked vibe and memories to reach her sexual climaxes. Those paled now in comparison to the hunger she saw reflected in his eyes. Had he, too, come since they'd seen each other last? Somehow the thought of him alone in the cottage, masturbating in the dungeon, set her blood pounding in her ears.

She shifted again and winced as she moved her arm wrong. Phillip's eyes narrowed. "Looks like I need to find a way to keep you still, slave."

The word ran like electricity through her veins. Her eyes flashed and a slow, sexy smile spread across her face as the slut inside awakened. She watched him rifle through a box against the wall, coming back with a silk scarf and several pairs of pantyhose.

"Sit up, slave."

He helped her to rise and she sat cross-legged on the bed.

"Cradle your cast with your good arm."

Sarah did so and tried to remain patient while Phillip fashioned a second sling out of the scarf. Using the pantyhose, he tied her arm to her body, effectively preventing her from moving either one. Looking satisfied, he laid her down with her head on the pillows and stood back to survey his work. The heat grew inside her and she spread her legs suggestively.

He didn't laugh. Her actions didn't even bring a smile. His cock stood fully at attention and Sarah longed to feel him enter her. Not even a full month had passed, yet she felt as needy as she had that first night she had allowed him to take her to his place. He simply stood, his hand seemingly absently running over the length of his cock as he stared down at her.

"Master, please...touch me." Her pussy creamed as she gave him his title and settled deeper into her own submissive sexuality.

"I like the way you beg, slave."

If she'd had hands available, she doubted she could have remained still. Her eyes focused on the object of her need — his cock. Thick veins wove over its length, bringing life and strength. The swollen tip, dark purple with blood, would be soft and velvety if she ran her tongue over it. Although she couldn't see it, she knew his pre-cum had already collected in the cloven spot and her mouth watered with the desire to taste it. She gave up more of her self-control and begged again even though she couldn't decide where she wanted it more, her mouth or her pussy. "Oh, please, Sir. Please let me feel your cock. Please?"

To be so near her and yet have to be so careful of her tormented him. Phillip wanted to give the monster inside him full rein and ravage her body, yet knew he needed to be careful. Her words, her submission, her bound body all combined... He mounted the bed, kneeling between her spread legs.

"Those pillows need to be somewhere else, slave." He reached up and took them from behind her raised head, his cock brushing her thigh in the process. Schooling himself, he refused to let her see the shock that shot through him. After three long weeks without her and with the animal rattling his cage inside him, Phillip knew he needed to master both if he didn't want to hurt her arm while seeking his own satisfaction.

Slipping the pillows under her ass, he raised her pussy and saw the cream gathered there. For the first time since he had walked into the bedroom, he smiled. "You are a very horny slave, aren't you?"

She nodded vigorously. "Yes, Sir, I am. I'm so damn horny, I could fuck a wine bottle! Now take me, damn it! Please?"

He laughed and the world settled back to rights. He wet his cock with the moisture from her pussy. "Nice begging, slave." His voice was dry but her words inflamed him. Supporting himself on his hands, he didn't hesitate further but pushed himself against her, forcing her pussy lips apart. Under him, she closed her eyes, her body relaxing.

"Yes, Sir...that's just right."

She didn't speak again but sighed and moaned as her body moved under his, pulling him in deeper with each push he made. Phillip watched her, unable to take his eyes off her. He had almost lost her in that accident and then, through the mistake of an eager officer, had been unable to comfort her all that time. The least he could do was to give her bliss to make up for it all.

He kept his rocking deliberately slow, even though it pained him to do it. The tightness wanted to explode but he held back. This was his gift to her. He gasped for air with the exertion and when her pussy muscles contracted around his cock and her moans became cries of fulfillment, he, too, groaned and let the tension go, to flood out of his cock and into her body in wave upon wave of pent-up deprivation.

And when he was spent, he pulled out and gathered tissues to clean her before cleaning himself, the tissues sticking to his cock. He grinned. There was plenty of time for a shower in the morning. For now, he pulled the pillows from under her ass and threw them to the floor. Reaching down, he pulled the sheet and blankets up over them and pulled her still-bound body into his arms.

"I love you, Sarah-my-slave."

"And I love you, Phillip-my-Master." Her good arm slipped around to gather him closer.

"Wait, I tied that arm…"

"Poorly," she chuckled. "You were trying to be too careful of my broken arm and the knots were loose." She snuggled into him. "I don't mind. Just more proof that you really do love me." He heard a muffled snort. "I'll even tell 'em that in court."

He leaned away so he could look into her eyes. "You're not my accuser, so you don't really need to be at the trial."

She looked at him like he'd lost his mind. "What are you talking about? Of course I'm going to be there. I kept trying to tell them at the hospital, and that detective who came 'round asking me questions—I told him too. You didn't beat me up and I didn't want that stupid order of protection."

"But I did beat you up."

"Only because I wanted it. And it wasn't really beating. There's a difference."

"Not in the eyes of the law."

"Yes, in the eyes of the law." Sarah set her jaw. Phillip had seen that determination before. His slave was no doormat, that was for darn sure. She pulled off the scarf and pantyhose ties and Phillip helped her as he let her continue her tirade. Obviously this, too, had been building for a while.

"The key word is 'consensual'. I wanted it...they can't punish you when I asked you to cane me." She glowered at him. "You bet yer booties I'll be at that trial. Right at your side."

He pulled her close and kissed her and when it ended, his eyes twinkled. "I couldn't have a better champion."

She didn't answer but only snuggled deeper into his arms. Feeling content, he wrapped his arms around her in protection, even though he wasn't sure who was protecting whom at the moment. He drifted off to sleep, finally at peace with the world.

* * * * *

Celebrating, Sarah and Phillip went out to breakfast after their first night together since the order of protection had been lifted. The small diner wasn't crowded so they had the entire end of the place to themselves. The sun hid behind the clouds and rain threatened to fall. In the soft light from the window, Sarah gazed across the booth at Phillip, her gaze drinking him in. In truth, she was half afraid this was another fever-induced dream and that he'd disappear into some drugged-out haze.

She loved the way his dark hair curled around his ears giving her just enough to run her fingers through. She loved how his eyes could twinkle with mischief or darken with desire, sometimes changing in a flash. And she loved his quiet strength, not only physically represented in those wonderfully broad shoulders of his but also living deep in his soul. Not being able to protect her these past few weeks had been torture for him and she understood that.

Still, what he had just told her had rattled him, she could see it in his eyes. "So let me get this straight…" Her own eyes narrowed as she rephrased and digested his latest piece of information. "The court wants you to plead guilty to some misdemeanor charge, pay a fine and be done?" She looked at him askance. "Why? Not that I'm not grateful they don't want to throw the book at you," Sarah hurried to qualify her question. "But it doesn't make sense to me."

"Ray says he thinks it's because they know they don't have a strong case. They can subpoena you and put you on the stand but apparently that detective you talked to doesn't think you'll help their case. As soon as you claim what we did was consensual, he thinks the jury will find in favor of us…of me."

"It was consensual. Does this lawyer of yours think you ought to plead guilty to this lesser charge? Why, if he's sure you can win in court?"

Phillip shook his head. "No, Ray wants to go all the way. But he wanted me to know that the district attorney is talking deal in order to save time and money."

"Well, I don't think you should take the offer."

She loved the little lopsided grin he got when she surprised him. He'd sat back in the booth as the waitress delivered two steaming cups of hot chocolate, both piled high with whipped cream out of a can. Sarah scooped off the maraschino cherry from the top and plopped it on Phillip's cup. "Here. I don't like them much."

"Good." He popped one after the other into his mouth, putting the stems off to the side. "I knew we made a good pair." But then Phillip's eyes did the twinkle-to-serious change and Sarah felt her chest tighten as his voice dropped. "Tell me, slave, why you think I shouldn't just take the plea deal."

When it was just the two of them, at home, playing by themselves, that word always gave her a warm glow. In public, a stab of pleasure mixed with embarrassment arrowed directly to her pussy. With a quick glance over her shoulder to make sure the waitress wasn't within hearing distance, she gave her answer.

"Because it'll send a message. There's a line between abuse and fun and the line changes all the time. That makes it difficult to legislate. But maybe a case like this can help create more guidelines so the cops won't jump in where they really don't need to and they can spend their time arresting *real* bad guys!"

She laughed as Phillip chuckled. Even to her own ear, her words sounded lame.

A new thought occurred to her. She sipped at her hot chocolate, choosing her words carefully. "On the other hand, Sir, you're an entrepreneur with a company to think of. I know you sold it off but the stock options you kept will plummet if the publicity gets out of hand. If pleading guilty to a misdemeanor and paying a few bucks now saves you embarrassment and more money down the line, I could understand if you choose the plea bargain.

"Of course, you will then have a record for a crime you didn't commit. Hell, there was no crime. And if you let them get away with it, then who's to stop the authorities from coming after all of us? After Will and Jill and Anton and Lady Aleshia and even me?" She sat up straighter as logic circled around again. "Phillip-my-Master, I love you and no matter what you do, I'll support you."

"And does that include postponing the wedding again?"

His eyes were dark and Sarah couldn't quite tell from them where he was heading. Deliberately setting her cup on the table, she'd sat back, a slight frown creasing her brow. "I'm not sure why we'd need to. We already missed our first appointment at city hall." The irony that he had actually been there while she'd been forced to remain away from him wasn't lost on her. He was getting to know that building on a much more intimate basis than either of them ever expected him to.

"In this state, a wife is not allowed to testify against her husband."

Sarah shook her head, not getting Phillip's point. "I wouldn't be testifying against you, I'd be testifying for you."

"Exactly! Ray and I want you to testify, because it's your testimony that will sway the jury in my favor."

"So why can't we get married before the trial?"

"Because, love, if we're not married, you can get up on the stand and clear my name. If we do get married, you can't testify at all."

Understanding came in a flash. "We can't get married!"

Phillip laughed and behind the counter, the waitress smiled to see two young people so in love.

"No, you're right, Phillip. We're just going to have to wait a little longer." Sarah thought of her apartment, with the packed boxes now half unpacked and of her lease. "I'll have to ask the landlord for another month's extension. I've been a good tenant so he didn't mind when I asked him for this month. Maybe he won't mind another…"

Phillip loved the way she bit the side of her lip when she puzzled out a problem. It gave her a pixieish air, like a little sprite trying to figure out how much mischief she could get into.

"Why not just move in with me?"

"Before we're married?"

He laughed at the shock on her face. "This is the twenty-first century, you know. People do sometimes live together before the wedding date."

Across from him, Sarah rolled her eyes. "I know. And it's not exactly like I'm saving myself for marriage…" Her cheeks turned a pretty pink color when the waitress came up from behind her at that precise moment. To the woman's credit, the server's face didn't change one iota as she delivered their meal, in spite of the fact that she had to have heard Sarah's comment. Phillip made a mental note to give the waitress an extra-big tip for her discretion.

Once alone again, he brought the subject back up. "I think it's fair to say we've established we're sexually compatible, slave." He loved watching her reactions when he surprised her. She wiggled on the vinyl seat and Phillip got a flash of an idea. Not for today, but for sometime in the future when he was feeling particularly wicked. He let it slide, content to watch her react to words alone.

"Yes, Sir," she finally murmured. "That's one thing that's a definite. We have compatibility. Lots and lots of compatibility." He watched a wicked grin try to spread across her lips. But she quelled it by biting off a piece of bacon and glancing to see the waitress's whereabouts.

"So then, move in with me."

She shook her head, apparently feeling on safer ground now that she was reassured their server was back behind the counter. "No. I know, it isn't logical." She put up a hand to stave him off and Phillip waited. "You've spoken before about symbols and how they're important reminders of who and what we are. Well, the marriage ceremony is a symbol as well. It's the moment our lives change. Legally we cease to be two separate individuals and we become one in the eyes of the law. It's momentous—an ending of one lifestyle and the beginning of another."

She paused, groping for the right words. "Living together before the vows, on a twenty-four/seven basis lessens the step. The ceremony becomes nothing more than an afterthought."

Phillip understood. "The collar ceremony has the same feel to it. When I fasten the silver torc around your neck, that's the moment I vow to be everything you ever need." He put his hand out and felt her warm fingers when she'd placed her hand in his. "It *is* a momentous moment...and I wouldn't have it any other way."

He'd felt her squeeze his fingers. "So no wedding and no living together until after the trial." That mischievous smile played about her lips again. "Of course, that doesn't mean I won't still be coming on weekends."

Phillip lifted her hand to his lips. "I expect you'll be coming a lot on weekends, slave." He watched her color again as his meaning hit home. Teasing her further, he tasted the back of her hand with his tongue, drawing little circles before giving her a kiss and releasing it. She might not wish to move in with him and he would respect her wishes, but there was no reason on earth why he couldn't pick up her training right where they'd left off.

Of course, neither of them had expected the trial to be postponed, not once but twice. The holidays, then New Year's came and went. Sarah often thought of that beautiful torc Phillip's uncle had made for her, wishing it were already welded around her neck.

Finally the trial date was set, the players assembled and life could begin to move on. Her arm had healed and only occasionally ached now, the stripes across her ass that had gotten them into this predicament had long since faded away. While each weekend made the wait bearable, both felt as if their relationship were stuck in a holding pattern, unable to move forward until the legal issues were resolved. Phillip even stopped pushing her limits for the time being, almost as if he couldn't go on until they had their lives back.

Chapter Twelve
The Trial

ॐ

"The court calls Sarah Simpson–Parker to the stand."

The bailiff's voice rang out in the small courtroom and Sarah stood, her chin high and her dander up. She'd been waiting weeks for this. The trial had been pushed back twice and now that it was underway, she was ready to tell anyone who would listen a thing or two, though her heart still beat hard and butterflies still threatened to take flight in her stomach.

"Raise your right hand and repeat after me." The bailiff held out a small black book and Sarah put her left hand on top. Her mind took in small details even as she repeated the words of her oath to tell the truth, the whole truth, so help her God.

The bailiff, fairly tall and looking official in his crisp uniform nodded to her and she sat in the old-fashioned wooden chair. To her right, the judge in her black robes kept a neutral face as the prosecuting attorney stood and came forward. To Sarah's left, the twelve members of the jury sat in comfortable chairs, more modern in appearance than the one she sat in now. A brief thought flitted through her mind. Was there was some psychological reason for their sitting in comfort while she sat ramrod-straight, her hands demurely clasped on top of her conservative gray skirt?

Phillip hadn't picked out this outfit today — she had. Not that she didn't trust him. She wouldn't be here as a hostile witness if she didn't. The modest skirt came to just above her knees, the blazer cut wider at the shoulders to accentuate her still-narrow waist. She wore a cream-colored silk blouse that buttoned high but not so high they couldn't see the strap of leather she wore tied around her neck.

She'd debated about the going-out collar. Would it be too much? It wasn't the same leather strap she'd worn that fateful Monday. That had been lost at the hospital. Phillip had bought this strip at the fabric store shortly after the order of protection had expired and she'd worn it every day since.

Ray Miller, Phillip's lawyer, had already told her to say as little as possible about their sexual preferences, forbidding her to use the word "slave" at any point. "Juries get funny when words like that are brought up," he had explained to her yesterday. "Just keep referring to your sexual lives as private and your kinks as exactly that. Stay matter-of-fact and nonjudgmental because that's exactly the way we want the jury to be."

The prosecuting attorney stepped up to her now. "So, Mrs. Simpson–Parker, what is your relationship with the defendant?"

Sarah kept her voice level and calm. She'd show them just how strong a woman she was and that she wasn't a spineless little wimp to be pushed around—not even by Phillip. She answered the question with no embellishment. If he wanted more, the damn lawyer would have to ask her.

"Phillip Townsend is my fiancé."

"And do the two of you currently live together?"

"No." She said nothing of the fact that she spent weekends at his cottage.

"Are you sexually involved with him?"

"Objection, Your Honor."

Sarah kept her face impassive, but she couldn't help the tiny smile that turned up a corner of her mouth when the judge proclaimed, "Sustained."

The prosecutor nodded at the judge before turning to her again. "Mrs. Simpson–Parker, when you were taken into the hospital, you had several wounds across your..." The lawyer paused as if searching for a proper word he could use in a courtroom. "Derrière."

He didn't fool her. She knew exactly what he was doing. By seeming to have to search for a delicate term, he denigrated the action into the realm of pornography. She remained still, not taking the bait. Only when he asked her a direct question did she have to answer him, though her blood began to boil.

"Please tell the court who gave you those wounds."

Sarah glanced over at Ray who nodded. Knowing full well her words were damning without a qualifier, she spoke a little quicker than she meant to. "Phillip gave me the three stripes across my...derrière...at my request."

"You requested them?"

"Yes, I did." A note of defiance crept into her voice.

"Why?"

"That's none of your business."

"Your Honor, I would like to submit to the court Exhibit A...a photograph of Mrs. Simpson–Parker taken at the hospital at the time of her admittance." With a theatrical flourish, the prosecutor held up an eleven-by-fourteen photo showing her on her side, the three red stripes across her ass glowing in full color. He made sure the jury got a good look before he turned back to her.

"Are you telling me that you asked to be beaten?"

"Objection! Three lines across her rear end scarcely qualify as a beating. Your Honor, Mrs. Simpson–Parker is not on trial here, and what her reasons were are not important."

"Do you object to Exhibit A, Mr. Miller?"

"No, Your Honor. Only to the question."

A tense ten seconds passed as the judge considered before finally nodding toward Ray and Phillip. "Sustained. Mrs. Simpson–Parker's reasons are not germane to the case."

She breathed a sigh of relief, even though she would have enjoyed telling this lawyer just what he could do with his questions prying into her sexual preferences. Her cheeks flamed, mostly in anger, but with a little embarrassment mixed in to have her kink so nearly exposed.

The prosecutor barely gave her time to finish her sigh, however, before he attacked again. "That wasn't the only time he beat you...you bear older marks on your breasts, similar marks." The damn lawyer picked up another photo from his table and held it for the jury to see. Phillip started to rise in protest and Ray pushed him back down into his seat. Sarah's cheeks burned in anger and shame. She didn't need to see the picture to know her breasts were on display for the world to see. The prosecutor rounded on her. "How often does he beat you, Mrs. Simpson-Parker?"

"He doesn't beat me." The words came out in anger. Out of the corner of her eye, she saw Ray look at her in warning.

"And yet you admit he gave you those marks?"

"Yes. He gave me those because I asked for them."

"How did you ask for them? On your knees, begging? Or did you simply do something that, in your eyes, was wrong? You did something you felt you needed punishment for, isn't that right?"

"No, that's not right. That's not it at all." Her voice rose as she defended the man she called Master. "I asked him to cane me because I wanted to know what it felt like. I wanted to feel the rush. It's my kink, counselor, and it's none of your business."

Her cheeks burned with embarrassment as she realized the lawyer had gotten her to admit her kink after all, but she was damned if she was going to sit here and insinuate that either of them had done something wrong. She stuck her chin out in defiant pride. Her journey with Phillip had taught her so much and she was not about to let some lawyer demean her life just because she liked her sex accompanied by whips and chains.

The prosecutor seemed to sense she wasn't going to be the dishrag he hoped she would be. Turning away from her, he addressed the judge. "No further questions, Your Honor."

Ray shook his head and the judge turned to Sarah. "You may step down."

Her hands shaking, Sarah stood, partly relieved, partly disappointed. In some ways, she felt like a kid who'd been promised a ride on the roller coaster and gotten a ride on the merry-go-round instead. Somehow she had envisioned her giving a rousing speech that totally exonerated Phillip — a speech that would cause the courtroom to erupt in applause and instant exoneration. But the prosecutor hadn't asked her the right questions. He'd focused on her instead of on Phillip and she felt she'd tripped over her own tongue in trying to answer him. Giving Phillip a searching look as she passed his table, she took her place between Will and Jill in the spectator seats.

* * * * *

Waiting for the jury to return had to be the absolute worst part of the trial. Phillip sat up front with his lawyer beside him. Until the trial, Sarah realized she'd never seen him in a full suit before. His everyday wear tended to be casual, though he rarely went for the jeans and a sweatshirt look. Sarah liked that. Mostly he wore dark pants and plain white shirts that ended up looking anything but plain on him because he had them tailored to fit his wide shoulders and narrow waist. Phillip might be pushing forty in a few years but he kept the shape of a much younger man.

The three-piece he wore today was a gray Hickey–Freeman. Sarah only knew because he'd left the suit hanging from the beam of the four-poster last Friday. He'd told her to hang it in the closet as he had prepared the bed for playing. That night he'd tormented her with a feather in some spots she never even knew were ticklish. When she had hung the suit, she hadn't been able to resist sneaking a peek at the label.

He looked so calm compared to Ray, who sat drumming his fingers on the wooden table. Sarah knew the calm wasn't just for effect. They'd kissed that morning before leaving separately for the courthouse and he'd shown not a single sign of nerves when he'd said, "Remember, Sarah-my-slave — I love you always. Tell the truth and set me free!"

She bit her lower lip to keep from smiling in the courtroom. It might not be seemly to sit there grinning like a fool, remembering her intended's sweet embraces as they waited for a decision that would plot the course of their lives. The same quiet confidence he brought to their sexual lives, he brought to the courtroom and Sarah had long ago realized it was simply a part of his dominant nature.

Not arrogance, though. Confidence. She watched Ray stop the drumming and pick up a pencil to twirl between his fingers instead. Impatience was a trait Phillip had never shown with her. He didn't show it now and according to Will, he had never shown it with anyone but himself.

How long was that jury going to be out? Sarah checked her watch. Only half an hour so far? Well, the judge hadn't dismissed the court, so even though the afternoon wore on, she must have hopes that they'd reach a verdict fairly quickly.

Her mind began to drift again, going over her testimony, then floating around to when she should tell her boss she was finally going to take that vacation and go on her honeymoon, then jumping back to the apartment and the landlord's goodwill in letting her go to a month-by-month lease until things got settled. She was just starting a mental grocery list when the door to the back opened and the bailiff called out, "All rise."

Phillip did not feel as calm as the picture he projected. In fact, he was quite nervous. Ray's finger-drumming wasn't helping. Was he doing that because he wasn't sure how things were going to go? Or because the man just had excess energy?

"All rise."

Phillip stood immediately, watching the judge return to the bench, followed by the jury filing into place. He tried to read faces but they were as impassive as his own. He thought he saw a smile from one of the two middle-aged women who sat near each other in the line but didn't dare count on it.

"Has the jury reached a verdict?"

"We have, Your Honor. We find the defendant not guilty."

Phillip heard a small squeal from behind him but couldn't tell if it was Sarah or Jill. He barely heard the words of the judge dismissing the case as Ray shook his hand. The prosecuting attorney approached and offered his congratulations. Phillip shook hands, hearing only the words "not guilty" playing over and over in his head.

And then Sarah was beside him. Sarah, the woman he loved, the woman he'd been forced to wait for. He swept her into his arms and right there in front of God and everybody he kissed her hard and long and deep.

Later, Sarah would remember the events of the next hour only in glimpses. Kissing Phillip, the joy in her heart, the race down the corridor to the judge's chambers, the look on her face when Phillip asked her to marry the two of them right there.

Sarah had produced the paperwork from her purse, all signed and ready to go months before the untimely interruption. Jill and Will stood up for them and Phillip and Sarah officially tied the knot in the eyes of the law.

Chapter Thirteen
Bound

෨

Sarah thought they'd never get home. Well, back to Phillip's cottage, anyway. Now her home as well. With the sun already low on the horizon when they left the courthouse, it was full dark after their celebratory supper with the group Sarah was beginning to affectionately think of as "Phillip's gang".

Finally the two of them sped through the darkness to pull into the cottage's long driveway. A bitter wind blew and the two hurried to the house, anxious to be out of the elements and in where it was warm and safe.

Her sigh was explosive. Sarah sank against the closed front door as she finally rid herself of all the pent-up tension she'd been carrying for weeks. She shivered and sighed again, blowing out the last of her worries as Phillip hung their coats.

Coming over to her, he gathered her into his arms, the small lamp on the side table casting alluring shadows over his face. "Come here, woman."

She clung to him, breathing deeply of his cologne, caressing the heavy wool of his suit coat with her cheek. Her hands slid beneath his coat and around his back to pull him closer. Under her fingers, she could feel the warm broadcloth of his shirt and beneath it, the hard muscles that had wielded that cane long ago. That cane that had given her the most extreme orgasm of her life had also been the cane that caused them so much trouble.

Pulling away, she looked up with concern. "Sir, please promise me one thing?"

"What is it, slave?"

"Promise me you'll someday use that cane again." She put her fingers on his lips to stop his protest. "I liked it. It was a misunderstanding by outside people that the courts have now rectified. But I liked it." Heat blushed in her cheeks as she admitted she liked the sharp pains that had blossomed into ecstasy and her voice trailed away in embarrassment. "I thought it was...fun."

Phillip took her chin, pulling her face back up to him. "Fun? Interesting word choice, my slave." But then he grew serious again. "Someday we'll get the cane out again, I promise. Just not quite yet."

Sarah saw a trace yet lingered of some phantom deep in his psyche. He had put her in danger and still hadn't forgiven himself. She smiled and deflected his angst with a sexy waggle of her eyebrows. "Then I do hope my Master has some other wonderful activity planned for tonight?" She stood on her tiptoes so she could whisper in his ear. "Your slave wants to celebrate!"

Phillip's laughter filled the room and happiness swelled inside her. She loved it when she could make him laugh. He stepped away from her, his eyes twinkling. "Show me how much you want it, slave."

With only the small light of the lamp to light her, Sarah did a striptease worthy of Gypsy Rose Lee. Swaying her hips to imaginary music, she flung her hair back and tossed her head as her fingers slowly unbuttoned her blouse. The matching jacket she had taken off before putting her coat on and as she pulled the blouse out of the waistband, Sarah realized she'd left it in the car. Dropping her head so her hair covered half her face, she smiled coyly and decided it could wait until morning. Especially when Phillip raised an eyebrow at her antics and shifted, though not before she noted the growing bulge in his pants.

With a shimmy of her shoulders, she let the blouse fall, catching it neatly in her hands. She held it out to the side, then decided she didn't really want to drop it on the floor of the hallway. Turning the situation to her advantage, she sauntered to where he now leaned against the archway that led to the living room. Waggling her eyebrows again, she tossed the shirt over his shoulder, making sure to bounce her breasts enticingly as she did so.

He didn't move but his grin was all the encouragement she needed. Feeling brazen, she moved back only a little before turning and bending at the waist, her legs spread wide. She ran a hand from the back of her knee up her thigh, pushing the skirt up as she did so, letting him see the tops of her stockings and the garter that held them in place. When he shifted his weight against the doorframe, she knew she had scored.

Still keeping her back to him, she tossed her head again, looking over her shoulder and watching him watch her as she slid down the zipper of her skirt. The garters and stockings had paid off. Since it was a weeknight, she had dressed and gone to court from her apartment, her natural optimism hoping even then for the evening celebration they were about to have.

Sliding the skirt off and making sure he got a good look at her ass before she stood again, she tossed it over her shoulder, keeping it hooked on her finger. When she turned to face him, she dropped it in front of her, covering her shaved pussy from his view. Teasing him, she spread her legs and pulled the skirt slowly up through, pressing it against her mound as she threw her head back, closed her eyes and let her remaining inhibitions go.

Phillip watched her gyrate in the hall, his cock throbbing as she teased him with glimpses of her body. It didn't matter that he knew every inch of her skin, that he'd taken possession of her pussy and her ass and her mouth. When they'd met, he'd been looking for a woman who would sexually submit to him, someone who would obey his commands and let him play with her body as he saw fit. He'd also wanted someone he could give his heart to, though he wasn't sure he'd known that at the time. Standing there watching Sarah's mind slip into her sexy, submissive state made him realize he'd found so much more than his fantasies had ever dreamed.

Her eyes had gone dreamy and when she threw the skirt over his other shoulder, he could smell the scent of her arousal all over the fabric. He remembered her first entrance into this hall, how scared and nervous she'd been because he had asked then for her compliance. And oh, how she'd given it to him that night!

As she wrapped her bra around his neck like a scarf, he grinned and wondered just who had trained whom. He'd opened the door for her but she'd embraced that part of her sexuality with a passion even he had never expected. His cock rose, pressing against his pants with increasing urgency.

"That's enough, slave. Leave the stockings." His voice was calculatingly rough, knowing the tone would settle her deeper into her role as his submissive. She didn't disappoint him. With her foot, she pushed the shoes she had just kicked off to the side, then came to stand before him, her legs spread, her arms behind her head and her breasts pushed out in offering.

Her eyes still held a twinkle, a sprightly reminder of how much she enjoyed submitting to his will. Even as he watched, however, she closed those beautiful brown eyes and took a deep breath. Letting it out slowly, he watched her shoulders relax and her head bow. When she reopened her eyes and reset her gaze, the pixie she could be was gone, a waiting slave in her place.

Phillip's cock moved in his pants. God, what this woman did to him! A simple act of submission and he was ready to throw her to the ground and take her right there in the hallway. He needed to master himself before he could Master her.

Turning on his heel, he gestured for her to follow him to the bedroom. Tonight would be special. He was a free man once more and intended to celebrate.

Bidding her to kneel in the doorway, he took a moment to blindfold her so she could not see the preparations he made. Phillip closed the curtains against the night and lit several candles around the room. Jarred candles, long tapers, short tea lights—all lent their flames to cast a magical spell over the room.

Finally done, he turned to survey his work before going over to Sarah—his slave, his pet—who waited on her knees in patience.

Phillip wasn't making any attempt to be quiet with whatever he was doing but Sarah still couldn't figure out the details. He moved several times from the closet, where she knew he kept whatever toys weren't in use in the dungeon. But what he was getting out or putting away, she couldn't tell. She could, however, smell the perfumed scent of the candles and she smiled. The soft light they spread around the room always made her feel as if she'd stepped back into another century.

She heard him approach and his fingers untied the knot of the scarf he'd tied around her eyes. Still without saying a word, he gave her back her eyesight and she blinked several times as her eyes adjusted. Amazing how well-lit a room could become just from a dozen or so candles.

Phillip held his hand out to her and she accepted his help in standing. The sheet and blankets had been stripped almost completely off the bed, forming a luxurious pile that cascaded over the intricate wrought iron footboard to puddle on the hardwood floor. Several coils of thick black rope lay in a neat row on the top of the bed.

He still held her hand and a gentle tug pulled her around to face him. There was nothing gentle in his look, however. Candlelight reflected from his eyes and in their depths, Sarah saw the hungry beast she knew he could become. Held in check now, she knew how he devoured her when the beast took control. Her eyes narrowed as the woman she kept caged stirred in response.

"I will bind you tonight in a special webwork, my slave." Phillip's low voice murmured a spell to enthrall her and Sarah followed willingly. She let his words hypnotize her, her desire to please him coupling with her deeper desire to be devoured by him.

He draped a length of heavy cord over her shoulders, letting the weight center her. "There's magic in these black ropes, my love, magic that will take your breath away." Another length of rope across her shoulders made her pull in a breath. "Magic that will bind your soul to mine." A third length made her bow her head in submission.

"Yes, my Master." Her voice, barely a whisper, gave him the title from the depths of her being.

"Kneel."

The weight of the ropes around her shoulders pushed her down. Sinking to her knees, she absorbed the heaviness and used it to help her find the quiet places inside her mind. Only by stilling her thoughts could she let the cage open tonight. The touch of Phillip's hand on her hair made her look up.

"I love you, Sarah."

His tone, quieter, more serious than she had ever seen before, made her breath catch in her throat. Phillip stood before her, his psyche bared to the core. A core of quiet strength formed inside her, a core that understood she could do anything with him at her side.

"I love you, Phillip."

And then the beast was back, his eyes darkening with hunger she knew only she could feed.

"Down on all fours."

Willingly, she went down, her rear pressed against the bed, the ropes draped like a scarf across her shoulders. Phillip stepped back and Sarah's gaze fell on his shoes—black shoes with the laces neatly tied—just peeking out from the hem of his cuffed pant leg. The slow smile spread across her cheeks as she reveled in the symbolism.

If he'd hoped to humiliate her, it hadn't worked. The woman on all fours before him was a fiercely independent woman who graciously bowed to his commands because she chose to. His cock, which had grown soft as he made preparations, stirred again to see her bow to his will under the ropes he would bind her with tonight.

He turned the growl that formed in his chest into a clearing of his throat. Tonight was not a night to rush. Capricious as they sounded, he had intent behind his commands. His voice deep, he now moved her to yet another position with but two words. "Stand, slave."

She trembled as she did so but Phillip did not offer his hand to steady her. Once she was standing, he removed the weight of the ropes, one by one laying the coils on the bed until she stood nearly naked again before him, only dressed in only her garters and stockings.

That was soon to be remedied. He still wore his tie and now he undid it, pulling it through his buttoned-down collar. "Put out your hands," he instructed her and was pleased when she brought them forward, palm to palm, without needing to be told. She was learning.

With quick, deft twists, he tied her wrists together, then threw the remaining length over the top support of the four-poster. He pulled her arms up so that she had to stand on her tiptoes, yet he wanted her comfortably so. All he really needed was to get her hands out of the way for the next part but forcing her up a bit would help her mental journey that was all about control.

He noted the warmth of her skin, running his hands down her arms and over her breasts. The last thing he wanted was an unforeseen chill that would ruin his work by bringing her mind back to mundane matters. He left her and went to check the thermostat in the living room. For good measure, he nudged it up a few degrees.

Phillip paused in the doorway, blessing all the powers in the universe that had brought Sarah into his life. She hung there, patiently waiting, her even breathing making her breasts move in the most enticing manner.

"Are you ready to be bound, slave?"

She looked at him with a steady gaze, understanding the question's many levels. Her voice quiet, she gave the one reply that would answer them all. "Yes, Master."

Phillip wasted no more time. Picking up a coil of black rope, he passed one end around her body, tying it just under her raised arms. Satisfied the knot wasn't too tight, he wound the rope around and around her body, pulling it taut and snug against her skin. Bit by bit her breasts were flattened under the rope's unceasing descent.

"With each circle of the rope, I ensnare you further." Phillip wound another length. "Feel how the rope becomes a second skin, both a corset that binds and a garment that covers, giving not even a glimpse of your skin underneath."

Sarah closed her eyes as Phillip continued to encircle her with black rope against her white skin. Her mind reeled and she relaxed into her bondage, feeling the tie bite into her wrists.

A sharp tug of the rope made her eyes fly open, however and sent her up on her toes.

"Do not go to sleep on me, slave."

"No, Sir…just enjoying it." Feeling dreamy, she thought she smiled but couldn't be sure.

Phillip had run out of rope but tied another length to the first, or was it the second? Her breasts were tight to her body now, the nipples purposely pinched between two coils. Heat darted from those two points straight down to her pussy. She wanted to rub it—her pussy, the heat, her nipples—all of them. Phillip had been smart to tie her hands out of the way.

"Deep breath in."

She took in as much air as she could but the coils didn't give her much room. Phillip quickly passed the rope around her waist several times as she held the breath as long as she could. And when she exhaled, she discovered she couldn't pull in another deep breath. The ropes forced her to breathe in shallow draughts. Her pussy twitched so violently, she was afraid she'd come right then and there.

Phillip tied the end off, bringing the last coil tight against her skin. With a deft pull on the tie that held her hands, he released her, letting her pull down her arms unfettered. The change in pressure around her midsection as she dropped her arms to her sides made her feel as if her shoulders floated on top of the rest of her body.

Gesturing to the long pier mirror that hung on the wall opposite the foot of the bed, Phillip directed her gaze. Sarah gasped in pleased surprise.

The candlelight softened the lines of her body, casting shadows that complemented her curves. The stark contrast of her white skin against the thick black rope astonished her almost as much as the beauty her figure took when pressed into such an hourglass shape. She ran a palm over the corded corset, feeling the bumps made by the tightly packed ropes. Like being encased in tight corduroy, she thought as she turned sideways and examined her reflection.

From this angle, her ample breasts all but disappeared. Phillip had wound the coils tightly across her chest, forcing her breasts to stretch downward. A small gap showed where her nipples jutted out, supported by a half-moon of flesh the rope had rolled away from. Experimentally, she ran the palm of her hand over her nipples, delighted at the tingles her touch produced.

As she twisted and turned to get a good view of Phillip's binding, the ropes loosened a little and she found she breathed easier. Either that or her body was simply getting used to its new condition. Whichever way it was, the ropes felt like a second skin. Delighted and feeling naughty, she turned to face Phillip, standing with her feet apart and her hands up behind her head in an attitude of submission she thoroughly enjoyed.

Phillip stepped to her, putting his hands on her waist. "I like how this makes you look, my beautiful slave." He bent to capture her mouth with his. For a moment, Sarah was off balance, the suddenness of his tongue against her lips taking her by surprise. Her hands slipped apart and she almost grabbed his shoulders before his hands steadied her even as he took possession of her mouth.

His tongue swirled inside, caressing and playing with her tongue and she couldn't stop the response of her body. Not that she wanted to stop. He staked his claim on her and she accepted his dominance, her tongue returning his caresses, reveling in his taste and in the scent of his cologne. With an effort, she returned her hands behind her head, even as he still kissed her and her head swam.

Was the room spinning because of the ropes around her chest? Or because Phillip took away what breath she had with his kiss? His fingers lightly pinched her exposed nipples and a low moan of need welled up, becoming audible only when his lips left hers. She leaned into him as he pulled away, reluctant to give up the passion of his lips on hers.

He gave her a critical going-over as she stood recovering. "Your cuffs would make the picture perfect."

The four wide strips of black leather lay in the top drawer of his dresser, their home when they weren't around her wrists and ankles. He slipped one around each wrist, fastening each with its small golden lock. Kneeling like a knight of old, he uttered a single word "Up" and she complied, using the post of the bed to steady herself since putting her foot on his knee so he could lock the cuff on her ankle threatened to overbalance her. The rope encircling her dug into her waist and she blushed as the released scent of her arousal filled the room.

"Look again, slave. Model yourself for me."

He had been right. The cuffs completed the picture of her submission.

"Lie on your back on the bed."

The terse direction, uttered with a strained voice of passion, whirled around in her head as she leaned toward the bed, grace quickly replaced with desire. She set her rear on the edge of the bed, pausing a moment to watch him take off his shirt and drop it to the floor. She never tired of looking at his strong shoulders or the way his chest hair tapered in a neat line down his abdomen. When his fingers began unbuttoning his pants, she quickly lay down, bringing her knees to her chest but keeping them spread open so he could see what he had done to her.

His cock touched her pussy and her moan was more than just breath this time. Flinging her arms over her head, she gave herself to him, inching down the bed, wanting to feel him fill her.

She wasn't at the right angle, however. The bed wasn't high enough for Phillip to stand beside it and take her. Should they move to the dungeon? Surely that table was high enough.

Phillip had the solution, however and Sarah settled back into the comfort that she was in good hands when he picked up two shorter lengths of black rope and wrapped each of her ankles in a mock-corduroy cuff. Throwing the ends over the corner of the bedposts, he spread her legs wide and lifted her ass off the bed. Satisfied, he dropped one end and tied down one suspended leg, then fastened the second.

Sarah still had use of her hands and in a fit of mischievousness, she reached down to her pussy, spreading her lips wide and fingering her clit. The bend in her body, strained against the ropes, made it difficult for her to breathe as her fingers played but it was worth it to see the look on Phillip's face.

So intent on getting Sarah positioned exactly the way he wanted her, Phillip had momentarily ignored the wonderful musk revealed by her spread legs. He would get to that in due time. Tying off her ankle, he turned to face her, intending to prolong her anguished desire a little longer.

But her look of total enjoyment and teasing took him by surprise. A few minutes earlier she had been well on her way to that place of bliss that was his target. Her eyes had lost focus and she had been putty in his hands.

Now, however, the wanton she hid inside had come to the fore, challenging him and his authority by playing with herself and teasing him along. His cock stiffened sharply in response. The animal he kept on a short leash, pulled hard, wanting to show this little slut a lesson in who was boss.

The still-sane part of him gloried in this power exchange. Tied, Sarah held more power over him than she realized. Tied, she let loose the wanton that threatened his control. Tied, she became the controlling one who, in turn, let him let loose his animal to ravage her.

He pulled off his clothes, his engorged cock swollen, needing to be satisfied. This was what he wanted—a ready pussy just waiting for him to take what belonged to him. He rubbed the shaft, feeling the raised veins and prolonged the agony.

"Do you want this, slave? Do you want me to fuck you?"

Sarah nodded, running her finger along her slit and opening her pussy lips invitingly. "Yes, Sir. I want this. Please, Sir, take me." A small whimper came from the back of her throat. Phillip loved the noises she made when she pleaded with him. He put his cock at the entrance to her pussy, pushing away her fingers and taking over.

"Beg me."

Two simple words, but they shot through her system like liquid fire. Pressing her palms on the bed, she tried to leverage herself to get his cock inside her. "Please, Sir...Master. Take me. Fuck me!"

Her nipples, caught between the loops of the rope, sent pricks of pleasant pain each time she moved. She moved anyway, letting the stabbings take her even deeper, deeper than the spot where the wanton lived, to a spot she could only reach if the wanton led. From far away, she heard her voice pleading over and over, "Please, Master...fuck me...use me!"

His huge cock entered her—relentless, forcing, pushing inside her aching pussy to fill her. Someone cried out. The pressure eased, then came on again, eased and came as he pumped his cock into her pussy. His body slammed against hers and Sarah welcomed him, pulling him in with urgency, needing him to press harder, deeper, faster.

And Phillip obliged, his hands on the bed on either side of her, supporting himself as he took control of her, playing with her body and sending her mind and spirit flying. Her hands flew up and rested on his forearms, not to push him away but to urge him in, her sounds gone to wordless cries as her mind shut down all processes but the wish for him to take her.

Below him, she whimpered, her hands now gripping his forearms, her brow creased, her breath in short, ragged gasps. Suddenly her eyes flew open, though he realized she couldn't see him. Her body convulsed and her whimpers turned to grateful cries. Her hands fell from his arms as she gave herself up to her orgasm, letting the waves take her mind where they would.

Phillip could hold back no longer. With a roar to match his slave's, he let loose the pent-up tension in his cock, the seed inside spurting out in relief to fill the pussy of the woman he loved. She cried out beneath him as she came again, her muscles milking him of every precious drop he could give her. Together they rode the waves of passion, their souls entwining, becoming one. He would stay with her in this bliss forever if he could.

But humans are made only to touch heaven, not live there. Phillip's breathing slowed now that he was empty. Slowly, he opened his eyes to look at the beautiful woman beneath him. Her silky brown hair lay arrayed around her head like a tangled halo. Her cheeks were flushed and warm with life, her eyes opening reluctantly, just as loath to leave the dream-world where they both were one being, and forced to become two separate individuals once more.

Sarah tried to take a deep breath but the ropes didn't let her and he felt her pussy twitch around his cock. He slid a hand down so he could finger her clit, knowing he wasn't hard enough to thrust into her again. She gasped as he pinched that tiny organ with his fingers and he was rewarded when her pussy contracted around him again. No great cries this time, though, only small whimpers. Did she have one more orgasm in her?

Pulling out, Phillip knelt down next to the bed. Her pussy dripped with their combined juices. Inserting two fingers into her sopping pussy so he could tell if she came or not, he captured her clit between his lips, gently squeezing it.

His slave's response was immediate. Her hands clutched the sheet and she cried out. He nibbled on her clit, swirling his tongue around it, enveloping it in warm, moist heat before sucking it into his mouth, pressuring and tormenting that little bud.

She came around his fingers and Phillip took pity on her. Each time, her cries were weaker as her body skated closer to exhaustion. With a tired grin, he helped her though this one, giving her the opportunity to enjoy every last spasm. Only when her body quieted did he remove his fingers and go into the adjoining bathroom to wash his hands.

Sarah felt the warm wet washcloth and almost came again. If her body hadn't been so incredibly satiated, she might have. Phillip lowered her ankles to the floor and she felt the blood flow back into her feet, making her plenty warm enough for the moment. Idly she watched him coil the short black ropes, her thoughts drifting without any direction.

"Give me your hand, slave."

She latched onto his command as if it were a port after a long time at sea. He pulled her to a sitting position, not letting her stand.

"Let's get these ropes off, shall we?"

Feeling a bit like a small child, Sarah just sat there, letting Phillip do all the work. She raised her arms when he told her to, held her breath when he instructed and lay back on the bed, all while her mind wrapped in a warm cocoon of satisfaction.

Not until he had blown out all the candles and pulled the covers over the two of them did she stir from her contentment. Spooning into his arms, she snuggled tight. His whispered words in her ear made her smile. Turning her face to him, she murmured, "I love you too, Sir." A moment more and she was fast asleep.

Chapter Fourteen
Permanence

ॐ

"She'll be here, Sarah. Stop worrying." Jill inadvertently tugged on a strand of Sarah's hair. The collaring ceremony was set to begin in less than half an hour and she still didn't have the slave-to-be's hair upswept to her liking.

Sarah shook her head, hardly realizing she pulled the strand clear of Jill's fingers again. "I don't know, Jill. Beth's been pretty distant since the accident. And she was pretty hurt to think I'd get married without her."

"Stop fidgeting!" Jill laughed. "You're going to look beautiful for the collaring ceremony if it's the last thing I do on this earth!"

Sarah grinned and took to twisting her fingers on her lap to rid herself of the nervous energy that threatened to overwhelm her. Had she been this antsy when waiting for her wedding to Tom? Biting her lip, Sarah decided her first wedding was a whole different beast altogether. Then she'd been a naïve virgin starting off a new adventure, without much of a clue about what would happen.

While she still wouldn't call herself worldly, this time around Sarah knew exactly what she was getting into. Two days ago, she and Phillip had been legally married by the same judge who had presided over his court case. Tonight's ceremony in the cottage wouldn't be legally binding but that didn't matter. This ceremony held another purpose entirely.

"I don't think Beth's coming." A tone of finality crept into her voice. "I told her about the ceremony and all it entailed." Sarah's fingers touched her still-bare neck.

"And?" Jill twirled another strand of Sarah's golden-brown locks, pinning it into place.

"And she said she'd be here to show her support for me, even though she still thinks I'm making a mistake marrying a man who beats me."

"When are you going to tell her otherwise?" A hard note sounded in Jill's voice and Sarah felt obligated to defend her best friend, or the woman who had been her best friend up until a few months ago. Since the accident and all it had revealed about her sex life, Beth might as well have been living in another city altogether for the amount of time they'd spent together. Sarah missed the long talks on the phone but had given up calling when Beth's haranguing got to be too much.

"I did try to tell her, several times. She just doesn't want to hear that I like...pain." Even to her ears it sounded sick and disgusting, two words Beth had used in their conversations, though Beth had turned them around and used them on Phillip.

Jill's look softened. "The vanilla world often doesn't understand. From what you told me of her before, I had thought she might be able to see the Dom side of a D/s relationship or at least the Domme one but apparently not?"

"Not. Definitely not."

Sarah glanced at the clock on Phillip's dresser, then clutched her stomach and took a deep breath as she realized the time. "Jill, we can't wait much longer. It's almost time. Do you think Phillip's as nervous as I am?"

She swallowed several times as a fist of iron suddenly grabbed her stomach and squeezed. Despite how anxious she'd been for this day to arrive, despite the fact that she'd longed for it, despite the fact that, in the eyes of the law, she and Phillip were already married, she still needed several deep breaths to keep the meager contents of her stomach inside where they belonged. A huge change in her life sat right outside the bedroom door. Was she truly ready to commit to being a sexual slave for the rest of her life?

The warmth that spread up from her pussy gave her the answer. After months of waiting, months of talking and discussing what fell under Phillip's dominion and what did not...the moment was here. Jill stepped back and made a low sound of appreciation.

"You are spectacular, Sarah. Stand up and take a look."

Sarah moved her head experimentally, making sure none of Jill's careful work would fall. Her hair had been upswept into several curls and ringlets, piled high and out of the way. Running her hand from her bare neck down, she felt the stiff bones of the corset that narrowed her waist and turned to see the view from the side. The cream-colored hose and garter continued the line all the way down to her shoeless feet.

"Let's tighten those laces and get you into your dress, shall we?"

Sarah nodded, glad for Jill's calming presence. As Will's slave, Jill actually held no part in the ceremony other than to get Sarah ready—a big enough job, Sarah decided—and to bear witness along with the other guests to the vows soon to be spoken. Obediently, Sarah turned around and held her breath as Jill firmed up the corset, forcing her breasts up almost as if they were sitting on a shelf, then she held up her hands so Jill could slip the peasant-style blouse over her head, settling it off her shoulders and showing the tops of her breasts. Despite the play she and Phillip had done in public on only two occasions, showing this much cleavage still made Sarah blush.

Jill held out the full-length skirt and Sarah stepped into it, taking a moment to zip it up in the back before stepping into the low-heeled slingbacks that completed her outfit. With a final tug to tighten her blouse under her skirt, she turned to the pier glass mirror that hung at the foot of the bed.

"You look beautiful!" Jill flounced Sarah's wide skirt, watching it settle in graceful folds. She didn't mention the fact that Sarah's nipples raised her tightened blouse. No sense it making her more nervous. Jill glanced at the clock. "And with ten minutes to spare!"

Sarah opened her mouth to say something but a quiet knock on the door interrupted her. For a moment, panic clutched her stomach. Phillip wasn't supposed to see her yet. She had an entrance all planned out. How she'd walk the length of the living room to where he stood at the far end and how she'd gracefully kneel beside him.

But it wasn't Phillip Jill let in the door. A familiar face, wreathed in brown curls, almost timidly poked her head around the door.

"Beth! You came!" Sarah squealed and ran to throw her arms around her friend. She nodded at Jill, who discreetly left, closing the door behind her.

"I decided I didn't want to miss it." Beth disengaged herself from Sarah's hug. "Look, Sarah, there's something I need to say before you decide if you want me to stay or not."

Afraid that whatever Beth was going to say would ruin things forever, Sarah tried to head her off. "It doesn't matter, Beth. You're my friend and you're here. It was important to me to have you here. I think because you've known me forever. You even knew Tom. I don't want that part of my life to end just because a new part of my life is beginning."

Beth took a deep breath. "Well, I've thought a lot about this whole thing, believe me and I need to tell you I can't agree with it all. No, don't interrupt." She held up her hand to forestall Sarah's protest. "Let me get through this. Please?"

Sarah nodded, forcing herself to let Beth have her say, even through the fear that their friendship was ending in spite of her words.

"I've been doing a lot of research on the web about your particular…kink. I know, when you showed me that list of sites to visit, I swore I never would. But I did. I always knew that stuff existed but to realize you were into it to the point of wanting to do it always? I guess I've just been so shocked by that, I couldn't think straight." She ran her hand through her short hair in a gesture Sarah recognized. Whenever Beth was working at solving a problem, from where they should go for dinner to dealing with crisis situations, the habit was ingrained. Suddenly Beth dropped her arm and grinned. "Hell, I'm not sure I'm not still shocked."

Sarah opened her mouth and again shut it without uttering a single word when Beth held up her hand.

"I've decided, however, that we've been friends far too long to let something like this come between us. I'm still not totally convinced you're not brainwashed or something." She gestured to the four-poster bed where a pair of cuffs still dangled from one corner and shuddered.

"Sarah, I came because you're my friend and I love you. And friends don't abandon friends, even if they really don't understand the road they're on." She dropped her hands to her side.

"So. If you still want me to stay, knowing I don't really understand it or agree with it, I'd love to witness the ceremony and stand by your side."

Sarah took Beth's hands. "I just need to know you're going to be happy for me. I don't want to have you watch over my shoulder all the time, waiting for some catastrophe to happen. Phillip is a good man. I both love and trust him. All I ask is for you to love and trust me."

Beth smiled, tears in her eyes. "I can do that, Sarah. I really can. If you'll still have me?"

Sarah threw her arms around her best friend. "Thank you! I love you too, Beth! Please stay!"

* * * * *

Sarah had left the particulars of the ceremony to Phillip. Now he stood at one end of his living room, the furniture pushed back against the walls, waiting for the woman who would soon vow to live her life as his slave. On either side of him stood the two men who had guided his life—his Uncle Irv Anberg, who had first explained the facts of life to him and Will, his best friend and mentor. In a few moments, Sarah would enter, kneel before him and take vows that would make her his slave forever.

The very thought of all the responsibility he was assuming settled on his shoulders like a cloak of lead. Sarah was the one, of that he was sure. But was he up to the task? The charges brought against him by an eager intern and rookie cop had shaken his confidence more than he'd let anyone know. He hadn't meant to hurt Sarah, in fact, he hadn't hurt her. The stripes he'd given her had moved her to a higher plane, giving her an incredible orgasm. How did one explain to the vanilla world what that did to him? How it made him expand with power and satisfaction and just plain old joy to see the woman he loved writhing in sexual ecstasy? How he gloried in her submission, not to lord it over her, but to bring her to those heights over and over and over? He shook his head as he waited for his soon-to-be slave to emerge from the bedroom, where currently she was closeted with her vanilla best friend. Phillip knew Beth had approved of him right up until the secret of Sarah's submission came out. Glad for the two steadying presences on either side of him, Phillip resisted the urge to cross the length of the living room, stride to the bedroom door and demand his woman.

Will leaned in to mutter something in his ear that Phillip didn't catch. He turned to his best man with a puzzled expression and Will repeated himself. "Jill just gave me the okay sign."

"What does that mean?" He hadn't even seen Jill reenter the room and as he looked around, he saw no sign of her now. Apparently she'd given her message and disappeared.

"She's been listening at the door and Sarah and Beth have made up. Give it another minute or two and we can get started."

Phillip nodded and curbed his impatience. If Beth was on her way to accepting Sarah's choices, that was a good sign. He smiled at the others gathered to witness the collaring ceremony. They hadn't invited very many, since most of the world really wouldn't understand what was about to happen. Paul, Beth's mostly on-again boyfriend, stood chatting amiably with Anton as Lady Aleshia looked on and Phillip wondered if the two of them had more in common than they might suspect, based on what he knew about Beth.

The woman in question hurried into the room, coming to stand beside Paul, giving Phillip a teary-eyed nod as she took her place. Apparently all was well between Sarah and Beth. That made Phillip feel good. Taking Sarah away from her friends was something he had never intended to do. He liked her independence. Just not where sex was concerned.

All thoughts of the guests fled, however, when Jill took her spot in the center of the arch leading from the hall to the living room. Will turned to the stereo system against the front wall and a moment later, the deep sounds of Pachelbel's *Canon in D* filled the room. Wearing a simple pink shirtwaist dress with a matching wide belt, Jill moved forward, her steps slow and steady, her eyes twinkling and a delighted smile dimpling her cheeks. In her hands she carried a small nosegay of holly and evergreens to symbolize Sarah and Phillip's everlasting love.

Jill stepped to Will's side and Phillip's breath caught to see the vision that graced the archway now. Dressed in a tea-length skirt and matching blouse of ivory muslin, her upswept hair cascading little curls around her face, Sarah stood poised and calm and waiting for his signal. In her hands, she held a small blue velvet pillow and resting on top, the collar Phillip's uncle had designed, its silver gleam catching the last rays of sunlight.

His heart pounded to see her, so ready to make a commitment that would change their lives. Although legally husband and wife for two days, the ceremony getting underway now would bind them much more thoroughly than any court of law could ever hope to achieve.

Phillip nodded and Sarah moved forward, her step sure and graceful, her eyes fixed on Phillip's face. Later she would realize she should have acknowledged the witnesses but so caught up in the moment, she barely remembered their existence at the ceremony. Phillip's eyes held hers and she glided gracefully to him, paused a moment until she heard the right beat in the music, then knelt before him. With a long-practiced gesture, she held up the blue pillow and waited.

The *Canon* ended and Phillip's uncle asked the question they'd written for him. "Who is this woman and what does she want?"

Sarah answered, her voice clear and sure. "I am Sarah Townsend, wife of Phillip Townsend and I wish to be his forever-slave."

His uncle turned to Phillip. "You are my nephew, yet an independent man who makes his own decisions. Do you wish to accept Sarah's offer to become your forever-slave?"

Uncle Irv was extemporizing somewhat but Phillip didn't mind. The older man had presided over hundreds of collaring ceremonies in his life and certainly knew better than either of them. He'd given Phillip several templates to choose from but had told them this was a ceremony of the heart and the words they wrote needed to be their own.

So he and Sarah had spent the better part of the last two days putting the final touches on the short ceremony that would bind them more strongly than any law could do. He knew his answer and gave it now, his voice strong and commanding.

"I call upon the witnesses present to hear Sarah's request and to hear my answer. She wishes to be my slave." Phillip looked down at his wife kneeling before him, her face turned up toward him with a look of self-assured entreaty. She begged but with incredible dignity and sure of his answer. It took all the willpower he had not to reach out and touch her as he gave his answer.

"I accept Sarah as my forever-slave."

Relief flooded Sarah, even though she had known what his answer would be. When Phillip took the pillow from her hands, she dropped her arms to her sides and waited as his uncle accepted the pillow and Phillip lifted the torc.

"See the physical sign of Sarah's submission. In a moment I will place it around her neck, never to be removed." Phillip paused, his voice dropping a bit as he deviated from their written script. "We had originally planned at this point to have the torc welded around Sarah's neck. But recent events have shown me that might not be such a good idea.

"In the hospital, I saw the bloodstained leather that had been your going-out collar lying on a tray after they had cut it off you. Had it been welded steel, medical care would have been delayed as they waited for a welder to remove it." Phillip's voice dropped again and the love he had for Sarah came through every impassioned word.

"I will never put you in harm's way, my forever-slave. Ever. Do you understand?"

Sarah felt tears of joy welling behind her eyes but blinked them back. She nodded and at his raised eyebrow, found her voice. "I understand, my forever-Master. Thank you."

Phillip stood straight again, barely realizing he'd bent over in his admission of love. Going back to the script, he proclaimed his intent. "I place this collar around your neck as a sign of your service and submission."

Sarah bent her head so he could fasten it and Phillip both rejoiced and marveled at her long slender neck bowed before him. His uncle had designed a special lock in the two ends of the torc so it fastened together with a quiet click, leaving almost no seam. He stood and nodded to Uncle Irv, who continued the ceremony.

"You have been collared, slave, and are now the property of your master. You are his to do with as he pleases, when he pleases. You give him all rights over your body. Do you so swear to honor this commitment?"

"I do so swear," Sarah replied.

Uncle Irv turned to Phillip. "You have collared a slave and she is now your property. She is yours to protect, yours to do with as you wish. You are responsible for her well-being and health. Do you so swear to honor this commitment?"

"I do so swear," Phillip answered.

"Then in the presence of these witnesses, I acknowledge you both as Master and slave. Go forth to love and prosper."

With a grin, Phillip held out a hand to Sarah and she placed her hand in his. He pulled her gracefully to her feet and he stood for a moment, loving the look of silver around her slender neck. Then he turned and presented her to their friends. "Everyone? May I present to you, Sarah, my forever-slave."

The tension broke as Jill squealed and dashed around Will and Phillip to hug her tightly. Everyone laughed and crowded around, congratulating the couple. Sarah's favorite moment afterward came when Phillip's uncle boomed out to Paul that he'd love to design a collar for Beth. Paul grinned and seemed to consider it and Beth turned a wonderful shade of pink. Only Sarah heard Beth mutter, "'Cept it would be you who would be wearing it, slave-boy."

Paul's grin only got wider.

Phillip and Sarah had worked much of the day to prepare a feast of hors d'oeuvres as a reception for everyone. There were several toasts given and glasses raised. Sarah and Phillip were perfect hosts but as the evening grew late, Phillip turned to Sarah.

"Slave, say goodnight to our guests. Go to the dungeon and prepare to be used."

Sarah had been in the middle of a conversation with Jill and Anton, explaining to Paul the intricacies involved in a life of submission, when Phillip gave his command. She blushed furiously. She didn't really want to leave the conversation but she loved the fact that he'd given her her first order as a forever-slave, even if it did embarrass her. Jill and Anton both bowed respectfully to her, something they had never done before. Even Paul seemed to catch on and sketched a little bow of his own as she excused herself from their conversation.

She hugged Beth, who looked confused, bowed to Lady Aleshia and Uncle Irv, who then pulled her into a big hug and welcomed her to the family again. Will stood beside Phillip and Sarah gave them her deepest bow before scampering off to the dungeon. There were still dishes to be done and furniture to rearrange but apparently that was no longer her concern. She hung up her skirt and blouse, rolled down the stockings and took off every piece of clothing, including her corset, before standing there, unsure what to do next.

Chapter Fifteen
Forever

ဢ

Sarah turned on the little light beside the door of the dungeon and glanced around the room for her cuffs. She felt naked without them. Absentmindedly at first, then with purpose, she fingered the new collar around her neck.

It lay flat against her skin, the thin silver band in the back widening to almost an inch in the front where the two sides came together in a graceful vee. There was no further decoration on the simple silver and Sarah's fingers traced the upper line of the torc where it dove beneath the little hollow of her throat before rising again on the other side.

The door to the dungeon had been shut when she entered and Sarah had shut it behind her. Muted noises from the still-continuing party came through the door. That puzzled her. Weren't they all going to take the hint that Phillip wanted to use his slave?

Unless Phillip wanted them all to use his slave. The thought gave her shivers and made her pussy spasm. He'd put her on display twice, though he'd only shared her once before, and she'd loved his use of her both times. Did he intend to share her again tonight? On the very night she'd sworn her obedience to him?

Several small pillows lay scattered in the corner behind the door. Phillip used them on occasion when he wanted her body cushioned against something particularly hard. She took two now and put them on the floor before the door, kneeling in position. When he entered, she wanted to be ready, whether he was alone or with all the others.

The noise in the other room quieted down but Sarah didn't hear the front door. That meant they were all still there, just quietly talking now. It was hard, not being out at the party. She enjoyed the company of all those present and loved to see how Beth and Paul fit in with everyone else. Being treated as a sex slave in front of them all was embarrassing.

And exciting. She couldn't deny that the warmth that spread across her cheeks when he had given the order was indicative of the warmth that spread through her pussy.

A noise just outside the door captured her attention. She put her hands behind her head and waited for the door to open.

It wasn't Phillip, however, who entered. Will came in first, followed by Uncle Irv and Anton. Paul came in next, looking a little sheepish but like a kid in a toy store. Phillip followed and closed the door behind him and stood before her. She was surrounded by men.

"Stand."

Feeling a little nervous and self-conscious, Sarah stood, dropping her hands to her side and putting her feet together, unsure how much of herself to reveal to these men.

"Hold out your wrists."

Without hesitation, she did so. Paul and Anton stepped closer to her, each with one of her cuffs in his hands. In unison, they wrapped her wrists and locked on the little gold locks she loved so much.

"Spread your legs."

Sarah knew what was coming now. She didn't hesitate, even though she knew her cheeks warmed. Uncle Irv and Will fastened her ankle cuffs and locked them home before standing beside her, their hands trailing up along her legs, Will's hand resting on her ass, Uncle Irv's on her waist. Anton and Paul stepped in again and Sarah felt almost intoxicated by the presence of so many men, all touching her, feeling every inch of her skin. Hands roamed and she could feel their cocks pressing against her skin, only the fabric of their pants keeping them from touching her.

A hand reached into her hair and pulled her head back, not forcefully but relentlessly, bending her backward. Phillip stood behind her and he turned her face toward his, claiming her mouth with his kiss.

He sucked her tongue into his mouth, his own dancing around her. She gave herself to him, wanting his touch to join the caresses of the others. His fingers traced the outline of her collar and she melted into the arms of the men who held her when he whispered into her ear.

"Slave, you will wear the cum of each of these men before the night is finished."

She would do him proud, of that she was confident. Her body, however, was not hers to command as the men lifted her, carrying her to the table, turning her over and laying her down face first, her body nothing more than a tool for them to use. There was no need for her to express her arousal, the musky scent filled the room.

Someone pulled her arms up and fastened them down, another spread her legs and locked them into place. Still another gathered her hair, brushing it all to one side so her face was clear. Each ministration, lovingly performed, fed the wanton inside her.

And then the hands were gone. She felt them all withdraw, still surrounding her spread on the table but knew they had moved a respectful distance away. From somewhere down by her feet, Phillip's voice gave her instructions.

"Slave, you expressed a further interest in the cane. I have decided to give you that present as a gift for this occasion. Do you accept my gift?"

Did she accept it? Absolutely! A chance to prove her submission in front of all these witnesses? She didn't want to blow this chance. Or have Phillip lose face. Her voice a bit muffled by the leather top, she gave her acceptance. "Yes,

Master. Please let me give to you my submission as a gift in return."

"I accept the gift of your submission."

Phillip stepped back and nodded to his uncle, who already held the cane in his hands. Feeling a bit as if they were acting out some sort of ceremony, Phillip bowed to his uncle before moving to the side where he could see Sarah's face. A look of surprise briefly furrowed her brows but she said nothing, only clenched her fists in readiness.

But that would not do. She couldn't be tense—her body needed to relax. Anton and Paul stood up by her hands and he instructed each one to hold her hand, to stroke her arms and shoulders. Only when he saw her muscles relax under their touches did he nod to his uncle again.

Once, twice, three times Uncle Irv laid the cane gently on her ass cheeks, taking careful aim. Even though Phillip was ready for it, the smack of the cane on his beloved's skin still made him jump. A bright red streak appeared across her cheeks. Sarah didn't even make a sound. Phillip watched as her body relaxed its involuntary tightening. The men on either side continued to rub her shoulders and arms, helping her to a deeper state of submission.

Phillip's cock stirred. In a different man, seeing another man's hands on his wife would provoke a storm of jealous rage. Phillip found her willingness to submit to him even to the point of being shared, to be a tremendous aphrodisiac. He watched as his uncle delivered a second blow and his cock grew harder still.

Paul's face had taken on a pained look, Phillip noted as Sarah's body recovered. He glanced over to Will, giving him an eyebrow to suggest he relieve the newbie. While Paul might not yet realize it, he had the makings of an excellent submissive male.

Right now, however, the man's cock strained at his pants so hard Phillip was sure the seam was about to burst. Tall as himself, Phillip suspected Paul was similarly endowed and empathized with his pain. Will stepped over to Paul, taking Sarah's hand and gave him a short command. Paul nodded gratefully, pulling down his zipper and letting his cock loose.

Phillip would have whistled, except the sound would have broken the mood he had worked so hard to craft. Paul's cock stood out at a total of ten inches, thick as a woman's wrist and ready to burst. Phillip nodded his permission and Paul rubbed his hand along his cock, taking only a few seconds before his cum spurted forth and covered Sarah's lower back.

The warm liquid gushed over her skin and a small moan from the back of her throat escaped. These men found her an object of desire and their use of her had caused at least one of them to lose control. Her head was turned away but she suspected Paul, since the others had training in how to hold their climaxes until the best possible moment.

The cum dripped down along her side and her pussy answered, oozing a creamy white liquid of its own. She squirmed on the table, not to get away but to get relief. A low chuckle from Phillip told her he was enjoying her predicament.

She could just see him out of the corner of her eye. Wearing a pleased grin, he glanced down and winked at her. Joy flooded through her, a joy she had never thought she'd ever experience. To be surrounded by men who wanted her, who came at the sight of her naked body being used — her eyes closed again as she savored the warm feelings coursing through her.

The cane tapped her ass again, lightly taking aim. Sarah pulled in a deep, cleansing breath, letting it out slowly. The hard thwack came before she could draw another breath and she gasped the air into her lungs, her body flinching before she could control it. A cold hand rubbed her ass, easing the pain away and turning the sharp sting into a dull ache. In her mind, she bowed her head and centered her thoughts on the touch of that hand. Was it Phillip's? Paul's? She didn't know and found it didn't matter when the hands parted her ass cheeks and a finger slid down to circle her hole, teasing her but not yet penetrating.

The finger was only a tease, however, stretching her a little but then withdrawing while her legs and wrists were unbound from the table. The men helped her to rise onto all fours, then helped her down from the table. She stood a little unsteadily as Will carefully piled the assortment of pillows in the corner. Apparently satisfied, he lay on top of them, his head higher than the rest of him, his rear end on the floor, his hard cock at attention. He slipped a condom over his cock and nodded to Phillip.

To her surprise, Phillip turned her so her back was to Will and moved her so she straddled his legs. His voice held the promise of something incredible when he instructed her. "Kneel on all fours, slave."

With her knees on either side of Will's thighs, Sarah knelt facing his feet. Paul was still recovering, so Anton scooped up her hair into a ponytail, cinching it off into a not-so-neat, yet effective bundle with a hair tie. Will took her hips and inched her back so she was positioned exactly to his liking. When something warm dribbled down between her ass cheeks, Sarah suspected what was going to happen and her pussy twitched in anticipation.

Will's finger penetrated her ass, working the lubricant around as he stretched her. Sarah closed her eyes and concentrated on relaxing her muscles, intent on allowing this use of her. When Will was satisfied she could take him, he guided her hips until the tip of his cock stood pressed against her hole. "Take me in, slave," he commanded her, his tone brooking no disobedience.

But disobedience was the farthest thing from her mind. Eager to show off her skills and eager to make Phillip look good, she wanted this as much as Will did. Anton came and lifted her arms, holding her upright so Will's cock could penetrate her ass, filling her with every inch she could take.

She slid down onto him like it was a well-greased pole, which wasn't so far from the truth.

Satisfied that Will was properly placed, Anton now took Sarah's legs, bringing each one forward in turn while she leaned back, her hands pressing on Will's chest. Briefly concerned she might be hurting him, the thought flew as she realized her dripping pussy was now open and available to their sight.

The four men who remained standing stood over her, their dominance of her obvious. She gloried in it, loving the fact that they found her beautiful and sexy. Anton bowed to Phillip and put a condom on his long shaft and Sarah let her head drop backward, reveling in what they were doing to her.

Anton had no need of lubrication to enter her, Sarah provided plenty of her own. He slid in, filling her in a way she'd never been before. Two cocks filled her. Two cocks rubbing against each other, separated by the mere membranes of her body. Her body expanded, her soul reaching out and accepting them into her, pulling them deep inside. Her moan was a sigh of contentment and she would have moved in her need had not Will taken hold of her upper arms and prevented her.

Phillip now straddled her upper body. His cock danced before her face, enticing. He gave her a single word command. "Open." She eagerly complied.

Slowly, Phillip took her mouth. No condom graced his cock and she licked the pre-cum from its slit. But Phillip was not in the mood for her to give him a long, extended blowjob today. He wanted possession and relentlessly he pressed over her tongue and slid down her throat. When she gagged, he pulled back and waited for her to relax, then pressed forward again until her nose was buried against his groin.

She couldn't breathe. In spite of her best intentions, her body tried to wiggle away from his cock in order to get air. Phillip took her by the hair and pulled out long enough for her to grab a breath before plunging deep again. He held her tight to him until her body rebelled once more, then released her, pulling his cock back so he could both take her and give her breath.

Some unknown signal must've been given, for now the three men moved in unison, their cocks plunging deep inside her in a slow rhythm designed to drive her wild. For a moment, Sarah saw herself as if her mind had separated from her body and stood watching. Paul and Uncle Irv stood off to the side, watching as Sarah, laid out like a feast, accepted three men inside her. Will beneath her, helping to support her as his cock thrust into her ass, Anton kneeling upright above, his fingers poised over her clit to add to her enjoyment and Phillip above them all, commanding them all as a maestro controls an orchestra. He set the pace, his hand moving up and down in small, timed movements. The sound of their groans as they fucked her added to the music of their motion.

Then Anton's fingers pinched her clit and Sarah's consciousness snapped back inside her as the wanton took over. She moved her body in concert with the men, her mouth, her ass, her pussy, all hungry and wanting to be fed. A growl came from the depths of her belly and forced itself around Phillip's cock.

Sarah felt larger than herself, her being swelled, encompassing all the world. The men used her body not for just their enjoyment but for hers. The tempo increased, the beat moving her faster along a dark land. Far from being afraid, she was surrounded by men who cared for her, whose arms protected her even as they thrust her forward.

Phillip's cock filled her mouth and she sucked it hungrily, Anton's fingers drove her insane as Will's hands held her up.

"Come for me, slave. Come now!"

She was his to command. They flung her headlong over the cliff and her mind fell into the depths as her body convulsed around three cocks embedded in her.

Her mind, still reeling, her body, not yet recovered, heard the tone change in Phillip's growl. Hot liquid gushed into her mouth and down her throat. Without thought, she accepted his gift and swallowed every drop he gave to her. Dimly she heard him give another command. "Again. I want her to come again."

The fingers on her clit pinched her again, rubbing and working magic. She was their puppet and her body responded, sending waves of pleasure coursing through her, making even her fingertips tingle.

Time had ceased to have meaning. How long had she been pinned by their cocks? Ten minutes? Twenty? An hour? She would stay here forever if that was their wish, her body their toy, her orgasms her gift.

She licked Phillip clean, loath to feel him leave her. Anton, too, pulled out, his cock still hard and the strain of not coming showing on his face. Paul helped her to rise off Will's cock, who also had not yet come, his cock still standing as proud and stiff as when she'd mounted him.

They laid her on the pillows and stood over her, watching her body shiver as she came down from the heights they had taken her to. Of its own volition, her hand stole down to her pussy, fingering herself in front of them, not wanting to descend yet, her body still wanting more of those precious heights.

Phillip nodded to the others and Sarah realized he commanded them as much as he commanded her. The thought sent a thrill through her—her Master as the Master of all. She closed her eyes and arched her back as her fingers sent another wave of ecstasy coursing through her. Soft drops of warm liquid along her belly and breasts let her know she wasn't alone. Cum pooled and dripped from her, their gift to her as much as her body was her gift to them.

Her mind blanketed by a thick, indulgent fog, she barely felt them bathe her when they were done, her mind only dimly registering the fact that the women had rejoined them and were bathing Phillip. Borne by the arms of several men, she found herself carried to bed and tucked under the covers.

Each man knelt by the bed and kissed Sarah's forehead before they left the room, each one giving her welcoming and gratitude for the use of her body. Uncle Irv was last. With tears in his eyes, he thanked Sarah. "I am too old to come, my dearest. But you took me back, you did. I have not seen such abandonment since my Tess died." From somewhere, Sarah found the strength to reach up and pat the old man's hand before he left.

The night's surprises were not quite done yet. Lady Aleshia said her goodbyes, bending and kissing Sarah's forehead and Jill did the same. But Beth knelt beside her, her eyes twinkling with new life. "I didn't understand before, Sarah. And I'm sorry I was a jerk about it. I had a very…informative…evening with the girls." Then Beth leaned forward and kissed Sarah on the mouth — not just a small peck but a deeper kiss that spoke of feelings long hidden. Beth, in her newfound dominance, broke the kiss, whispering to Sarah, "We'll talk later," and then was gone.

They all were. Phillip had nestled himself beside her, holding her as the guests left the room, seeing themselves out. Sarah turned into his arms, snuggling deep into his caress.

"You are mine, Sarah. And for me alone, you will come one more time."

Sarah didn't think she had another in her but when Phillip's fingers cupped her sex, toying with her clit, she understood just how good he was. Her body shook in a small climax, too tired to do more but loving every wave he coaxed out of her.

And when she lay still, her body sated and exhausted, he traced the collar with his finger. "I love you, Sarah-my-slave."

She put her face up and kissed him lightly, her body entwined with his. "And I love you, Phillip-my-Master."

Why an electronic book?

We live in the Information Age — an exciting time in the history of human civilization, in which technology rules supreme and continues to progress in leaps and bounds every minute of every day. For a multitude of reasons, more and more avid literary fans are opting to purchase e-books instead of paper books. The question from those not yet initiated into the world of electronic reading is simply: *Why?*

1. *Price.* An electronic title at Ellora's Cave Publishing and Cerridwen Press runs anywhere from 40% to 75% less than the cover price of the exact same title in paperback format. Why? Basic mathematics and cost. It is less expensive to publish an e-book (no paper and printing, no warehousing and shipping) than it is to publish a paperback, so the savings are passed along to the consumer.

2. *Space.* Running out of room in your house for your books? That is one worry you will never have with electronic books. For a low one-time cost, you can purchase a handheld device specifically designed for e-reading. Many e-readers have large, convenient screens for viewing. Better yet, hundreds of titles can be stored within your new library — on a single microchip. There are a variety of e-readers from different manufacturers. You can also read e-books on your PC or laptop computer. (Please note that Ellora's Cave does not endorse any specific brands.

You can check our websites at www.ellorascave.com or www.cerridwenpress.com for information we make available to new consumers.)

3. *Mobility.* Because your new e-library consists of only a microchip within a small, easily transportable e-reader, your entire cache of books can be taken with you wherever you go.

4. *Personal Viewing Preferences.* Are the words you are currently reading too small? Too large? Too... ANNOYING? Paperback books cannot be modified according to personal preferences, but e-books can.

5. *Instant Gratification.* Is it the middle of the night and all the bookstores near you are closed? Are you tired of waiting days, sometimes weeks, for bookstores to ship the novels you bought? Ellora's Cave Publishing sells instantaneous downloads twenty-four hours a day, seven days a week, every day of the year. Our webstore is never closed. Our e-book delivery system is 100% automated, meaning your order is filled as soon as you pay for it.

Those are a few of the top reasons why electronic books are replacing paperbacks for many avid readers.

As always, Ellora's Cave and Cerridwen Press welcome your questions and comments. We invite you to mail us at Comments@ellorascave.com or write to us directly at Ellora's Cave Publishing Inc., 1056 Home Avenue, Akron, OH 44310-3502.

erridwen, the Celtic Goddess of wisdom, was the muse who brought inspiration to storytellers and those in the creative arts. Cerridwen Press encompasses the best and most innovative stories in all genres of today's fiction. Visit our site and discover the newest titles by talented authors who still get inspired - much like the ancient storytellers did, once upon a time.

Cerridwen Press

www.cerridwenpress.com

*Discover for yourself why readers can't get enough
of the multiple award-winning publisher*

Ellora's Cave.

Whether you prefer e-books or paperbacks,

be sure to visit EC on the web at
www.ellorascave.com

*for an erotic reading experience that will leave you
breathless.*

CPSIA information can be obtained at www.ICGtesting.com
224069LV00003B/22/P